The Editor and the Text

In honour of
Professor Anthony J. Holden

The Editor and the Text

edited by
Philip E. Bennett
and
Graham A. Runnalls

EDINBURGH UNIVERSITY PRESS
in conjunction with
Modern Humanities Research Association

© Edinburgh University Press 1990
22 George Square, Edinburgh

Set in Alphacomp Garamond
by Pioneer Associates, Perthshire, and
printed in Great Britain by
Redwood Press Limited,
Melksham, Wilts

British Library Cataloguing
   in Publication Data
The Editor and the text.
1. French literature, to 1550.
   Linguistic aspects—Critical studies
I. Bennett, Philip E.   II. Runnalls, Graham A.
   (Graham Arthur), *1937*—
840.9001

ISBN 0 7486 0154 6

CONTENTS

INTRODUCTION

The essays contained in this volume, written by eminent specialists of Old and Middle French language and literature, reflect the widely diverse operations required of the textual editor. These operations lie at the intersection of a large number of different disciplines — palaeography, calligraphy, the nature and techniques of paper and parchment making, historical linguistics, dialect geography, topography, toponymics, lexicology, lexicography, *et j'en passe!*, and the editor cannot afford to be 'a jack of all trades and master of none'; he must be a master of them all.

The purpose of the present volume is twofold: to exemplify this diversity in the writings of scholars considering their speciality; and to form a collective tribute to one who is a true 'master' in the field — Anthony J. Holden, Professor of French at the University of Edinburgh. Tony Holden is a highly respected scholar, one of the most distinguished specialists of Medieval French in Britain today, and one whose reputation has always extended to France itself, where he has also, exceptionally for a non-native, taught medieval language and literature in a university French department. Virtually all Tony Holden's professional career has, however, been spent in Edinburgh, where he was first appointed to the Forbes Lectureship in Romance Philology in 1955, before becoming in turn Senior Lecturer, Reader, and Professor. At Edinburgh his career overlapped with the presence of such distinguished and colourful medievalists as John Orr, Duncan McMillan, and Dominica Legge. His teaching mostly concentrated on the interrelated disciplines of Romance Linguistics, the History of French, and medieval French and Provençal literature. As can be seen from the bibliography of his works published at the head of the volume, Tony Holden has devoted his career to the edition of medieval texts and to the complex series of philological processes which make the editing and understanding of those texts possible. Apart from his own masterly editions and articles, the greatest number of his published reviews deal with scholarly editions and discuss with invariable rigour and clarity the problems and issues involved. If, therefore, there is one word to characterise Tony Holden in his professional life it is 'philologist'.

For the textual editor is above all a philologist, not in the narrow sense of the word as it is, frequently disparagingly and wrongly, used in British university circles today (to indicate a particular approach to teaching history of the language) but in the broad sense of a scholar for whom the word of the text is the vital phenomenon. Certainly a fine knowledge of the varied disciplines listed in the first paragraph is vital, for in default of these no foundation is available on which to build the subtly complex intellectual structure of the new edition. Beyond even this extensive repertoire of technical expertise, however, the editor also requires a notable sensitivity to the historical and cultural context of the work he is editing, and to the literary habits and prejudices of the age producing the text. At this end of the spectrum philology as it is widely understood today blends into that literary criticism which has become more and more divorced from the basic operations of textual edition, but which was rightly understood to lie at the heart of that science by the Renaissance editors of Classical texts for whom the label 'philologist' was invented.

The diverse disciplines which go to make up the universe of textual edition are well represented in the pages which follow. The questions of manuscript reading, of understanding and interpreting scribal practice, and of establishing manuscript relationships are handled in a number of essays. For the theatre Graham Runnalls considers the typology of manuscripts in a corpus of largely single-manuscript works, throwing light not only on the transmission of individual texts but also on the life of the whole body of medieval dramatic literature in French. The work practices of a specific late medieval author, Christine de Pizan, are treated in a pair of complementary articles by James Laidlaw and Angus Kennedy, who are each able to elucidate the life and elaboration of the individual work, and, by passing from text to context, to show how the items relate to the political and cultural scene in early fifteenth-century France. Unlike Christine de Pizan the author(s) of the various branches of the *Roman de Renart* remain unknown, and even the attribution of the various parts of the *Renart* is at times uncertain. The way in which syntactic analysis and statistical method, if used with caution, can be applied to contribute to the determination of authorship, and hence to the organisation of the published edition, is tackled by Tony Lodge for the early branches of the corpus.

The knotty editorial problem of interpreting and representing scribal 'shorthands' is tackled in relation to the *Prose Tristan* by Philippe Ménard, who also considers the perennially sensitive issue of editorial intervention in the scribe's text, referring to a number of specific cases.

The sense of when the editor can restore a text, overriding the scribe's transmitted version, and when 'restoration' merely produces a new variant text with the modern editor taking the role of medieval copyist requires a fine balance of scientific knowledge and critical acumen to which Philippe Ménard's paper does full justice. Kenneth Varty poses the problem of the use and presentation of variant readings in that particularly complex series of related works generally known as the *Roman de Renart*. This apparently minute problem of technical presentation is of utmost importance since only its successful resolution will allow the modern reader to relate the editor's text to its source manuscripts and to re-integrate the twentieth-century page with the multiplex manifestations of the medieval work.

The question of variants and the positions of individual recensions within groupings of works which represent a wider constellation than that normally produced by the 'simple' manuscript transmission of a 'unitary' work such as a courtly romance is considered for the *chanson de geste* in relation to the late rhymed version of the *Chanson de Roland* found in the Cambridge manuscript by Wolfgang van Emden. This essay again reveals how the detailed preliminaries of textual edition throw a broader light on the history and nature of the 'work', that almost abstract essence in medieval literature, of which the manuscript is, in platonic terms, merely an accidental concrete exemplar. Another type of literature posing particular problems of transmission is the lyric, in handling which the editor has to cope not only with the vagaries of textual transmission *stricto sensu* but also with the complementary problems presented by the transmission of the music. The way in which the scholar can exploit musicological as well as textological expertise to improve editorial work on the lyric is ably demonstrated for the case of *Chansonnier T* by J. H. Marshall, who shows, as do many other contributors, that the mechanics of elaborating a text from the medieval page cannot be divorced from a sense of the aesthetics which first brought that page into being. In the case of the lyric the problem is further complicated by the need to keep in mind the dual demands of literary and musical 'texts' and the exigencies of performance, then and now.

Most of the 'works' treated in this volume have come down to us in multiple-manuscript versions of more or less closely related redactions. There is, however, a large group of texts from the French Middle Ages which survives only in unique manuscripts. These texts pose particular problems for their editors, and it is to these that Corin Corley addresses himself, taking *Le Bel Inconnu* as his example. In this instance the literary corpus of analogues, sources, and derivatives stands in for the manuscript family of multiple copy works, and the philologist must apply his skills in deducing evidence from autonomous texts, giving due weight to the creativity of each author in the process.

Beyond the strictest confines of handling manuscripts, their relationships, and the texts they transmit, the editor does need, as indicated above, to be able to extend himself into wider realms of linguistic and literary appreciation. In this sphere Philip Bennett looks at the help to be had in interpreting and establishing a text from toponymy and history in the broad sense, concentrating on a problematic passage from the *Pèlerinage de Charlemagne*. Gilles Roques's study of the evolution of an idiom throws light on the symbiosis that exists in philological work between literary (textual) and lexicological research. A similar study of the evolution of pronoun use within a corpus developed over time (that of the Grail stories) brings us to that boundary where editorial work and literary criticism meet, as Emmanuèle Baumgartner considers how misunderstandings provoked by linguistic change and scribal misreading produce modifications in the presentation of the Grail, its purpose, and the characters associated with it. Such elucidation, for all that it is far removed from the 'mechanical' consideration of faults and variants, is still an essential aspect of the work of presenting early literature to a modern audience, since the editor must also be a communicator on behalf of his text, enabling it to speak as clearly as possible to its new public.

All the essayists mentioned hitherto mix a greater or smaller degree of theory with practical exemplification. That the authors of the essays should concentrate on narrow areas and specific texts is an almost inevitable consequence of the format of the volume, leaving the reader to piece together the broader view from the sum of the partial considerations of each essay. The initial aim of edition, however, is to produce a text. We are, therefore, pleased to be able to offer as the last item in the volume a new edition by Tony Hunt of a short Anglo-Norman text, in which all the various skills which underlie the other essays are brought together.

The production and even the explanatory expostion of a text, faithful to such intentions on the part of its original producer(s) as can be determined, are, however, only an initial aim. For the text once elaborated re-enters the cultural stream, and becomes once more available for aesthetic commentary. Individual scholars may choose whether or not to pass from textual edition to literary criticism. However, the literary critic who deals with medieval texts cannot, whatever the theoretical fad of the moment, dispense with the tools of philology. Ideally the critic and theoretician will himself have at his command the expertise of the philologist. Failing that he needs at his disposal a corpus of reliable editions, such as those Tony Holden has devoted his professional life to producing. For, in the absence of sound philological work, there can be no valid or enduring criticism.

PHILIP E. BENNETT
GRAHAM A. RUNNALLS

BIBLIOGRAPHY OF
PROFESSOR ANTHONY J. HOLDEN

The items within each section of this bibliography are presented in the chronological order of their publication.

Books

Le Roman de Rou de Wace, ed. A. J. Holden, [S.A.T.F.], Paris: Picard, 3 Vols, 1970–73, Prix Lagrange de l'Académie des Inscriptions et Belles Lettres, 1973.

L'Ipomédon de Hue de Rotelande, ed. A. J. Holden, Bibliothèque Française et Romane B 17, Paris: Klincksieck, 1979.

Richars li biaus, roman du XIIIe siècle, ed. A. J. Holden [C.F.M.A. 106], Paris: Champion, 1983.

Le Roman de Waldef (Cod. Bodmer 168), ed. A. J. Holden [Bibliotheca Bodmeriana Textes 5], Coligny-Geneva: Fondation Martin Bodmer, 1984.

Chrétien, *Guillaume d'Angleterre,* ed. A. J. Holden [T.L.F. 360], Geneva: Droz, 1988.

Articles

'L'authenticité des premières parties du *Roman de Rou*', *Romania,* 75(1954), p. 220–33.

'Un maître des études romanes (John Orr)', *Les Nouvelles Littéraires,* 1–ix–1966, p. 8.

'Du nouveau sur le vers 3 du *Roman de Rou*; à propos de deux articles récents', *Romania,* 89(1968), pp. 105–15.

'Note sur la langue de Beroul', *Romania,* 89(1968), pp. 387–99.

'André de Coutances, *Le Roman des Franceis*', ed. A. J. Holden, in *Etudes de langue et de littérature du Moyen Age offertes à Félix Lecoy,* Paris: Champion, 1973, pp. 213–33.

'Ancien français *tresoïr,* "entendre bien", "entendre mal" ou autre chose?', *Romania,* 97(1976), pp. 107–15.

'A propos du vers 220 de *Boeve de Haumtone*', *Romania,* 97(1976), pp. 268–711.

'Nouvelles remarques sur le texte du *Roman de Rou*', *Revue de Linguistique Romane,* 45(1981), pp. 118–27.

'La géographie de *Guillaume d'Angleterre*', *Romania*, 107(1986), pp. 124-9.

'L'édition des textes médiévaux', in *Critique et édition des textes. Actes du XVIIe Congrès International de Linguistique et de Philologie Romanes* [Publications de l'Université de Provence 9] Aix-en-Provence, 1987, pp. 337-82.

Reviews

Nicaise Ladam, *Mémoire et épitaphe de Ferdinand d'Aragon*, ed. C. Thiry, Paris, 1975: *Romania*, 97(1976), pp. 277-9.

Trubert, fabliau, ed. G. Raynaud de Lage, Geneva, 1974: *Modern Language Review*, 71(1976), pp. 911-12.

Fouke le Fitz Waryn, ed. E. J. Hathaway *et al.*, Oxford, 1975: *Modern Language Review*, 72(1977), pp. 940-2.

Micha, A., *De la chanson de geste au roman*, Geneva, 1976: *Romania*, 97(1976), pp. 577-8.

Le Roman de Tristan en prose, les deux captivités de Tristan, ed. J. Blanchard, Paris, 1976: *Romania*, 98(1977), pp. 412-17.

La Vie de saint Laurent, ed. D. W. Russell, London, 1976: *Modern Language Review*, 73(1978), pp. 902-3.

Le Voyage de Charlemagne à Jérusalem et à Constantinople, traduction critique par M. Tyssens, Ghent, 1978: *Romania*, 100(1979), pp. 417-19.

Le Roman de Tristan en prose, Vol. 2, ed. R. L. Curtis, Leiden, 1976: *Modern Language Review*, 74(1979), pp. 451-3.

Le Rider, P., *Le Chevalier dans le 'Conte del Graal' de Chrétien de Troyes*, Paris, 1978, *Romania*, 100(1979), pp. 281-3.

Odenkirchen, C. J., *The Life of Saint Alexis*, Leiden, 1978: *Les Lettres Modernes*, 34(1980), pp. 393-5.

Ménard, P., *Les Lais de Marie de France*, Paris, 1979: *Romania*, 101(1980), pp. 124-7.

Benedeit, *The Anglo-Norman Voyage of Saint Brendan*, ed. I. Short and B. Merrilees, Manchester, 1979: *French Studies*, 34(1980), pp. 436-7.

I Fatti di Bretagna, ed. M. L. Meneghetti, Padua, 1979: *Le Moyen Age*, 87(1981), pp. 507-8.

Voorwinden, N. and de Haan, M., *Oral Poetry, Das Problem der Mündlichkeit mittelalterlicher epischer Dichtung*, Darmstadt, 1979: *Romania*, 102(1981), pp. 268-70.

Philippe de Thaon, *Le Livre de Sibile*, ed. H. Shields, London, 1979: *French Studies*, 36(1982), pp. 455-6.

Le Conte de Floire et Blancheflor, ed. J. L. Leclanche, *French Studies*, 37(1983), pp. 326–7.

Benoit, *Chroniques des Ducs de Normandie*, ed. C. Fahlin, Vol. 4, Notes by S. Sandqvist, Stockholm, 1979: *Modern Language Review*, 78(1983), pp. 443–5.

Busby, K., *Gauvain in Old French Literature*, Amsterdam, 1980: *Romania*, 104(1983), pp. 125–6.

Zink, M., *Roman rose et rose rouge*, Paris, 1979: *Romania*, 104(1983), pp. 265–8.

La Chanson d'Antioche, ed. S. Duparc-Quioc, Paris, 1979: *Romania*, 104(1983), pp. 546–52.

The Life of Saint John the Almsgiver, ed. K. Urwin, 2 Vols, London, 1980–81: *Modern Language Review*, 79(1984), pp. 696–7.

Holzmayr-Rosenfield, K., *Historicité et conceptualité de la littérature médiévale*, Munich, 1984: *Romania*, 105(1984), pp. 580–1.

Pensom, R., *Literary Technique in the 'Chanson de Roland'*, Geneva, 1982: *Cahiers de Civilisation Médiévale*, 28(1985), pp. 273–5.

Guillaume le clerc de Normandie, *Fergus*, ed. W. Frescolm, Philadelphia, 1983: *Modern Language Review*, 80(1985), pp. 710–12.

The Continuations of the Old French 'Perceval', V, The Third Continuation by Mannessier, ed. W. Roach, Philadelphia, 1983: *Modern Language Review*, 81(1986), pp. 193–5.

Nouveau recueil complet des fabliaux, ed. W. Noomen and N. J. H. van den Boogaard, Vols 1 & 2, Assen, 1983–4: *Modern Language Review*, 81(1986), pp. 996–8.

Medieval French Textual Studies in Memory of T. B. W. Reid, ed. I Short, London, 1984: *Medium Aevum*, 55(1986), pp. 139–42.

van den Boogaard, N. J. H., *Autour de 1300; études de philologie et de littérature médiévales*, Amsterdam, 1985: *Modern Language Review*, 82(1987), pp. 950–2.

Philippe Ménard

1. PROBLÈMES DE PALÉOGRAPHIE ET DE PHILOLOGIE DANS L'ÉDITION DES TEXTES FRANÇAIS DU MOYEN ÂGE

Les éditeurs de textes restent souvent très discrets sur les difficultés qu'ils rencontrent dans la lecture des manuscrits et sur les problèmes qui se posent à eux dans la compréhension et la transcription des graphies du Moyen Age. Sans prétendre épuiser ici toutes les questions, je voudrais soulever un certain nombre de problèmes, attirer l'attention sur des points qui méritent examen et qui, dans certains cas, appelleraient des recherches spécifiques.

La lecture u ou n

Parfois les copistes distinguent avec soin dans leur écriture les lettres *u* et *n*. Dès lors le lecteur moderne est enclin à transcrire ce qu'il voit. Il n'a aucune envie de retoucher çà et là, de régulariser, d'uniformiser. Certes, il constate des variations de graphie. Le ms. 2542 de la Bibliothèque nationale de Vienne en Autriche, qui nous a conservé le *Tristan en prose*, écrit habituellement *preudome* (Ph. Ménard, 1987, t. I, § 30, 9), rarement *preudoume* (§ 2, 1). De même, il dit couramment *estonné* (§ 54, 36), peu souvent *estouné* (§ 50, 9). Mais les variations graphiques sont monnaie courante dans les textes. A quelques lignes de distance, on trouve *vilonnie* (§126, 37-8) et *vilenie* (§126, 38), *esranment* (§ 38, 7) et *esraument* (§ 37, 23), etc. Compte tenu du fait que les formes *preudoume, estouné* sont normales dans un manuscrit teinté de picardismes, puisque *o* fermé suivi d'une nasale aboutit fréquemment à *ou* en picard (Gossen, 1970, p. 83, § 28a) et que l'on y rencontre des formes comme *houme, persoune, preudoume, Roume*, il serait incongru de faire disparaître du ms. ces particularités intéressantes.

Mais ailleurs on est en droit de s'inquiéter. Des éditions modernes impriment des formes curieuses: par exemple des noms de lieu, où *u, n* et parfois *v* sont fâcheusement permutés. Le problème se pose de savoir, en premier lieu, si le copiste distingue toujours nettement le *u* et le *n*. Ensuite, il convient de prendre parti. Même s'il s'avère que le copiste ignore la géographie et déforme le nom, un éditeur raisonnable hésitera à imprimer une forme complètement extravagante. En pensant à l'auteur, qui sans doute connaissait le toponyme en question, il opérera une retouche minime pour retrouver la forme authentique du nom.

Ainsi dans *Ami et Amile*, Dembowski (1969) v. 59, on préfèrerait lire *Tranes* (adaptation de la ville italienne de Trani) plutôt que *Traves*, qui n'a aucun sens. Certes, il faut tenir compte des genres littéraires. Une géographie imaginaire existe dans les chansons de geste et d'une manière générale dans les récits de fiction. C'est même une des composantes de l'esthétique de ces textes. On peut donc hésiter parfois sur la conduite à tenir. En revanche, dans un texte de caractère historique, il n'est pas permis, me semble-t-il, d'imprimer *Fontevrant* ou *Andenarde* (Buridant, 1978, p. 4, § 269). Il faut lire *Fontevraut* et *Audenarde*. La confusion entre *u* et *n* est facile dans les manuscrits médiévaux et aussi sous la plume d'un seul et même copiste. Voilà pourquoi il ne faut pas porter une confiance aveugle à ce que l'on voit écrit, car on risquerait d'imprimer des formes monstrueuses. A suivre fidèlement les copistes, on propagerait des aberrations et l'on répandrait des formes inconnues de l'auteur.

Il faut pousser la réflexion plus loin pour éviter de croire naïvement à tout ce que l'on voit. Dans l'édition récente *The Old French Crusade Cycle*, vol. VII, *The Jerusalem Continuations*, Part 2, Grillo (1987), l'éditeur du texte imprime le pronom-adjectif indéfini *tout* sous la forme *tont*. Certes, le copiste du manuscrit abrège le mot et écrit un tilde sur le *o*. Mais je crains que l'éditeur moderne s'abuse en imprimant ici une nasale. Pour ma part, je transcrirais *tous* au vers 361 (*je le sai tous de fi*) et *tout* au vers 537 (*Mahoms qui tout forma*). Une preuve en est donnée au vers 1895, où le mot *trestout* est écrit en toutes lettres. N'est-ce point l'indice que la barre dite de nasalisation et parfois à interpréter comme l'abréviation d'un *u* et non d'un *n*? Ni Godefroy (1880–1902) ni Tobler-Lommatzsch (1915–89) ni le *FEW*, von Wartburg (1922–88) n'enregistrent une forme *tont* avec nasale. De surcroît, au plan phonétique on serait fort en peine d'expliquer une semblable évolution. Il est donc permis de penser qu'il s'agit là d'une fausse lecture et qu'il faut interpréter tout autrement le tilde d'abréviation placé sur la voyelle.

Sur cette question importante, il faudrait assurément poursuivre des recherches. On me permettra ici d'attirer l'attention sur des faits voisins: le problème de la notation du *e* sourd par *e* + *n*. La question a été abordée par J. Lanher dans un important article (1972) et aussi par Cl. Régnier (1973). Jean Lanher transcrit par *n* la barre de nasalisation sur *e* et imprime *Huens, freren, renceveront, englise*, etc. On pourrait ici aussi estimer que le tilde doit être transcrit par un *u* et imprimer *Hueus, frereu, reuceveront, euglise*, etc. Je me contente de poser la question. Le problème mériterait un examen approfondi. S'agirait-il d'un *e* dialectal qui se serait nasalisé? La nasalisation affecterait-elle tous les mots relevés par J. Lanher ou seulement quelques-uns? Même si les chartes en question appartiennent à une région de 'forte nasalisation' comme le dit J. Lanher, on observera que pour les mots cités plus haut il n'y a pas du tout de nasale pouvant exercer une action ni progressive ni régressive. On peut donc se demander si ici encore le tilde ne serait pas à interpréter comme je l'ai fait précédemment.

La lecture u, v et w

On laissera de côté les questions qui concernent seulement le moyen français, comme de savoir s'il faut écrire *pouoir, aura, saura*. Sur ce problème on se reportera à O. Jodogne (1966) et A. T. Baker (1937). Regardons seulement la présence de *u* double dans les manuscrits. Comment faut-il transcrire? Chez les éditeurs la tendance à transcrire par *w* est assez répandue. Il ne s'agit pas ici de contester le *w* d'origine germanique, si courant dans les graphies du Nord et de l'Est (Gossen, 1967). Le problème est autre: doit-on transcrire par *w* ou par *vu* des mots comme *widier* (*Chansons et Dits artésiens*, R. Berger (1981), 19, 65) ou *weil* (Gerbert de Montreuil, *Continuation du Perceval*, Oswald 16970)? La pratique d'user en pareil cas de *w* semble discutable. Autant il est normal d'écrire *wiscier* 'huissier' *Ille et Galeron*, Lefèvre (1988) v. 4100) ou *wi* 'aujourd'hui' *Lancelot en prose*, Micha (1978–1983), XII, 5), car aucune autre transcription n'est possible, autant il paraît naturel de transcrire *vuidier* ou *vueil*. Rien ne prouve, en effet, que dans ces formes qui appartiennent à des séries verbales la prononciation soit *w*, et non *vu*. Si, comme il est vraisemblable, l'ensemble des formes a la même prononciation à l'initiale, il convient d'opter dès lors pour la transcription la plus simple, la plus claire, celle qui ne prête pas à équivoque, c'est-à-dire pour le digramme *vu*. A l'intervocalique, on peut hésiter quand on rencontre *uu* dans un manuscrit. Doit-on écrire *ewangile* ou *euvangile*? Comment prononcer? Les éditeurs de textes littéraires transcrivent constamment *ewangile*, comme le montre le Tobler-Lommatzsch (III, 1526). Ont-ils raison? Je trouve une forme *euvangele* dans une charte de 1275, citée par Godefroy (IX, 574). Je me contente ici de poser la question et de suggérer qu'il ne faut peut-être pas continûment écrire avec *w*.

La transcription du y

Quand un éditeur de texte rencontre dans un manuscrit un *y*, il a tendance à le conserver tel quel. Dans la plupart des cas il a raison. Mais il faut éviter d'oublier la vraie nature du *y*. Ce n'est rien d'autre qu'un *i* un peu plus long, un peu plus majestueux. Autrement dit, le *y* équivaut parfois comme le *i* à notre *j*. Ainsi dans le *Tristan en prose*, le nom de lieu qui apparaît sous la forme *Tyntayol* sous la plume du copiste du manuscrit 2542 de Vienne doit être transcrit *Tyntajol* (Ph. Ménard 1987, t. I. § 24, 28). De même, on trouve parfois dans les manuscrits le nom de Jules César écrit *Yulius*. Il convient ici encore d'écrire et de prononcer *Julius*. Le développement du *y* s'est fait surtout en moyen français. Des toponymes qui ont toujours été pourvus d'un *j* dans la prononciation, se trouvent alors parfois écrits avec un *y*. Je ne crois pas qu'il soit licite de conserver cet *y* et d'imprimer, par exemple, *Castelbayac* comme le fait D. Lalande dans sa bonne édition du *Livre des fais* de Boucicaut (1985, p. 170, 204). La petite ville de Castelbajac ne doit pas avoir son nom déformé et devenir méconnaissable.

L'hésitation entre c et t

Il arrive que le lecteur moderne hésite et ne sache pas si le copiste a écrit un *t* ou un *c*. Dans le doute il est obligé de choisir et de se fonder soit sur l'étymologie, soit sur l'usage le plus répandu dans le texte. Même si le copiste distingue avec soin *c* et *t*, il peut arriver qu'il faille ne pas le suivre. Ainsi dans le *Tristan en prose* le copiste écrit indifféremment l'adverbe *adont* et *adonc*. Il serait déplacé d'opérer le moindre changement de graphie. Mais il lui arrive aussi d'écrire le relatif *dont* sous la forme *donc*. Pour des raisons de clarté il semble alors indispensable de faire une petite rectification de graphie et d'écrire toujours le relatif *dont*.

Il semble indispensable pour des noms de lieu de suivre également la graphie autorisée par l'usage, et ne pas imprimer une forme fantaisiste, due soit à l'ignorance du copiste soit à une déformation fâcheuse du toponyme. Ainsi dans la *Chanson de Du Guesclin* de Cuvelier, dont j'utilise l'édition dactylographiée de Jean-Claude Faucon (1985), il convient de rectifier ce qu'on voit à première lecture et d'imprimer *Condat*, et non *Condac* (v. 24130), *Bregerac*, et non *Bregerat* (v. 24140). Si l'on respectait aveuglément ce que l'on voit, on aboutirait à des monstruosités. Toutes les confusions ne sont pas également respectables. Toutes ne doivent pas être conservées.

Graphies simplifiées et graphies inverses

Des problèmes délicats se posent parfois au sujet de graphies simplifiées. Par exemple, la réduction, d'ailleurs tout à fait épisodique, du mot *criee* 'la huée' en *crie*. Un cas se présente dans le ms. 2542 du *Tristan en prose* au f. 190 v° c pour un passage encore inédit. Le texte nous dit *On n'espargnoit nul autre cevalier de la crie, ains crioient tout comunaument aprés lui.* Faut-il corriger pour la raison que l'exemple semble unique et que le copiste écrit ailleurs *criee*, y compris dans la même page? Doit-on estimer que la terminaison *-iee* s'est réduite à *-ie*, bien que le mot soit dissyllabique, par analogie de tous les participes passés féminins picards qui dans le texte se présentent sous la forme *-ie*, comme *laissie, esragie, detrenchie*? J'inclinerais, pour ma part, à suivre cette voie et à conserver la forme. Moins on touche une graphie, plus on permet aux philologues de progresser dans l'histoire de la langue.

On a parfois l'impression qu'une graphie réduite répond à un principe, et non à une banale faute. Ainsi il semble que certains copistes n'aiment pas écrire à la suite trois fois la lettre *e*. Prenons le participe féminin du verbe *veer*, qui devrait apparaître sous la forme *veee*. Le mot se rencontre parfois à la finale d'une laisse en *-ee*, sous la forme *vee*, qui attire immédiatement l'attention, qui introduit une dissonance et qui surprend le lecteur moderne. Voici un exemple emprunté à la *Chanson de Du Guesclin* de Cuvelier:

> Et li roys de Navarre ot la chose accordee,
> De Navarre leur fist abandonner l'entree
> Et commanda sa gent a icelle journee
> Que li ost qui venoit ne fust point empiree
> Et que pour leur argent ne fust chose vee.
>
> [v. 12012–16]

Le compte des syllabes et la nature de la rime imposent la forme *veee*. On ne maintiendra ici la forme réduite que si un nombre important d'autres exemples confirme que c'est une habitude du scribe de réduire ainsi les trois *eee* à deux. Sinon, on corrigera.

Dès la seconde moitié du XIIIe siècle les graphies inverses, d'ailleurs en nombre réduit, apparaissent dans les manuscrits. Ce serait, me semble-t-il, fâcheux de les faire disparaître, tant qu'elles ne compromettent pas gravement pour le lecteur moderne le sens du passage. La disparition de la consonne finale du pronom personnel *il* est bien connu devant la consonne initiale du mot suivant. Ce trait de phonétique syntactique doit être conservé. Il suffit de le signaler dans l'introduction linguistique du texte et de prendre quelques précautions pour éviter la confusion du relatif sujet *qui* et du relatif complément ou de la conjonction *que* suivie de *i* à valeur de *il*. Dès qu'on imprime *qu'i*, on peut savoir aussitôt qu'il ne s'agit pas du relatif. Ainsi le passage suivant du *Tristan en prose* (Ph. Ménard, 1987, t. I. § 88, 4) ne souffre d'aucune ambiguïté: *conme cele ki tout certainnement quidoit k'i s'en fust alés u roiaume de Logres.*

L'usage s'est répandu parmi les éditeurs de texte de conserver ces graphies, sans rajouter le *l* qui était tombé. Inversement, il serait opportun de ne pas retoucher les graphies inverses où apparaît *quil* au lieu du relatif *qui*. Ces formes sont intéressantes. Elles témoignent que les copistes avaient le sentiment que dans les graphies *qui* (que nous écrivons *qu'i* pour raison de clarté) un *l* manquait. Leur désir de rajouter le *l* manquant leur a fait commettre, sans doute, des erreurs. Il ont ajouté à tort un *l* à un *qui* relatif. Mais ici encore, si l'on supprime ces variations et ces graphies inverses, si l'on rectifie tout selon les usages du français moderne, qu'est-ce qui restera de l'histoire des graphies médiévales? C'est pourquoi il semble préférable de conserver non seulement *qu'i* à la place de *qu'il*, mais aussi *quil* au lieu de *qui*. Il suffit d'écrire en un seul mot *quil* pour que le lecteur moderne, déjà prévenu par les remarques faites dans l'introduction, reconnaisse qu'il s'agit d'un relatif. Ainsi paraît-il convenable d'imprimer *Signeur, or sachiés tout vraiement k'il n'i a nul de vous kil n'ait mout grant cose emprise sour soi* (Ph. Ménard, 1987, t. I, § 22, 6–8). Ou encore *Et kil puet de peril escaper par sens il ne fait mie trop a blasmer* (Ménard, 1987, § 124, 26). Le maintien de ces graphies inverses ne gêne pas la compréhension et restitue la vérité des graphies médiévales.

La lecture du é tonique dans les noms propres

Pour éviter de moderniser les formes médiévales il faut aussi prendre garde à la prononciation de la voyelle finale. Certains éditeurs écrivent *Achiles, Socrates*, tel le savant érudit qui a publié le *Livre des fais* de Boucicaut (100, 170 et 396, 34), ou encore *Placides*, comme fait l'éditeur du texte qu'il dénomme *Placides et Timeo* (Thomasset, 1980, p. 5 et *passim*). Je doute que ces formes soient admissibles. Pour ce qui est du dernier nom il apparaît avec un -*s* final, y compris au cas régime précédé d'une préposition (Thomasset, 1980, 420, 1). Signe qu'il faut écrire *Placidés*. De surcroît, ces noms s'inscrivent dans une série de termes à finale en -*és*: *Placidés, Achilés, Socratés* doivent être rapprochés d'*Ulixés*, de *Diomedés* ou encore de *Palamidés*. Ce dernier personnage est un des héros de premier plan du *Tristan en prose*. Il est fâcheux que dans son édition du manuscrit de Carpentras Mlle R. Curtis n'ait pas accentué le nom. Des rimes très éclairantes dans les textes en vers permettent de savoir comment l'on prononçait dans les oeuvres en prose du XIIIe siècle. Par exemple, dans le *Roman de Troie* on voit *Herculés* rimer avec le mot *pais* (24850), *Diomedés* avec *adés* (5211), *Ulixés* avec *Darés* (5201), *Achillés* avec *prés* (5659). Dans le *Roman de la Rose* on trouve *Alcipiadés* rimant avec *adés* (Lecoy, 1965-70, 8913). Dans le *Roman de Thèbes* (v. 22) on doit lire *Pollymnicés* et *Etÿoclés*. La graphie *Polinices* est une erreur de l'éditeur du *Roman d'Eneas* (2670). Un autre problème serait de savoir à quel moment de l'histoire la prononciation moderne s'est répandue et s'est imposée. La question sort des limites de mon enquête. Au vu d'un rapide sondage, il semble que l'ancienne prononciation en *-és* soit toujours vivante à la fin du Moyen Age. *Le Joli Buisson de Jonece* de Froissart, daté de 1373 par son dernier éditeur (Fourrier, 1975), fait rimer *Achillés* (v. 4785) avec *Moysés, souhés, pes,* etc. Plus tard, presqu'au milieu du XVe siècle, chez Michault Taillevent, dont Robert Deschaux nous a donné une très soigneuse édition (1975), il faut lire encore *Ulixés* (*La Bien Allée*, v. 17). La place du mot avant une pause le suggère:

> Penelope oncques n'ot amy;
> Ne daigna amer nullement
> Ulixés, sy non a tourment.

On pourrait dire la même chose de la forme du mot Alcibiade chez Villon. Il reste *Archipïadés* dans le *Testament* (éd. J. Rychner et A. Henry 1974, v. 331). Il semble donc qu'aucune hésitation ne soit permise, à plus forte raison, pour les textes écrits en ancien français au XIII siècle.

Problèmes de coupe des mots

La coupe des mots dans les manuscrits pose parfois des problèmes délicats aux éditeurs. Les enclitiques qui s'appuient sur le mot précédent, les proclitiques qui se soudent au mot suivant doivent être séparés selon les usages modernes. Les groupes médiévaux seraient intéressants à étudier selon les époques et les habitudes des divers scribes. Mais regardons seulement ici les conséquences qui résultent de la simplification d'un groupe de consonnes ou au contraire de la réduplication des consonnes à l'intérieur d'un groupe.

Exemple de réduction consonantique. Le ms. 2542 du *Tristan en prose* dans un passage encore inédit parle d'un personnage (il s'agit d'une jeune femme) que la reine Yseut avait nourrie *des enfance* (fol. 145 a). Il faut naturellement comprendre 'depuis la jeunesse de cette jeune femme'. La graphie *des enfance*, dans ce ms. picard ou les groupes *dessus* ou *ses sire* deviennent *desus* et *sesire*, doit être interprétée comme une simplification de *des s'enfance*. C'est ainsi qu'on pour rait corriger, en ajoutant la marque de l'adjectif possessif.

Inversement, à l'intérieur d'un groupe formé d'un élément proclitique et d'un élément accentué, on observe dans beaucoup de textes une tendance à redoubler la consonne initiale du mot accentué. L'éditeur moderne ne peut guère conserver ces groupes qui obscurciraient parfois la compréhension ou bien qui contredisent nos habitudes de séparer chaque mot l'un de l'autre. Quel parti prendre dès lors? Faut-il faire disparaître ces consonnes doubles? Mais on supprime un phénomène de graphie intéressant. Doit-on les maintenir à l'initiale? Mais on donne un aspect barbare au mot en question. Aucune solution n'est pleinement satisfaisante. La moins bonne semble la conservation du groupe. Imprimer *Il est assavoir* (Lalande, 1985, p. 65, 77) revient à unir deux éléments distincts et à adopter la coupe des mots médiévale, sortie d'usage. Au début du *Roman de Renart* (Roques 1948, t. I, branche 1, vers 1–2) l'éditeur écrit fâcheusement:

> Perroz, qui son engin ess'art
> Mist en vers faire de Renart . . .

On ne saurait compliquer davantage la lecture. Mieux vaudrait écrire *e ss'art* pour faire comprendre que l'on a affaire à la conjonction *et* sous la forme *e*, puis l'adjectif possessif avec consonne répétée, enfin le substantif *art*. Le même éditeur use ailleurs d'une autre pratique: Dans le *Roman du Comte d'Anjou* (Roques, 1931) il imprimait *a fforce* (v. 6516) ou *a rrire* (v. 5169). La séparation des deux éléments du groupe a pour elle l'avantage de la clarté: ainsi *a ssenestre* (Ménard 1987, t. I, § 23, 23). La présence de deux consonnes en tête du substantif suggère au lecteur expérimenté que le copiste médiéval avait rassemblé le mot et l'élément proclitique qui précède en un seul groupe.

On pourrait poursuivre encore ces réflexions et signaler d'autres problèmes. Arrêtons ici le cours de ces premières observations. Plusieurs idées directrices président à l'activité de l'éditeur de texte. D'abord, le désir de préserver des particularités de graphie ou des faits dialectaux intéressants. Ensuite, une certaine réserve à l'égard du copiste, qui n'est jamais infaillible. A le suivre aveuglément, on s'exposerait à des mécomptes. D'autre part, le souhait de faciliter la lecture et la compréhension du texte. Tout ce qui risque d'égarer le lecteur est fâcheux. Enfin, parfois une certaine prudence, une légitime incertitude sur la nature des phénomènes invitent l'éditeur à ne pas prendre parti. Lorsqu'il y a conflit entre ces différents principes, l'éditeur de texte est mal à l'aise. Il ne sait plus à quel saint se vouer. Le plus dangereux est peut-être de prendre obscurément parti sans le dire, sans mettre en pleine lumière les embarras que l'on éprouve ou les difficultés que l'on rencontre. Il n'est pas toujours possible de résoudre les problèmes que l'on se pose. Il suffit de les exposer pour que les lecteurs soient informés. En tout domaine rien ne vaut la clarté.

Références

Baker, A. T. (1937) 'Le futur des verbes *avoir* et *savoir*', *Romania*, 63, pp. 1–30.

Berger, Roger (éd.) (1981) *Chansons et dits artésiens*, Arras.

Buridant, Cl. (1978) *La Traduction de la Philippide de Guillaume le Breton, ms. Vatican Reg. 624*, thèse dact. Lille, pp. 44 et 269.

Constans, L. (éd.) (1904–12) *Le Roman de Troie de Benoît de Sainte-Maure*, Paris.

Dembowski, Peter F. (éd.) (1969), *Ami et Amile*, Paris.

Deschaux, R. (1975) *Un Poète bourguignon du XVe siècle, Michaut Taillevent, édition et étude*, Genève: Droz.

Faucon, Jean-Claude (éd.) (1985) *La Chanson de Du Guesclin*, thèse dact. Paris-Sorbonne.

Fourrier, Anthime (éd.) (1975) *Jean Froissart, Le Joli Buisson de Jonece*, Genève: Droz.

Godefroy, F. (1880–1902), *Dictionnaire de l'ancienne langue française et de tous ses dialectes*, Paris.

Gossen, C. Th. (1967) *Französische Skriptastudien*, Wien.

—— (1970) *Grammaire de l'ancien picard*, Paris.

Grillo, Peter (éd.) (1987) *The Old French Crusade Cycle, VII, The Jerusalem Continuations, Part 2, La Prise d'Acre, La Mort Godefroi and La Chanson des rois Baudouin*, University of Alabama Press.

Jodogne, O. (1966) '*Povoir* ou *Pouoir*? Le cas phonétique de l'ancien verbe *pouoir*', in *Mélanges P. Gardette, TLL*, 6, pp. 257–66.

Lalande, Denis (éd.) (1985) *Le Livre des fais du bon messire Jehan le Maingre dit Bouciquaut*, Genève: Droz.

Lanher, Jean (1972) 'Une graphie curieuse dans les chartes des Vosges antérieures à 1270', in *Les Dialectes de France au Moyen Age et aujourd'hui*, Paris, pp. 337–45.

Lecoy, Félix (éd.) (1965–70) *Guillaume de Lorris et Jean de Meun, Le Roman de la Rose*, Paris: Champion.

Lefèvre, Yves (éd.) (1988) *Gautier d'Arras, Ille et Galeron*, Paris.

Ménard, Philippe (éd.) (1987) *Le Roman de Tristan en prose*, t. I, Genève: Droz.

Micha, Alexandre (éd.) (1978–83) *Lancelot*, Genève: Droz.

Oswald, Marguerite (éd.) (1975) *Gerbert de Montreuil, La Continuation de Perceval*, t. 3, Paris.

Raynaud de Lage, Guy (éd.) (1966) *Le Roman de Thèbes*, Paris.

Régnier, Cl. (1973) 'E sourd final en lorrain du XIIIe siècle', in *Etudes . . . offertes à F. Lecoy*, Paris, pp. 514–17.

Roques, Mario (éd.) (1931) *Jean Maillart, Le Roman du comte d'Anjou*, Paris.

—— (éd.) (1948) *Le Roman de Renart*, t. I, Paris.

Rychner, Jean et Albert Henry (éds) (1974) *Villon, Testament*, Genève: Droz.

Salverda de Grave, J. J. (éd.) (1929) *Le Roman d'Eneas*, Paris.

Thomasset, Claude (éd.) (1980) *Placides et Timéo*, Genève: Droz.

Tobler-Lommatzsch (1915–1976) *Altfranzösisches Wörterbuch*, Berlin et Wiesbaden.

Wartburg, W. von (1922–1988) *Französisches Etymologisches Wörterbuch*, Berlin et Basel.

C. Corley

2. EDITING *LE BEL INCONNU* AND OTHER SINGLE-MANUSCRIPT TEXTS

Editing any Old French text involves finding solutions for a particular set of problems. While specific textual problems are bound to vary from text to text, there is generally a basic similarity in the questions of method and approach which have to be faced. For example, the various manuscripts have to be studied, the relationship between them has to be defined, and one of them has to be chosen as the base manuscript. The editor has to decide how conservative or free to be in his approach to the text, and whether to make abundant use of emendations or whether to use extensive notes.

Editing a text which is found in only one manuscript is necessarily a special case; there is no choice of base manuscript to be made, no manuscript tradition to be studied, no decision to make on whether to produce an eclectic or a conservative version of the text. The editor's task is thus in many ways very much simpler than in the case of other editions. At the same time, however, he has very little to help him in resolving the inevitable textual problems. In short, editing a single-manuscript text is a peculiar challenge, one which I shall examine here with particular reference to the *Bel Inconnu*, of which I am currently preparing a new edition.

Manuscript transcription

The editor's transcription of his manuscript should be painstakingly accurate. That may appear to be a statement of the obvious, but we shall see, with reference to *Rigomer*, that the smallest error can completely distort the text. One should not hesitate to compare one's reading with those of previous editors of the text, and check any divergences. One has, after all, no other manuscripts to help point up errors. Equally, one should be prepared to check and recheck any instance where one feels the reading is remotely suspect. If working from photographic reproductions — alas, all too often an unavoidable evil — the editor must endeavour to compare his transcription with the original manuscript, at least in cases of difficulty. While an ultra-violet lamp can help with deciphering faint or partly erased readings, I have found the most useful tool to be a magnifying-glass.

To underline the need for accurate transcription it is perhaps worth noting that in transcribing the *Bel Inconnu* I found over 200 errors in G. Perrie Williams's text (1929), itself very much more accurate than her first transcription (1915). Many of them might be considered trivial, and some are probably the result of misprints, rather than errors of transcription, but they include the name of Blonde Esmeree's father, consistently given by Perrie Williams (and Hippeau [1860] before her) as Gringras, but which I read, in every instance, as Guingras. In the same way, any 'new' edition based on an old transcription — such as T. B. W. Reid's annotated version of W. Foerster's *Yvain* (1942) — runs the risk of perpetuating mistakes which a genuinely new edition might eliminate; even Foerster made errors of transcription, as we shall see, while his 'regularisation' of forms to give them the Champenois flavour he thought suitable for Chrétien's works hardly accords with modern editorial practice.

Tools

With the transcription completed, the task of editing begins. Here, the editor should make use of anything which may possibly be of assistance: having only one manuscript to work with, he needs all the help he can get. Three aids come to mind: later versions of the text, such as Claude Platin's sixteenth-century prose version of *Bel Inconnu*; parallel or cognate versions — in this case, *Erec, Libeaus Desconus, Carduino,* and *Wigalois*; and the habits of the scribe or scribes.

Of these three possible sources of help, it is the last which perhaps requires the fullest explanation. Every editor is aware of the way 'his' scribe writes, his use of abbreviations, his level of care and accuracy, his language. I am suggesting here that it can be beneficial to study his habits in a broader sphere: in texts other than the one under consideration. Clearly, this is not always possible, but in our particular case, that of *Bel Inconnu*, the same scribe was also responsible for copying *Hunbaut* and the versions of *Fergus* and *Lancelot* found in the Chantilly manuscript. There is some disagreement concerning the attribution to the six or seven different scribes of the various texts in the manuscript. I believe the *Bel Inconnu* scribe probably copied *L'Atre Périlleux* as well as the four texts mentioned, but two or three of the hands in the corpus are very similar. By studying the pattern of errors found in these other texts, we give ourselves another tool for the work of editing our text. For example, consider ll.55–6 of *Bel Inconnu*:

Tant en i ot nes puis conter
Ne la dame ne puis nonmer.

(The *Bel Inconnu* quotations in this article are from my own transcription unless stated otherwise. The line numbers are those of the Williams edition). These lines follow an enumeration of some of the knights present at King Arthur's court. Perrie Williams emends 1.56 to 'Ne *les dames* ne puis nommer'. This makes sense of the couplet, but a better correction would seem to be 'Ne la *dime* ne puis nonmer' (nor can I name one tenth of them). There is no support for either change, but a study of the scribe's 'error pattern' shows that he not infrequently writes *a* for other vowels, which makes my proposed correction that much more likely — although in this instance it is conceivable that he misread the *-is-* of *disme* as *-a-*. Another example is found in 1.4767, where the manuscript reads:

Poisson, torgon, n'oissel volant

which Williams emends to 'Poisson, *dragon*, n'oissel volant'. This plausible correction is lent support by the fact that in line 4369 of *Fergus* the same scribe writes *tormont* for *dromont* (and, indeed, by his frequent interchanging of voiced and unvoiced consonants).

Familiarity with another text copied by the same scribe could also be helpful when we look at 1.3606 of *Hunbaut*, which reads:

Il me dist quant de moi pardi   3605
Qu'il serroit ci *aluimedi*.   3606

Neither Breuer (1914) nor Winters (1984) appears to have understood the apparently mysterious *aluimedi*: the former emended to [*dusc'*]*a lundi* while the latter read *a lunnedi* — the manuscript reading is clear, but there is no hair-stroke on the *i*. As well as the clue in ll.3575-8, when Gavain says:

'Et se li di que la venrai
Au plus tost que onques porrai,
Mien ensïent, dusqu'a huit jors,   3576
En quel liu que soit ses sejors.'   3578

the editor might look to *Fergus* line 5574, where this same expression occurs, to confirm that we have here 'a l'uime di' (on the eighth day, i.e. in a week's time). Had the reading of the other manuscript (P) of *Fergus* been more useful, it might have shed light on this. In fact, the *a hui vespri* of P, adopted by Frescoln (1983), is a markedly inferior reading. Again, there is a clue earlier in the text, in 1.5366, where the character in question states '*D'ui en huit jors ert la bataille*'.

The usefulness of a later version depends to a great extent on its fidelity — and possibly its chronological proximity — to the text in question. For instance, the sixteenth-century prose *Perceval* is close enough to the thirteenth-century versions to be of some use to an editor, although there are enough manuscripts to make reference to it largely unnecessary. In the case of the *Bel Inconnu*, on the other hand, the sixteenth-century version is a very free adaptation, of much less use, though it should still be consulted.

Similarly, the usefulness of cognate texts tends to be limited, but should not be discounted. For *Bel Inconnu*, the evidence of *Libeaus Desconus, Carduino*, and *Wigalois* is virtually useless. It is *Erec*, a more distant relation, which is the most helpful. This is in fact because, as W. H. Schofield (1895) and others have pointed out, Renaut de Beaujeu — or Renaud de Bâgé, as we should perhaps call him, in the light of A. Guerreau's article (1982) — made extensive borrowings from Chrétien's text. In fact, whether these parallels are borrowings or, less probably, common inheritance from an earlier version is irrelevant; what matters is that they are sufficiently numerous to rule out such explanations as coincidence or the common stock of romance formulae. We may contrast this with the relationship between *Bel Inconnu* and *Ipomedon*. Although there are many elements of the Fair Unknown story in the second part of the latter text, and some textual parallels (notably *BI* l.145 cf. *Ip.* l.7969, l.155 cf. l.7945, l.182 cf. l.8034, l.207 cf. l.8055, l.221 cf. l.8060, l.223 cf. l.8088, l.249 cf. l.8083, ll.258–9 cf. ll.8093–5, ll.267–9 cf. ll.8124–5 and 8128, l.271 cf. l.8129 and l.311 cf. l.8344) there is insufficient evidence to assume any direct or indirect link between the two. Thus, in certain instances, it seems legitimate to use *Erec* for emendation of *Bel Inconnu*. Consider, for example, ll.1793–4 of the latter:

> Li convient dire et otroier:
> 'Conquis m'avés, nel puis soufrir'.

Whatever possible changes might correct the rhyme and still make sense, only one emendation is possible: ll.1791–4 are essentially the same as *Erec* 6007–10, and so we can confidently follow *Erec* and, like Perrie Williams, emend to '"Conquis m'avés, nel puis *noier*"'.

Editorial practice

Here the editor's task is similar however many manuscripts he has at his disposal. He must decide how he is going to treat the text, how much to alter, how much to conserve, how much work to do for, how much to leave to, the reader. In short, he has to decide on his approach and the presentation of his critical apparatus.

In a single-manuscript edition, this largely boils down to two problems: should an individual emendation, or proposed emendation, be put in the text or confined to the notes?; and how are divergences from the manuscript reading to be signalled to the reader? In the latter case, printing costs and publishers' stipulations may play a major part. The use of italics to show emendations, as in Professor Holden's edition of the *Roman de Rou* (1970–3), is an excellent idea, and would be of particular value in editions where the rejected readings are not shown on the same page as the text, but it may be ruled out by external factors. On the other hand, the use of brackets to indicate words or letters which have been introduced to the text is widely accepted. Probably the best solution in a single manuscript case is to print all variations at the foot of the page, except such additions as can be shown by the use of brackets.

The former problem is more complex, and is hardly susceptible of prescription. Each editor will adopt a more or less conservative approach to the text, according to his nature. I believe the editor should incline towards conservatism: as Professor Holden says (1984 p.50), '[for an emendation to be made] . . . il faut d'abord que la leçon du manuscrit soit une faute évidente, et ensuite que la correction adoptée s'impose à l'exclusion de toute autre solution'. Taking the examples we have already considered in *Bel Inconnu*, at l.56 I would leave *la dame* in the text, and propose *la di(s)me* in a note, since the emendation is (*a*) wholly unsupported and (*b*) only one possible solution (cf. that of Perrie Williams). As for the correction to l.1794, I would incorporate it into the text, with a note justifying it on the grounds of the parallel with *Erec*. Line 3848 offers another instance where such a decision is required. The scribe wrote

> Hanas, copes d'or et d'argent
> Et molt rice vaillement   3848

leaving a hypometric line. Williams restored the syllable count by emending to 'molt rice *autre* vaillement'. I believe that the model must have read

> Et molt rice vaissellement

and the scribe's eye jumped from the -*sse*- to the -*lle*- of *vaissellement*. However, as this remains conjecture I would maintain the scribe's text and confine my suggestion to a note.

To sum up, I believe the text should be left unchanged, where possible, and extensive notes should be used, preferably with asterisks to show which lines have notes, as in W. Roach's edition of Manessier (1983). This solution is not ideal, and may not always be possible. A better approach in many ways is that of the parallel text, as used in A. Bayot's edition of *Gormont et Isembart* (1931), in which the manuscript transcription and the edited text are printed on facing pages. Even when that (expensive) approach is adopted, however, extensive notes will probably be necessary to explain and justify many of the editor's decisions. Furthermore, in cases where the manuscript is very good the editor may need to make so few changes that such a layout is totally unjustified.

Lacunae

To some extent, the treatment of definite and possible lacunae in the text is a special instance of editorial practice. Where definite lacunae are concerned, the question is how, if at all, the gap is to be filled. W. A. Nitze's use of the prose version of the *Joseph* springs to mind, in his edition of Robert de Boron's *Roman de l'Estoire dou Graal* (1971): the prose is based on the verse text, and is in broadly similar language. The editor has only to decide whether to include his borrowing in the text or whether to relegate it to a note. In the case of *Bel Inconnu*, the cognate versions or the sixteenth-century prose are possible sources, but any borrowing from them would have to be left in the notes, and perhaps even given in summary, as the language used is in each case so markedly different from that of the main text. Of course, there may be no possible source to 'combler la lacune', and the editor will be reduced to the familiar row of dots and a note.

In the case of possible lacunae, that may also be all that is possible, but the editor must first decide whether or not he is in fact dealing with a lacuna. This is often extremely difficult: the case of triplets, for instance, is a contentious one. While most editors believe that a triplet represents a line omitted (or conceivably added, in some cases) by a scribe, others maintain that mediaeval authors may not have been so scrupulous in their versification. Here, while we must remain suspicious of the evidence of even close cognate versions, we can at least consult our scribal 'error patterns', although their usefulness will depend on the texts and numbers of manuscripts involved. For example, the evidence of *Hunbaut* and *Fergus* suggests that all the triplets in *Bel Inconnu* are the result of scribal errors. The editor should also be particularly suspicious when he meets two triplets 'back to back'. It is highly likely that they represent a scribal alteration of the rhyme of one of the two middle lines, so turning a quatrain and a couplet (or the reverse) into two triplets.

Another point to consider in relation to triplets is the precise point at which the putative lacuna occurs. For instance, ll.2093 ff. of *Bel Inconnu* read:

Cil li respont: 'Or oi folie!	a (2093)
Par ci ne passerés vos mie;	b
Cest casement tieg de m'amie.'	c (2096)

Not unreasonably, Perrie Williams puts a lacuna at 2094, and treats lines b and c as a couplet. However, looking at ll.405–6:

| 'Par ci ne passerés vos mie | |
| Que bataille n'en soit furnie.' | 406 |

we might equally be inclined to posit a lacuna at 2095, resulting from the omission of a line like 406:

Cil li respont: 'Or oi folie!	2093
Par ci ne passerés vos mie	
[*Que bataille n'en soit furnie*;]	
Cest casement tieg de m'amie.'	2096

No firm conclusion is possible, of course, but this example shows how carefully we should consider such instances, as well as the use one can sometimes make of other parts of the text when considering emendations and lacunae.

Similarly, the editor should examine any possible lacunae very attentively. In some cases, a lacuna may not be immediately obvious, but can be shown to be present. A good example is found at l.2161:

As espees souvent s'asaillent.	
Sor les elmes tes cols feroient	
Que estinceles en voloient.	2160
A genillons souvent se metent;	
Nostre Signor del ciel proumetent	
Aummones et vels plenteïs,	
Que lor sires i fust ocis.	2164

where the knights must surely be forcing each other to their knees, and then the populace are on their knees praying for the success of the Bel Inconnu. It seems likely that the scribe jumped from one line beginning 'A genillons' to another. The editor should be particularly wary of assuming that every textual difficulty implies the presence of a lacuna, and should always remember that an apparent lacuna can sometimes be 'removed' by a small change to the text. This struck me on reading the opening lines of *Rigomer*:

> Jehans qui en maint bien s'afaite
> Et pluisor bele rime a faite
> Nos a un romanç commenchié.
> Assés briément l'a romanchié
> Des aventures de Bretaigne.   5
> Bien cuic que des mellors ataingne.
> Del roi Artu et de ses houmes
> Est cis roumans que nos lisoumes . . .
> Si est tels chevaliers le roi,
> U plus ot sens et mains desroi.   10
> Quant plus ot sens, de desroi mains,
> Dont fu ço mesire Gauwains.

The editor, W. Foerster, assumed a lacuna at the end of line 8, as indicated, printing in the rejected readings 8 *Handschrift keine Lücke* and 9 *tel chevalier*. However, it seemed to me that simply changing *tel* to *del* in line 9 would remove the need for any such assumption. Lines 9–12 would then mean, approximately, 'And it [the *roumans*] is about the knight of King Arthur in whom there was the most *sens* and the least *desroi*. That being the case [that he had the most *sens* and the least *desroi*], we are obviously talking about Sir Gawain.' Compare ll.2399–408 of *Yvain*. It is worth noting that *Rigomer* may be seen partly as an attempt to restore Gauvain to his former pre-eminent position in the Round Table 'pecking order', a position undermined by the rise of such heroes as Lancelot and, to a lesser extent, Perceval. Interestingly, when I had the opportunity to examine the Chantilly manuscript, I found that the manuscript reading was indeed *del chevalier*, although the scribe's *d*'s and *t*'s were similar enough to explain the editor's misreading.

Should the editor suggest a line or piece of text to fill a lacuna? Only, I feel, if he can do so by borrowing a piece of the same text from elsewhere, or if there is a very close cognate which contains the relevant passage. The former would be the case for ll.2093–6 of *Bel Inconnu*, mentioned previously. The latter might apply if the passage in question was a borrowing from *Erec*, for example. It would seem prudent to confine any such suggestion to the notes.

These brief observations are not intended as a blueprint for editing single-manuscript texts but rather as points which the editor of such a

text might consider. In conclusion, I feel compelled to remark that
anyone intending to undertake an edition of an Old French text, whether
it is found in one manuscript or in many, could hardly do better than to
study Tony Holden's exemplary work in the field.

References

Bayot, A. (ed.) (1931) *Gormont et Isembart*, Paris: Champion.
Breuer, H. and Stuerzinger, J. (eds) (1914) *Hunbaut*, Dresden: Gesellschaft
    für romanische Literatur.
Foerster, W. (ed.) (1908 and 1915) *Les Mervelles de Rigomer*, Dresden:
    Gesellschaft für romanische Literatur.
—— (ed.) (1890) *Kristian von Troyes: Erec und Enide*, Halle: Niemeyer.
—— and Reid, T. B. W. (eds) (1942) *Chrestien de Troyes: Yvain*,
    Manchester: Manchester University Press.
Frescoln, W. (ed.) (1983) *Guillaume Le Clerc: The Romance of Fergus*,
    Philadelphia: W. H. Allen.
Guerreau, A. (1982) 'Renaud de Bâgé', *Le Bel Inconnu*, structure
    symbolique et signification sociale', *Romania*, 103, pp. 28-82.
Hippeau, C. (ed.) (1860) *Le Bel Inconnu*, Paris, Repr. Geneva: Slatkine.
    (1969).
Holden, A. J. (ed.) (1970-73) *Le Roman de Rou de Wace*, Paris: Picard.
—— (ed.) (1984) *Waldef*, Berne: Fondation Bodmer.
Nitze, W. A. (ed.) (1971) *Robert de Boron: Le Roman de l'Estoire dou
    Graal*, Paris: Champion.
Perrie Williams, G. (ed.) (1915) *Li Biaus Desconneüs*, Paris, Oxford: Fox.
—— (ed.) (1929) *Le Bel Inconnu*, Paris: Champion.
Roach, W. (ed.) (1983) *The Continuations of the Old French* Perceval *of
    Chrétien de Troyes*, V *The Third Continuation by Manessier*,
    Philadelphia: American Philosophical Society.
Schofield, W. H. (1895) *Studies on Li beaus Desconus*, Boston: Harvard
    Studies IV.
Winters, M. (ed.) (1984) *The Romance of Hunbaut*, Leiden: Brill.

J. H. Marshall

3. THE TRANSMISSION OF THE LYRIC *LAIS* IN OLD FRENCH *CHANSONNIER T*

Copyists transcribing medieval strophic songs, in so far as they make provision for music at all, normally draw staves above the words of the first stanza only. Since the same music served for the succeeding stanzas, it would have been a waste of parchment to do more. But in non-strophic pieces such as lyric *lais* and *descorts* the usual procedure was to draw staves above the whole text. Because the music was through-composed, it was not enough for a copyist to supply music solely for the first strophe or versicle, since of necessity this could give no indication of the tunes to which the succeeding strophes were to be sung. But most *lais* and *descorts* do show musical repetitions: each strophe commonly displays at least a twofold musical symmetry, the music of the first half of the strophe being re-used for the second half (minor responsion). And some of the more complex *lais* also involve the recurrence of whole blocks of musical material at intervals within the structure (major responsion). A copyist was therefore not obliged to transcribe the whole of the music from beginning to end: just as no eighteenth-century composer wrote out every note of a minuet and trio, so the patterns of minor and major responsions in a lyric *lai* could be satisfactorily represented without the provision of notes for every part of the text.

This is precisely what the copyist of the Old French *chansonnier T* (B.n., f. fr., 12615) set out to do for a number of lyric *lais*. The difficulties he encountered in adopting this procedure pose many problems for the modern textual and musical scholar, over and above the ordinary hazards of medieval textual transmission so familiar to the recipient of the present essay. The copyist's problem stemmed from the difficulty of unambiguously laying out text and (partial) notation on the page, without the aid of such modern devices as repeat signs, *da capo al segno* directions, or the ordered disposition of several lines of text beneath a single line of music. He availed himself of only one simple procedure: the alternation of segments of notated text with blocks of unnotated text. To a medieval performer aware of performance conventions, this was no doubt all that was required. The modern scholar or performer finds himself obliged to deduce these conventions from the scribal procedures themselves. Our notion of the metrical structure of each text depends on an examination of the scribe's lay-out of words with and without notes. And our notion of the musical structure of each piece depends on the study of its metrical structure. Solutions to these interrelated problems require examination of the procedures which the scribe adopted in the accomplishment of his dual task.

The eleven *lais* grouped together in MS *T* are not set off from the surrounding material. Following directly on a motet by the Moine de Saint Denis (Raynaud, 1884, 33), the *lai*-section begins at the bottom of f.61^V with the rubric of the first piece (the text of which opens at the top of f.62^r) and continues as far as the first line of f.76^V, where the end of the eleventh *lai* is followed immediately by the rubric and notated text of a *chanson avec des refrains* by Pierre le Borgne (Raynaud, 1884, 824). The following table of rubrics will serve to indicate summarily the contents of the section, together with the short titles used in the present essay.

61v–63^V.	Ci comencent li lai Ernoul li Vielle de Gastinois, et cis est de Nostre Dame. [*Nostre Dame*]
63v–66^r.	C'est ci li Viés Testamens et li Noveaus. [*Testament*]
66r–67^r.	Li lais du Kievrefoel. [*Kievrefoel*]
67r–68^r.	Li lais de le Rose. [*Rose*]
68r–69^r.	C'est li lais d'Aelis. [*Aelis*]
69r–70^V.	C'est chi li lais des Amans. [*Amans*]
71r–72^r.	Li lais des Puceles. [*Puceles*]
72r–73^V.	Li lais Markiol. [*Markiol*]
73v–74^r.	Uns lais de Nostre Dame, contre le lai Markiol. [*Flors*]
74r–75^V.	Li lais Nompar. [*Nompar*]
75v–76^V.	De bel' Yzabel. Contredis. [*Yzabel*]

Seven of the texts (all except *Kievrefoel, Flors,* and the two Franco-Occitan pieces *Markiol* and *Nompar*) are *unica*. All are, or were intended to be, notated, with the exception of *Flors*, which, as its rubric indicates, was sung to the tune of *Markiol*: the scribe therefore copied it without any provision for music. The text of *Markiol* is notated throughout, that of *Nompar* has staves throughout, although the notation breaks off at the foot of f.74^V. Of the remaining eight texts, the first seven have partial notation; *Yzabel* is ruled for partial notation (i.e. only some sections of the text have staves) which has not been inserted.

The importance of the *T*-copyist in the transmission of the lyric *lais* would justify a study of his scribal practice far more ambitious than the present essay which has a more limited aim. After an examination of the scribe's methods of setting out the words and music of the *lais* on the page, some of the editorial problems encountered in establishing a readable and singable text of the notated Old French *lais* (i.e. the first seven pieces) are illustrated with specific reference to the relation of text, music, and metre: neither purely textual issues not involving the music nor purely musical issues not involving the text are raised here. Line references refer to Jeanroy, Brandin, and Aubry (1901), which, despite its serious textual and musical shortcomings, is likely to remain the only complete edition until replaced by that at present in preparation by Miss Ann Buckley. For many of the points raised in this chapter I have profited from discussion with Miss Buckley. I am grateful also to her for allowing me to see her transcriptions of the music, which are far more accurate than any hitherto available. Reference is also made to other editions and musico-metrical analyses of the *lais*; but purely textual editions and studies are not discussed.

    It is possible to follow in some detail the copyist's operations. He first ruled in dry-point thirty-six lines per page. He then copied the texts, leaving two lines blank above each line of text wherever the latter was to be notated; but copying the text on consecutive lines wherever it was to remain without notation. Where an unnotated segment of text came to an end in the middle of a line, he left the remainder of the line blank, starting the next portion of (notated) text at the beginning of the next line but two, i.e. after leaving the appropriate space in which a stave could later be drawn. At intervals, he left a blank of appropriate size to accommodate a coloured initial. These are in general intended to mark out the musico-metrical sub-divisions of the texts, though they do not do so in any absolutely consistent way.

    These procedures, if followed through without forethought, would sometimes have left the copyist with one or two blank lines at the bottom of the page. This he avoided. Where a single empty line would have been left over at the foot of the page, he contrived to leave a line blank at a more appropriate point higher up the page. Thus, on f.63$^\mathrm{V}$ (after the end of *Nostre Dame*) and on f.74$^\mathrm{r}$ (after the end of *Flors*) he left three (instead of two) blank lines to accommodate the first stave of the following piece. Where two blank lines would otherwise have been left over at the foot of a page, he resolved the difficulty by continuing his text on to a supernumerary (37th) line, thus following his usual practice of leaving two lines blank (the 35th and 36th) to accommodate the stave. This occurs six times (at the bottom of ff.64$^\mathrm{r}$, 68$^\mathrm{V}$, 69$^\mathrm{r}$, 70$^\mathrm{V}$, 71$^\mathrm{r}$, 71$^\mathrm{V}$).

In each of the spaces left blank for the purpose, the copyist then drew a five-line stave. His normal practice was to draw the stave the full width of the page, as far as the right-hand margin, regardless of whether the whole of the text beneath it needed (or was intended) to carry notation. Even at the end of *Kievrefoel, Nompar,* and *Yzabel* (ff.67^r, 75^v, and 76^v), where the last word of the text fell in the middle of the line, he prolonged the stave to the right margin, so that the rubric of the following piece had to be placed under a superfluous portion of blank stave. It was only at the end of *Testament, Amans,* and *Markiol* (ff.66^r, 70^v, and 73^v) that the scribe chose to end his stave above the last word of the text, leaving a blank space three lines deep which, in the first and third instances, was subsequently filled with the rubric for the next piece. This disposition of text, stave, and rubric demonstrates that the staves were drawn only after the texts were complete and that the rubrics were inserted (apparently by the same copyist) only after the staves had been drawn. It was at this stage that an illuminator inserted the coloured initials in the spaces which had earlier been left blank for them. The fact that ff.75^r–76^r, which have empty staves, do not lack rubrics and coloured initials suggests that the work of rubrication and illumination preceded the insertion of the music.

It was only now that the notes were copied on to the staves. It is impossible to determine whether the music was inserted by the text-scribe himself. Since the latter had enough musical knowledge to execute the quite complicated lay-out of the text in preparation for the insertion of the notes (even if, as is probable, he was copying from an exemplar with a similar lay-out), it is quite possible that he was responsible for text and music. But there is no sign that he profited by this opportunity to rectify mistakes or omissions in the text, even where he must have been aware of a textual deficiency. This might be held to indicate that the music-copyist was *not* identical with the text-copyist and regarded a defective text as no business of his. For simplicity's sake, however, I refer throughout this essay to 'the copyist'.

Where a stave offered more space than was strictly necessary, the copyist had a choice of two procedures: he could leave the superfluous portion of stave unfilled; or he could insert as much of the next musical phrase as it would accommodate, the incomplete series of notes serving as a useful cue for the musical repetition. His procedure seems to have varied from text to text. In the first four *lais* copied, there is only one instance of the right-hand portion of the stave being left blank (*Nostre Dame,* 124–5). But in *Aelis* there are six (17–18, 31, 45, 61–6, 69, 98), in *Amans* two (12–14, 145), and in *Puceles* two (40–4, 206–9).

As he proceeded with his work the copyist seems to have cared less about the appearance of the written page (which is not enhanced by partially empty staves). He may simply have become increasingly lazy.

Three types of scribal error involving text and music are conceivable: those in which a musical error stems from a mistaken scansion of the text; those where the presence of a textual error is indicated by the music; and cases where both text and music are faulty. In addition, the fitting of music to unnotated portions of text can present considerable difficulty.

Even where the text is correctly copied, the copyist is guilty of one recurrent musical error which, since it affects our perception of the metrical structure of the text, requires mention. In lines containing an elided vowel (usually a final -*e*), he was sometimes misled into providing an extra note, thereby falsifying not only the musical phrase but also the scansion of the text. It is only by reference to parallel lines within the musico-metrical structure that we can deduce the correct syllable-count. An example will make the procedure clearer. Lines 242–9 of *Testament* are eight masculine heptasyllables each sung to the musical phrase

but for l.244 (*Chascuns par le monde ala*), the copyist, scanning *mondë ala*, provided eight notes by repeating the final B of the phrase. In l.247 (*Sainte Eglise comença*), he scanned *Saintë Eglise* and provided eight notes by writing the initial C of the musical phrase four times instead of three. The same error recurs a number of times in the *lais*, e.g. *Testament* 60 (scanning *li avoit* instead of *l'avoit*), 81 (*balancë adés*) and 174 (*presencë et*); *Kievrefoel* 91 (*jovenes* counted as three syllables instead of two); *Rose* 9 (*m'amië a*); *Aelis* 7 (*folië ou*); *Amans* 119–20 (*afairë em*); *Puceles* 155–6 (*droiturë ens*) and 194 (*bellë amer*). In many of these passages, failure to recognise the scribe's mistake led Jeanroy into misguided textual corrections and Aubry into musical errors. Once the reason for the presence of a superfluous note is recognised, restitution normally presents no problem.

Where the scribe found himself placing the music above a line that was already textually deficient, he nevertheless quite often copied the music correctly. We must suppose that in many such cases he was aware of the textual error, even though he did not bother to correct it. Thus at *Nostre Dame* 83, though the text has *saintisme* for *saintismement*, he correctly gave the seven notes the line required. At *Nostre Dame* 223 he omitted the word *nos* but did not omit the note which went with it. Similarly, a textual defect does not give rise to a musical error in *Testament* 58 (hypometric, with *deseur* instead of [*de*] *deseur*) and 87 (hypermetric by one syllable); in *Amans* 31 (where *leuree*, printed as *l'eüree* by Jeanroy, is a mistake for *l'eure*), 33 (hypometric: read *De ce ki* [*mais*] *m'atalente*) and 102 (hypermetric: read *s'el* for *s'ele*); in *Puceles* 10 (where the copyist wrote *prex* instead of *pitex*) and 190 (where *lai baillie* is no doubt a mistake for *l'assaillir*). Two other cases involve a mechanical slip of which the scribe was obviously aware. At *Testament* 5 he wrote *est* twice and even placed two notes above the dittography, but he spaced out the rest of the musical phrase so as to give only the correct number of notes above the whole line. Similarly, in *Aelis* 1, where he had written *de parfont trop* instead of *trop de parfont*, he placed the eight notes of the line in such a way that the eighth lay above *-font*, with the misplaced *trop* having no note above it.

In a number of lines not obviously dissimilar to those just discussed, the copyist allowed a textual error to lead him into musical error. Such cases require a twofold restoration, which can be substantiated only by the convergence of textual, metrical, and musical evidence. Correction therefore involves a particularly delicate reconciliation of the claims of philology and musicology. Prudence causes me to limit myself to a couple of examples. At *Rose* 11–12, the MS offers the textual reading:

> Diex, ki iés la clés
> A tos biens mais,

the second line being summarily corrected by Jeanroy to *De tos biens*, which constitutes the first three syllables of his l.12. Maillard (1963, p.259) simply reproduces the MS readings. Two other lines occupy a place in the metrical scheme analogous to that of 12, namely 67 (*Ki me soit remés*) and 141 (*Nule autre n'est tex*). These clearly indicate that at 12 the metrical pattern demands a five-syllable line rhyming in -*és* (with *e* < tonic free *a*), as is supposed in the schema offered by Spanke (1938, pp.190–1). The correction to *A tos biens només* ('God, who art named the key to all that is good') is an obvious restoration of rhyme, syllable-count, and sense. But what of the music? Line 141 is without notation. At 12, the copyist offers us

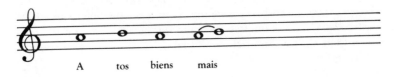

at 67

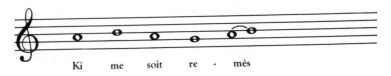

Clearly, at l.12 the copyist was induced by the deficiency of his text to truncate the musical phrase in order to accommodate it to a line of four syllables. If my transcriptions are accepted, suppletion of the missing note G above the missing syllable *no-* gives a satisfactory solution. What I have transcribed as an A–B ligature is written by the scribe as an ordinary *podatus* in 12 but as a *quilisma* in 67. The only other passage in the *lais* where he uses this latter note-form (f.71^r, staves 1 and 2: *Puceles* 1–12) strongly suggests that for him the *quilisma*, the *epiphonus*, and the ascending *plica* were interchangeable.

At *Amans* 10, another scribal reduction of a five-syllable line to four syllables occurs. The text is readily restored as *Cil s'[en] entremet*, the scribal error being a simple haplography. That the line should (as Jeanroy already thought) have five syllables is confirmed by the following line (*Ki son cuer i met*) and by the four unnotated lines which conclude strophe II and which are — quite mistakenly — reduced by Jeanroy to two:

21   Mon cuer vers li tor,
21a   Si ke sans retor
21b   Ke plus n'i demor
22   Li otroi m'amor.

Again, what of the music? At 7 the copyist offers

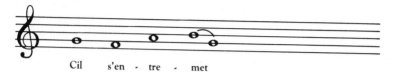

Cil   s'en - tre - met

but at 8

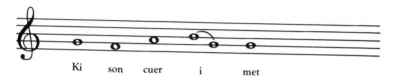

Ki   son   cuer   i   met

The correction, by suppletion of the final G, is obvious.

Not all cases are so easily restored. Nevertheless, it is possible, by balancing the probabilities of error in the music or in the text, to arrive at a satisfactory solution of a high proportion of musico-metrical problems, providing one has regard to the copyist's habits. A particularly relevant example occurs in ll.48, 52, 72, and 76 of *Testament*. In Jeanroy's text, all four lines are octosyllabic, although the first three are made so only by editorial interference:

    48   Des Noé, si come j'ai dit [com MS]
    52   Ysaac son enfant petit [son fill petit MS]
    72   Assés de teus [lors] i avoit
    76   Et tel i ot ki conissoit.

Lines 48, 52, and 72 are written out with their music, in each instance the same seven-note phrase

the only musical variant being the use of a C–D ligature instead of the D in l.48. The consistency of both music and scansion in the first three instances clearly indicates that a heptasyllabic line, sung to the musical phrase quoted, was what was intended here. Typically, it was when writing out text without music that the copyist mistook the scansion. It requires no greater ingenuity to correct l.76 to *Tel i ot ki covissoit*, 'there were some who were covetous'. Jeanroy, by choosing to correct

the other three lines on the pattern of 76, falsified the metrical pattern
four times over; and Aubry, slavishly following him as usual, botched
the musical phrase four times over. A balancing of the claims of text
and music is evidently not guaranteed by such collaboration between
philologist and musicologist, however eminent. Nor does Maillard
(1964) resolve the problem: he follows his predecessors in taking ll.72
and 76 as octosyllables sung to an eight-note phrase, although he
maintains 48 and 52 as heptasyllables.

Where a whole line of text is omitted, the copyist's normal practice is
to omit the whole of the corresponding musical phrase. This is the case,
for example, in *Kievrefoel* 7 and in *Nostre Dame* 87. Restoration
presents no great problem here: in the former passage, it is easy to
restore the missing line (as Jeanroy silently does) from the other
complete MS, the missing music (as Aubry does) from that of l.1; in the
latter (where the text is left blank by Jeanroy), one may readily conjecture
the suppletion [*Virge esperitable*] and, with Aubry, Jeanroy *et al.*,
(1901) and Maillard (1964), fill the musical lacuna by re-using here the
recurrent musical phrase which the copyist provided for ll.2, 4, 9–13,
16, 18, and 20. It ought to be stressed, however, that this musical
suppletion, plausible though it is, cannot be substantiated in any absolute
way from the text as we have it. The metrical unit

    a b a b c   ent, ié, able
    7 7 7 7 5'

which occupies ll.83–7 (87 being the missing line), is repeated three
times, to form three more five-line units, at 88–102; the fifth line of
each unit is an invocation consisting of *Virge* plus an adjective in *-able*,
whence my proposed textual restoration. And the same fourfold
repetition of the five-line metrical unit recurs, with new rhyme-endings,
at 124–43. Since, however, ll.90–102 and 124–43 are transmitted by
the scribe without notation, not one of these seven five-line units can
provide the musical material which would serve to complete the defective
first unit with absolute certainty. Aubry's suppletion, though accepted
without comment by Spanke (1938, p.195) and by Maillard, must
remain an unsupported hypothesis.

This last instance illustrates the dilemma which faces those who seek
to restore a textually and musically defective passage. Suppletions can
be regarded as entirely reliable only when a parallel passage, i.e. a unit
which we deduce to be metrically and musically identical, is transmitted
in a textually complete form with all its music. But if one unit is
defective, how can we know that the supposedly 'parallel' unit, itself not
defective, is actually a repetition of the same pattern? How, indeed, do

we know that one unit *is* defective? If a metrically aberrant passage is also semantically or syntactically deficient (i.e. it does not 'make sense'), we may reasonably regard its defectiveness as established beyond doubt. But in many cases it is an irregularity in the metrical pattern alone which alerts us to the likelihood of a textual deficiency. The best that can be hoped for in such cases is that a posited correction should achieve at one and the same time textual, metrical, and musical sense. An example will illustrate the precariousness of such arguments. Strophe XVII of *Testament*, which deals with the humanity of Christ, appears in Jeanroy *et al.* (1901) as follows:

> C'est la fois, c'est la creance,
> Ce doit on croire et savoir,
> 168 Ke sa saintisme naissance
> Fu faite por nos valoir,
> Car il fu en tel estance,
> Chil ki velt le puet veoir,
> 172 Moult nos valoit s'acointance
> . . . .
> Sa presence et sa poissance
> . . . .
> 176 Mais la honte et la viltance
> . . . .
> La presence k'en soffrance
> . . . .
> 180 Reçut sa chars, ke poissance
> Contre mort ne vaut avoir.

Jeanroy, postulating the omission of four lines, was content with the laconic observation: '173, 175, 177, 179 manquent: le sens et le rythme le prouvent'. Despite the sheer improbability of a copyist skipping four non-contiguous lines out of eight and nevertheless arriving at a text which (*pace* Jeanroy) more or less makes sense, this conception of the passage passed on into Aubry's reconstruction of the music, as well as into Maillard (1964). And yet the metrical assumption on which Jeanroy's four lines of dots are based is entirely false. He assumed that ll.172–9 must be metrically identical with the six lines which precede and the two which follow them, i.e. that they must consist of an alternation of feminine and masculine heptasyllables on the rhymes *-ance* and *-oir*. But the presence of internal rhymes in 174 and 178 might have alerted him to the fact that the lines which are actually parallel with 172–81 occur in his strophe XX, namely ll.214–19 (though here Jeanroy chose to print the two heptasyllables with internal rhyme as four trisyllabic lines, thereby disguising the near-identity of the two metrical units). What ought, above all, to have alerted him to the parallel structure of 166–81 and 206–19 is the near-identity of the music of 206–8 with that of 166–8 (after the first syllable of 209 the text is unnotated). In other words, the music of 206–8 acts as a cue for a large-scale repeat, the music of strophes XVII–XIX serving for XX–XXII.

Jeanroy's misconception about the metre led Aubry into an equally misconceived regularising of the music of 166–81, whereby each of the eight couplets reconstituted by Jeanroy (twelve lines of text and four lines of dots) is sung to an identical reconstituted pair of musical phrases, which the MS attests in precisely this form only for ll.96–7. Such generalising of one form of a musical phrase at the expense of all variant forms is constant in Aubry's handling of the music of the *lais*. On many occasions, as here, he gives an utterly misleading picture of the MS transmission of the music. Cf. the well-founded protestations of Maillard (1963, p.280, n.701). Nevertheless Maillard (1964), though he largely restored the MS readings for the other lines, followed Aubry exactly in the music which he gave for the four ghost-lines.

What, then, of the text which was the starting-point for these musical misunderstandings? With one small emendation (in 178) and some modification of Jeanroy's punctuation, it makes perfectly acceptable sense:

172   Moult nos valoit s'acointance,
174   Sa presence   et sa poissance.
176   Mais la honte et la viltance,
178   La pesance [presence MS]   k'en soffrance
180   Reçut sa chars, ke poissance
181   Contre mort ne vaut avoir,

XVIII

182   Ne ne vaut ne ne dut mie,
183   Car nature le requiert:
184   C'est çou ki nos rendi vie [. . .]

('. . . His frequenting of men, His presence on earth and His power brought us great profit. But the shame and the degradation, the grievous burden that His flesh patiently bore, for He would have no power over death, nor did He wish to nor ought He, for so human nature requires —

this it is which gave us life . . .'). Even the awkward repetition of *poissance* (174, 180) and of *vaut* (181, 182) may be ascribed to the author's clumsiness of expression, rather than to the copyist's carelessness. Certainly, he was less inattentive than editors have supposed.

Problems of 'restoration' are at their most acute when one attempts to match the incompletely notated music to the totality of the text. It is reasonable to make one basic assumption here, namely that the copyist (barring unintended slips and omissions) gave enough music to allow the unnotated portions of text to be sung. Where the metrical forms are simple no problem arises. The middle strophes of *Kievrefoel* (III–XI) are all eight-line structures showing a fourfold metrical symmetry. The scribe notates the first two-and-a-half, or three, or three-and-a-half lines of each strophe. Since, at the beginning of the third line of each strophe, the music begins to repeat the tune of the first line, it is safe to assume that each of the nine strophes in question had the musical form ABABABAB.

But not all *lais* display so straightforward a musico-metrical structure. Problems occur when the analysis of the component metrical units is not clear to the eye of the researcher (especially if the eye is not guided by a musical ear). I propose to conclude this essay by offering a solution to one such problem which has, in my judgement, never been satisfactorily resolved. Of the last four strophes of *Rose* (X–XIII, ll.148–225) only X and the first one-and-a-half lines of XI are notated, the music for the opening of XI being an exact repeat of the opening of X and therefore clearly indicating that from the beginning of XI the music is to repeat. And yet XI is not identical in form with X (it is in fact twice as long); XII, though the same length as XI, does not repeat its metrical structure; and XIII is not identical with any of the previous three strophes. Three different reconstructions, which it would be tedious to discuss in detail, are offered by Aubry (Jeanroy *et al.*, 1901), by Spanke (1938, pp.193–4), and by Maillard (1963, pp.257–8). All are fatally flawed by their mistaken analyses of the metrical structure of strophe X. Jeanroy's puzzlement over strophe XII is abundantly clear from his desire to replace the rhyme-words of four lines (191, 193, 198, 201) and by his 'correction' of two perfectly good pentasyllabic lines to trisyllables at 199–200. Each time, as so often in the *lais*, it is the copyist who is right! The key to a solution lies in the fact that XI is exactly twice as long as X. The musico-metrical form of the twelve lines of X may be represented schematically as

A	B	C^1	C^2	D		E		C^3	C^3	F	C^4	C^5	G
a	a	b	b	a		a		c	c	d	e	e	d
5'	5'	3'	3'	5'		5'		3'	3'	5'	3'	3'	5'
	(unit 1)					(unit 2)			(unit 3)				

Provided one analyses the structure of the twelve lines asymmetrically as indicated above (5 + 1 + 6 lines), the way in which the author of *Rose* constructed the twenty-four-line strophe which follows becomes immediately clear: it consists of each unit twice (112233): 10 + 2 + 12 = 24 lines. Applying the same mode of analysis to strophe XII–plus–XIII (and ignoring all editorial interferences with metre and rhyme), one finds that this long concluding strophe offers unit 1 three times, unit 2 three times, and unit 3 four times (schematically 1112223333). The 'extra' repetition of the third unit is no doubt to be regarded as equivalent to an *envoi*, rounding off the whole *lai*. Viewed in this way, repetitions of the music of strophe X exactly fit the succeeding sixty-six lines of the text and bring it to a striking and musically satisfying conclusion. The analysis may appear excessively mathematical. But for that I make no apology: in the Middle Ages music and mathematics are closely allied. And the much maligned copyist, in providing so much music and no more, showed himself to be more aware of this point than modern scholars have been.

References

Jeanroy, A., Brandin, L. and Aubry, P. (1901) *Lais et descorts français du XIIIe siècle: texte et musique*, Paris. Reprinted Geneva: Slatkine Reprints, 1975.

Maillard, J. (1963) *Evolution et esthétique du lai lyrique*, Paris: Centre de Documentation Universitaire.

—— (1964) *Lais et chansons d'Ernoul de Gastinois*, Rome: American Institute of Musicology.

Raynaud, Gaston (1884) *Bibliographie des chansonniers français des XIIIe et XIVe siècles*, Paris: Vieweg. Revised by Spanke, H., *G. Raynauds Bibliographie des altfranzösischen Liedes, neu bearbeitet und ergänzt*, Leiden: Brill 1955 repr. 1980.

Spanke, H. (1938) Sequenz und Lai, *Studi Medievali*, n.s. 11, pp.12–68. Reprinted in Spanke, H. *Studien zu Sequenz, Lai und Leich*, ed. U. Aarburg, Darmstadt: Wissenschaftliche Buchgesellschaft, 1977, pp.146–202. Page-references are to the reprint.

4. ON THE VARIANTS, AND THEIR
PRESENTATION, IN SCHOLARLY EDITIONS OF
THE *ROMAN DE RENART*

We have three scholarly editions of the *Roman de Renart*: Martin (1882–87), Roques (1948–63), and Fukumoto *et al.* (1983 & 1985). They present, respectively, the three families of mss., alpha, beta, and gamma. As yet we have no edition of any of the so-called independent, non-family, full-length *Romans de Renart*.

Manuscripts of the *Roman de Renart* (A, B, C, etc.) are described in Fukumoto (1983, vol. 1, x–xii). For MS r, see Fukumoto (1987); for MS s, see Rossi and Asperti (1986); for MS t, see Suzuki *et al.* (1988); for an edition of n, see Harano (1987 & 1988); for an edition of part of the variant form of br.IV in MS H, see Chabaille (1835); for a discussion of this, see Varty (1989); for MS I, see Nieboer (1989).

Martin used A as his base ms. for branches I–XIV because he thought it was the nearest to the original *Roman de Renart*, filling the numerous lacunae from D. He used N for XV–XVII since A ends with XIV. For XVIII–XXII and XXIV he used B, the best representative as he saw it of the beta family (the next oldest family and therefore next nearest to the original); and for the remaining branches he used the one ms. in which each makes its unique appearance — M for XXIII, H for XXV, and L for XXVI. At the time he established his text, the alpha family was composed of MSS A, D, E, F, G and N; the beta family of B, K, L and the fragments a, b, c, and d as well as the half-related fragments e, h and q; and the gamma family of C, M and the extensive section of N known as little n. Martin was also familiar with the full-length, independent MSS H and I, and the independent fragments f, g, and i. MS O was discovered too late to be included in his list of variants, but he mentions it in his preface. He deliberately excluded F and G as being too close to E to be worthwhile separate mention. He also deliberately excluded I as being too divergent to cope with, and as a very inferior *Roman de Renart*. He quietly passed over the second appearance of branch IV, 'Le Puits', contained in H: it, too, would probably have been too divergent for his system of presenting variants to cope with. A pity, for these — MS I and the variant branch IV of MS H — are two of the most fascinating variants in the whole of the *Roman de Renart*. Furthermore, Martin excluded the variant readings of all fragments except a, e, and n. In spite of these omissions and exclusions, his list of variants is formidable. Within his self-imposed limits and those due simply to his ignorance of the existence of some MSS, his long list of 'variants (611 pages compared with 864 pages of established text) commands admiration and great respect. The text of each branch is compared with the corresponding text for all but the most minor (largely orthographic) differences thus: in branches I–XIV within the relevant range of B, C, D, E, H, K, L, M, N, a, e, and n; in branches XV–XVII within the relevant range of B, C, D, E, H, K, L, M, and n: and in branches XVIII–XXII within the relevant range of L, C, and M. The inadequacies of the omissions (deliberate or otherwise) remain as follows:

for branches		
Ia, V, Va, VI, XII	no reference to F, G, I or O.
I, Ib, VII, IX	F, G, I, O and little o.
II	no reference to F, G, I, O and little l, r, s, and t.
III	no reference to F, G, I, O, and little s.
IV	no reference to F, G, I, O and little s, t and (for the second version of IV), H.
VIII	no reference to G, I and little b, c, d, q, or p (but does, exceptionally, refer to F).
X	no reference to F, G, I.
XI	no reference to F, G, I and little h and k.
XIII	no reference to F, G, I and little q.
XIV	F, G, I and little l.
XV	F, G, I, O and little l.
XVI	I.
XXI	little r.

Roques used B as his base ms. for all the branches of his edition. He chose B because he felt the time was ripe for the appearance of a scholarly edition of the *Roman de Renart* from each of the remaining families, and there was more sense in beginning with the beta family as the second oldest of the three; and from within this family, B was the most complete. Furthermore, the other two members of this family suffered from serious defects — K being far from complete and L 'plus récent et partiellement composite'. Roques gave not only all the important variants from K and L but also, whenever useful in his view, from their cousins or, rather, independents H and (for branches I, Ia, and Ib) I, together with the fragments b, c, and d. He also referred to, on occasion, A, D, and N from the alpha family; and C, M, and n from the gamma family. As in Martin's edition, so in Roques's, much space is given to the inclusion of variants. The one volume in which he presents branches I, Ia, and Ib is typical: 109 pages of established text, 42 pages of variants. One might criticise Roques's failure to use the partially related fragment q for *Le Pèlerinage*, and H for the second version of *Le Puits*; but one cannot criticise his failure to use the partially related fragment e for *Renart médecin*, or I for parts of branches II, XIV, and XV, or m for parts of branches II and XIX since these had gone missing between the end of Martin's period of research and the beginning of his own. (And fragments r, s, and t have been discovered since the end of Roques's period of research.) The chief inadequacies of his edition therefore remain (where variant readings are concerned), the unfortunate absence of *Renart empereur*, unfinished at the time of his death and which he would have had to compare with L and H and little h; and his bypassing of the problem of presenting the variants of the second version of *Le Puits* in H. Little r would now need to be compared with part of the *Tiécelin* episode, and for part of that featuring *Patous*; and little s, also for part of *Tiécelin*, the *Vol des poissons, Le Puits,* and *Le Viol d'Hersent.*

Fukumoto *et al.* use C as their base MS. Evidently they decided that, between a choice of a representative of the gamma family and one of the independent MSS, it was time to edit a gamma MS; and they chose C, giving all the variants of M but not, sadly, those of the substantial section of N known as little n. It is Fukumoto *et al.* who have, since publishing their fine edition of the *Roman de Renart*, discovered and published the fragments r and t which are also relevant to the gamma family (Fukumoto, 1987); both for part of *Chantecler*, r alone for part of branch XXI (*Patous*), and t alone for part of branch IV (*Le Puits*). The half-related fragment k (relevant to branch XI, *Renart empereur*, has, like e, l, and m, gone missing.

We are left, then, without any scholarly edition of the important independents H, I, and O; and, from the alpha family, D, E, N, F, and G; from the beta family K and L; and from the gamma family, M.

Apart from the above-mentioned omissions (for whatever reason) from the editions of Martin, Roques, and Fukumoto *et al.*, the chief problem for the reader of the first two is the off-putting appearance of the variants and the difficulty of reconstructing a reading of any one line for which there are several readings. *Yet many of these variants are of great interest either to the philologist or to the scholar whose main interest is in evaluating the artistic and literary qualities of these stories.* They are difficult partly because the basic information is not only presented in a welter of abbreviations, letters, and numbers, but also because vital pieces of relevant information are given at different places in the edition: i.e., reasons for choice of base MS, the list of rejected readings, the variants themselves, etc. Above all they lack an introductory editorial comment with some detailed examples of the qualities and characteristics of the variant readings which would help the philologist and the literary commentator. They also lack notes (some of which could and should be coupled with entries in a glossary) in which particularly interesting words, phrases, etc. are discussed.

The way in which the variants are presented in Fukumoto *et al.* has much to recommend it. They have, of course, the easiest task since they chose to compare with only one variant MS. They make the most of this by presenting the variant reading at the foot of the page of established text in the second of two lower-margin registers. The first of these registers contains all the rejected readings and information about the source of their correction (mostly M, but occasionally A, B, D, H, and O are drawn on). The use of two lower-margin registers in smaller type than is used for the established text has the advantage of enabling the reader to reconstruct both the base MS's reading and that of the variant(s) quite easily. Furthermore they have many notes in their section of Notes on individual words, phrases, lines, and sentences, etc. of special interest to the scholarly reader — notes which make considerable use of variant readings and other scholars' views about them. Two of the best examples of this editorial practice are to be found in their notes on the lines numbered 5 and 8 in both their own and Martin's edition:

De Tristan qui la chievre fist

and

Romanz de lui et de sa geste.

(In passing, if anyone doubts what I say about the difficulty of reading Martin's and Roques's variants, of re-establishing the text of the variant MSS etc., let him reconstruct the second of the two lines quoted above — as well as the uncorrected readings of the base MSS; then let him compare with what Fukumoto *et al.* offer in their notes; and let him ponder in particular all the variants which each editor gives for *lui* and *sa geste*.) To return to Fukumoto *et al.*'s critical apparatus, it seems to me they could have improved on their presentation and discussion of the variants by including (either by a sign within the body of the established text, or in the margin, or in the second lower-margin register) a cross-reference to the relevant note. For example, the variants for *qui* in the first of the two lines quoted above are admirably discussed on p.398 of their second volume but one only discovers this by a systematic reading of their notes. All that was needed was the inclusion of a footnote 'C: 5 qui, *see note*'.

Could Martin and Roques have done the same as Fukumoto *et al?* For Roques, yes; he would rarely have needed to put more than one rejected reading per page of established text, and rarely more than five lines of variants per page. (And, if one were redesigning the edition to include two lower-margin registers, one for rejected readings and one for variants, there would be a little less text per page and therefore proportionately less critical apparatus per page.) The situation would have varied from branch to branch because Roques, though more often than not comparing with only two or three other MSS, does occasionally compare with five or six. Martin, however, juggles with even more MSS and compares with as many as nine for some parts of some branches. If we take as an example p.2 of Vol. I with its thirty-six lines of established text (i.e. ll.25–60 of Br. I) — a page on which Martin already prints two lines of rejected readings in a lower-margin register, he would have needed thirty-two lines for the variants he prints on pp.1–2 of Vol. III; and these thirty-two lines are already in smaller print than that used for the established text. However, if he had confined himself to comparing with other alpha MSS, had this been an alpha *Roman de Renart*, he would have got all his variants into ten lines. He would then have managed to present twenty-eight lines of established text per page *and* got almost all the information his reader needs to reconstruct the base and the closely related family mss on the one page. But then, Martin published all his variants in a separate volume, so all the reader has to do is open this at the relevant page and supply his own register of variants.

If such a similar massive editorial enterprise were undertaken anew, it would surely be best if (rather than decide that this or that full-length ms. should be used from one end to the other as the base) a decision were taken to publish the branches one by one, each in a separate volume with its companion volume of variant readings. Perhaps even smaller units still should be presented in each volume, units like those given by Fukumoto *et al.* who have presented Martin's branch II as IIa (*Prologue*), IIb (*Chantecler*), IIc (*Mésange*) etc. One could go even further than they do and break up some of the branches in ways I have suggested in two recent essays (1987, 1989). Thus, *Renart empereur*, branch XI, includes XIa, 'L'Amitié de Renart et d'Isengrin', XIb, 'Renart et les mûres sauvages', XIc, 'Renart et Roonel', etc. Such a branch-by-branch narrative-unit-by-narrative-unit edition might well use a different base MS for each branch or unit. In this connection, perhaps the MS to use is the one that requires the least correction. If this had been important to Martin he might well have chosen D instead of A + N; and similarly Fukumoto *et al.* might have chosen M instead of C. For example my analysis of three units from Martin's branch II as told in the gamma MSS produces the following results.

Chantecler: on fifty-nine occasions C and M agree against n; M and n agree twenty-eight times against C; C and n agree twenty-two times against M; on eight occasions each of C, M and n differ from each other. Little n is blatantly faultier than either C or M on nineteen occasions either because rhyme words do not rhyme, or syllables are missing or added, or lines are missing, or the grammar is faulty and the sense is lost, or the spelling is radically wrong, etc. Fukumoto *et al.* find it necessary to correct six times by using M; Professor Lodge and I have edited M and find it necessary to correct M six times by using C. Clearly, as far as this family of MSS is concerned, an editor will use either C or M for this unit, but not n.

Tibert: on thirteen occasions C and M agree against n; M and n agree six times against C; C and n agree against M twice. Once again little n is clearly faulty on ten occasions where it differs from C and M for mostly the same reasons that it is faulty in *Chantecler*. On one occasion only it is superior to both the other MSS. These statistics point to M as preferable to C, and indeed Fukumoto *et al.* correct C by M four times, but Lodge and Varty (1989) do not find it necessary to correct M by C at all for this unit.

Hersent (Le Viol.): this episode is complete only in M and n. MS C lacks one folio, i.e. more than sixty lines of verse. The three MSS have unique readings on six occasions only (curiously all of these are to be found within the first fifty-one lines). On five occasions these unique readings are acceptable from any of the three MSS. On one only M seems preferable to the other two. All relate to very minor matters. On thirty-one occasions M and C are identical in their opposition to n. On twenty-two of these occasions the readings of C and M are equally acceptable, but on nine M is preferable to C. All relate to minor matters. On twenty-eight occasions M and n are identical in their opposition to C. Of these variant readings, sixteen are equally acceptable, but ten times the common readings of M and n are marginally preferable to C, while C's reading is perhaps better on two occasions. All relate to minor matters. Only six times are C and n identical and opposed to M. Three of these variants are equally acceptable, but on the other three occasions, the C + n readings are marginally preferable. All relate to minor matters. It emerges that M is to be preferred twenty-three times, C fourteen times, and n scarcely at all. In those lines common to M and n only (i.e. those lines corresponding to the ones missing from C), there are twenty-four variants of which twelve seem equally acceptable but twelve are manifestly superior in M. For this unit, an editor would presumably use M if he were editing only a gamma version of it.

But whether a future editor of the *Roman de Renart* proceeds branch by branch or unit by unit with parallel volumes, one for the established text and one for the rejected readings and all or a restricted number of related variant readings, together with a full, reasoned section of notes (possibly — preferably — linked to a full glossary), it seems vital to me that the variants be introduced by an editorial survey of both their linguistic and artistic implications. Confining these comments once more to examples from Martin's branch two, an editor might begin with some remarks on *general* linguistic differences, and offer a precise example or two, to prove rather than simply assert that these are normally without any profound significance, that normally they do not affect the narrative, but bear testimony to a considerable degree of language variation within literary French in the Middle Ages — a variation which would probably pass unnoticed by the listener. To prove this he might compare, from the *Tibert* episode three versions of the account of Tibert's response to Renart's invitation to him to join forces against Isengrin, and take those versions from such different MSS as A in Martin's edition, B in Roques' edition, and C in Fukumoto *et al.*'s edition; (Martin vol. I, p.111, ll.709–22; Roques, CFMA 79, p.45, ll.4689–702; Fukumoto *et al.*, vol. I, p.57, ll.1699–712). An analysis of these lines shows that linguistic differences are frequent but minor. They mostly reflect irregularities in the Old French system of declension; verb forms — especially switches in the use of tenses, here a past, there a present; pronoun forms and use; and the fairly common substitution of one conjunction or adverb for another.

Comments on 'literary' differences would probably be made under three headings; variants which occur chiefly at the beginnings and endings of branches or units as the different anthologists rearrange the stories; substantial differences, usually the result of added or subtracted lines of verse; minor but interesting differences involving single words or phrases or sentence structures.

(a) *Beginnings and endings*. The editor of a gamma MS in particular might point to the extensive and skilfully managed new link passages at the beginning and end of the story of Isengrin's and Hersent's complaints at Noble's court. The gamma anthologist seems to have created an introduction of twenty-seven lines to what is branch Va (*Le Serment*...) in which Isengrin ponders over the humiliation he suffered when Renart raped his wife and, instead of battering and insulting her (as he does in the alpha anthologies) he calls his friends together to take counsel with them. The net result is to focus on the debate about rape which will follow, a fundamentally serious topic around which the author of Va burlesques his way. This new introduction also draws attention to Isengrin's real motive in taking Renart to court — revenge, not justice, and the desire for revenge is precisely what will lead to his undoing. Finally, through this new introduction, the gamma anthologist succeeds in making Isengrin's private shame become that much more public, a point which Noble himself will make, and which feeds his and his allies' vengeful determination. A particularly noteworthy difference between the alpha, beta, and gamma endings to this branch is the way in which, in the alpha tradition, Renart's backing away from the oath-taking ceremony is followed by a chase of epic proportions of about 125 lines, and ends with Renart escaping into the security of his castle. In the beta tradition, this ending is rejected and in its place Renart gets out of the ceremony by tempting Brun and Tibert to go on a new expedition with him in search of food — an expedition which results in further suffering for the bear and the cat, and brings disaster upon the crowd gathered to witness the oath. The former ending heightens the mock-epic flavour; the latter increases the emphasis on the mocking of justice. The gamma anthologist attempts the impossible and offers both endings, beta first and alpha second. Although this is obviously very clumsy, he follows them with a totally new ending which neatly balances his new beginning, an ending which depicts Isengrin once more consulting with his allies about the next step to take in his unending conflict with Renart.

(*b*) *Substantial differences within the stories.* In *Chantecler* there is only one major difference between the three families. Beta severely abbreviates part of the role given to Pinte and to the Goodwife. All three describe how Renart finally tricks Chantecler into crowing with his eyes closed, grabs him, and joyously makes off. From this point on both alpha and gamma describe Pinte's reaction ending with her lament:

> Lasse! Dolente! con sui morte
> quant je ainsint pert mon seignor!
> Trestote ai perdue m'amor . . .

By omitting this speech, and in particular lines which delightfully burlesque courtly language and situation, beta loses much of the comedy. The comic contrast with the Goodwife's realistic comment is also lost:

> Lasse, trop m'est mesavenu . . .
> Mon coc que cil gorpil enporte!

for these lines are also missing from B. For the aristocratic hen it is a major tragedy; for the peasant woman, it is rotten luck. Then, after Pinte's lamentations, all the families tell us that the Goodwife opened the gate to the henyard, but only alpha and gamma offer the next twelve lines before she shouts 'Harou'. These contain a fair amount of detail which build up an atmosphere of tension in mock-heroic manner. In all three families the Goodwife's loud 'halloo' brings some peasants on the scene, but then, in beta, all they do is shout 'Voi li gorpil' and then disappear from view. In alpha and gamma, however, they come up to the Goodwife, engage her in the liveliest of dialogues and give the loudest of chases over thirty-six lines, thereby increasing the comedy and the mock-heroic effects yet further.

(*c*) *Minor but interesting differences.* Only gamma pinpoints the real cause of Chantecler's downfall when Pinte calls out as Renart runs off with him: 'Vostre orgueil si vos a traï . . .' Alpha reads: 'Vostre senz vos a escharni.' In the same vein, gamma tells us that Chantecler returned to his position by the roof 'fierement' whereas alpha and beta say he did it 'seurement' . . . In the *Hersent* story a number of tiny details show that the gamma storyteller/copyist had a penchant for irony. Near the beginning he has Renart refer to Isengrin as his 'amis' where in beta the word 'anemis' is used. Similarly (and consistently) Isengrin is called Renart's 'bon ami' where both alpha and beta call him 'son anemi'. Another glimpse of gamma's irony occurs when Hersent is being raped and shouts out:

> Renart, c'est force, et force soit

for only in gamma is the fox's response described with the comically vulgar image:

> Renart se test, a cui est bel
> de ce qu'il li fet le cenbel . . .

If editorial comments of this kind, selectively, succinctly made prefaced each unit's list of variants, they would, I think, do much to encourage the reader to use them more than is usually done.

Finally, I feel that editors should be much more willing to tackle especially divergent stories, MS I, for example. It is not so divergent that it could not have been included even in Martin's list. I have transcribed MS I's equivalent of Martin's Brs. II/Va and found that, for the greater part, it compares very easily with his established text. Usually it abbreviates very considerably by straightforward omission. Martin could have done for MS I what he does for MS e at the head of Branch X. Here, for example is the list of omissions which would have to precede *Chantecler*: missing are the equivalents of ll.5-6, 13-16, 20-24, 33-4, 37-49, 53-62, 65-70, 83-4, 90-91, 109-10, 113-14, 125-6, 135-6, 145-60, 164-6, 169-70, 179-84, 187-93, 199-214, 221-2, 229-40, 243-4, 255-6, 265-8, 271-4, 278-83, 286-88, 299-302, 307-10, 317-18, 324-6, 337-8, 362-7, 381-2, 384-5, 391-408, 411-12, 439-40, 461-4. There are no additions. As for the effect of these omissions, and the extent of the differences within a line, the reader might like to compare the following version of the *Prologue* with that published by Martin, vol. I, p.91, ll.1-22:

> Seigneurs, oÿ avez maint comte,
> Que mainte hystoire vous raconte;
> Conment Paris ravi Helainne,
> Le mal qu'il en oust et la painne;
> Et fabliaux, et chansons de geste,
> Et mainte autre hystoire honneste
> Que on conte de mainte terre;
> Mais onques n'oÿstes la guerre,
> Qui tant fu dure de grant fin,
> Entre Renart et Ysengrin.
> Moult fu creüse (?) c'est la voire,
> Des or conmencerai l'istoire.

Occasionally, but rarely, there are additions. For example, in Va, between Martin's l.432 and 433, twenty lines are added — an exchange between Noble and Isengrin. The king actually goes so far as to forbid Isengrin to fight Renart, but Isengrin defends himself fiercely:

> Si li a dit: 'Se Diex me voie,
> Pour nulle riens ne sofferroie
> Qu'entre vous et Renars le court
> Vous combatissiés en ma court,
> Ne que vous eussiés guerre ensamble.'
> 'Sire,' dist Ysengrin,' moi samble
> Que vous soustenés sa partie,
> Mais foi que doi sainte Marie,
> Moult miex me deussiés aidier,
> Et ma parti consillier,
> Que je vous ai tousjours bien fait;
> Assés miex que Renart n'a fait;
> Mais se j'eusse estei boiserres,
> Faux et trait(r)es et tricherres,
> Miex m'amissiés par mon musel;
> Mais dehait ait cui il est bel
> Que je si bien servi vous ai
> Quant si malvais loier en ai.
> Mais on suelt dire en repuiner
> Que de tel seigneur, tel louier.'

To my mind we need an edition of MS I; it is a great deal more interesting than it has been given credit for. Perhaps its 500 and more miniatures become part and parcel of the storytelling as Ettina Nieboer (1989) has suggested, and that it is partly the victim of a censor whose sense of moral values has been outraged, here and there, by the unexpurgated versions of the *Roman de Renart*.

A scholarly edition of one of the oldest surviving *Roman de Renart* MSS, H, is also needed. A glance through Martin's list of variants for br. XIII (*Renart empereur*) is sufficient to show how divergent it can be, and interestingly so. We need at least an edition of branch IV (*Le Puits*) in its second, uniquely divergent form. Martin could so easily have included it in his variants in much the same way as he includes the 175 lines unique to MS M's version of *La Mort et Procession Renart*, pp. 586–9, vol. III. This is important, I think, because it seems to me to be an earlier form of the branch, one which reflects a *Roman de Renart* version of what was a fable, but a version composed before the famous story of Renart's seduction by Hersent, and his subsequent raping of the she-wolf. After all, both the now standard version and this variant one share the first 149 lines, and the variant version is concluded in only another 278 lines.

More scholarly editions of the *Roman de Renart*, both of the independent full-length anthologies and of some of the oldest branches in all their most divergent forms in a way that enables the reader to compare them easily (even in loose-leaf folders!) would, I think, help *Roman de Renart* scholars to get freer still from the influence of Foulet's thesis, and see the stories for what they are, *and* the anthologies, at different stages in their evolution, the products of a process of continuous artistic creation.

References

Chabaille, P. (1835) *Le Roman de Renart, Supplément, variantes et corrections*, Paris. (For the variant version of Br. IV in MS H).

Fukumoto, N., Harano, N. and Suzuki, S. (1983 & 1985) *Le Roman de Renart*, vols 1 & 2, Tokyo: France Tosho.

Fukumoto, N. (1987) 'Sur un fragment non-publié du Roman de Renart conservé à la Bibliothèque Royale Albert Premier', in A. Vitale-Brovarone e G. Mombello (eds), *Colloquio dell International Beast Epic, Fable and Fabliau Society*, Alessandria: Edizioni dell'Orso, pp. 15–22. (This treats MS r).

Harano, N. (1987 & 1988) 'Le Roman de Renart édité d'après le ms. n.', in *The Hiroshima University Studies*, 46, pp. 333–48, and 47, pagination not yet available.

Lodge, R. A. and Varty, K. (1989) *The Earliest Branches of the Roman de Renart*, Dundee: Lochee Publications.

Martin, E. (1882–87) *Le Roman de Renart*, vols 1, 2, & 3, Berlin, New York: Walter de Gruyter, reprint 1973.

Nieboer, E. (1989) 'Un regard nouveau sur le manuscrit I du Roman de Renart', in Varty, K. (ed.) *A la Recherche du Roman de Renart*, 2, Dundee: Lochee Publications, pagination not yet available. (Nieboer and Varty are preparing an edition of MS I).

Roques, M. (1948, 1951, 1955, 1958, 1960, 1963) *Le Roman de Renart* C.M.F.A. 78, 79, 81, 85, 88 and 90, Paris: Champion.

Rossi, L. and Asperti, S. (1986) 'Il Renart di Siena: nuovi frammenti duecenteschi', in *Studi Francesi e Provenzali, Romanica Vulgaria Quaderni*, 8/9, pp.37–64. (This treats MS r).

Suzuki, S., Fukumoto, N. and Harano, N. (1988) 'Sur le Manuscrit t du Roman de Renart', in *Reinardus*, 1, pp.156–62.

Varty, K. (1987) 'De l'Appellation des branches et des contes des Romans de Renart *and* Les Anthologies dans les Romans de Renart', in Varty, K.

(ed.), *A la Recherche du Roman de Renart*, 1, Dundee: Lochee Publications, pp.7–12 and 51–77.

—— (1989) 'La Datation des contes de Renart le Goupil et la branche IV: Renart et Isengrin dans le Puits', in Varty, K. (ed.), *A la Recherche du Roman de Renart*, 2, Dundee: Lochee Publications, pagination not yet available. (This treats the variant version of br. IV, *Le Puits*, in MS H.).

Anthony Lodge

5 SYNTACTIC VARIABLES AND THE
AUTHORSHIP OF *RENART* II–Va

Introduction

Lucien Foulet's authoritative study of the two dozen or so branches of the *Roman de Renart* (Foulet, 1914) was written with such insight, balance, and erudition that even after three-quarters of a century one feels almost churlish in criticising aspects of it. His achievement in 'rescuing' this collective masterpiece from the hands of the nineteenth-century folklorists still stands firm: whatever may be the debt of the *Roman de Renart* to an oral tradition stretching back to the mists of primitive Indo-European culture, the French text which we have come to know through the editions of Martin (1882) and Roques (1948–63) can be studied essentially as conscious art, created by individual artists writing at precise moments in the late twelfth and early thirteenth centuries. Foulet's dispersal of Sudre's 'foule anonyme' (Sudre, 1892) was as effective as it was necessary.

To substantiate his case in the debate then raging between the exponents of the old Romanticism (with its emphasis on the naturalness and spontaneity of medieval art) and the modernists (with their stress on convention and conscious authorial intent), Foulet was led to postulate a hypothetical 'first French poem about Renart'; he brought together as one poem episodes which did not occur together in that order in the medieval manuscripts (branches II and Va as numbered in Martin's edition of the *Renart*) and attributed them to a single author, Pierre de Saint Cloud:

> *Renard et Isengrin*, le plus ancien poème français qui ait traité de Renard, a été composé en 1176 ou 1177 par Pierre de Saint Cloud.
> [Foulet, 1914, p.217]

Such an expedient was most advantageous in the debate with the folklorists: the date of composition of such a poem was (according to Foulet) calculable, the presumed author had at least a name, and the conflation of the tales making up branches II and Va had a satisfying narrative shape. This provided a firm foundation with unimpeachable 'literary' credentials to support the vast and complex Reynardian edifice which, according to Foulet, grew up subsequently and which was so masterfully explained in later chapters of Foulet's thesis:

(46)

La vérité est qu'il [Pierre de Saint Cloud] a écrit Va et II tout d'une pièce, et ainsi il a composé un poème de plus de 2,400 vers, où le sujet principal est traité non pas en 370 mais bien en 1,382 vers. [Foulet, 1914, p.212]

Impressed by this idea of the unity of II–Va, K. Varty and I resolved some years ago to abstract from the corpus of Renart tales those attributed by Foulet to Pierre de Saint Cloud, and to produce a manageable edition of them for undergraduates. This edition is currently in press, and what follows here is a development of ideas adumbrated there. Unfortunately, as our editorial work on II–Va proceeded we became increasingly aware not of the homogeneity of II–Va but of the differences of tone and language between the various episodes. It is some of these differences that I propose to examine here.

Difficulties with Foulet's hypothesis

The episodes which Foulet brought together in II–Va are set out in Table 1. A glance at the MSS of the *Renart* will show that any unity which II–Va may originally have had was seriously masked by the activities of subsequent medieval anthologisers: the horizontal lines in Table 1 represent interruptions of Foulet's II–Va sequence in the

TABLE 1

		α MS A Martin		β MS B Roques	γ MS M Lodge and Varty
Prologue	(II)	1–	22	3733–3750	–
Chantecler	(II)	23–	468	4065–4458	23– 470
Mésange	(II)	469–	664	4459–4654	471– 674
Tibert	(II)	665–	842	4655–4796	675– 842
Tiécelin	(II)	843–1026		5551–5695	843–1004
Renart and Hersent	(II)	1027–1388		5705–6100	1005–1418
	(Va)	264– 288			
Isengrin's Complaints	(Va)	289–1146		6101–6958	1419–2306
Dénouement (1)		–		6959–7273	2307–2621
Dénouement (2)	(Va)	1147–1272		–	2622–2826

principal manuscripts. Foulet was particularly anxious about the break between 'Renart and Hersent' and 'Isengrin's Complaints', regarding the latter (which recounts the trial of Renart) as the logical and necessary continuation of the former (which gives the facts of the case). In Martin's edition this crucial point is reached towards the end of branch II and at the beginning of Va:

> Les manuscrits ADEFGHINO séparent II et Va par le groupe III (VI) IV et V, nous offrant ainsi la série II, III, (VI), IV, V, Va: les autres manuscrits, BCKLMn terminent II au vers 1390 ou 1394 (au lieu de 1396) et font suivre immédiatement Va. [Foulet, 1914, pp.24–5]

The α family interrupts the narrative during the 'Renart and Hersent' episode. Only the β family respects the continuity of 'Renart and Hersent' and 'Isengrin's Complaints', but it interrupts earlier sections of Pierre de Saint Cloud's poem between 'Tibert' and 'Tiécelin'. The γ family, contrary to what Foulet maintains here, separates 'Renart and Hersent' from 'Isengrin's Complaints' by some twenty-five folios: in MS M the end of the 'Renart and Hersent' episode occurs at f. 5a, while the beginning of 'Isengrin's Complaints' figures only at f. 30c. In fact, the medieval compilations of the episodes in II–Va differ at other points, too: the 'Prologue' occurs immediately before 'Chantecler' only in α ; it is separated from 'Chantecler' by the 'Creation of Renart and Isengrin' in β ; it is placed before 'Renart and Isengrin' in γ (although missing from M). Indeed, the compiler of γ feels free to re-order completely the episodes attributed to Pierre de Saint Cloud.

In the face if its obvious discontinuity in the MSS, Foulet nevertheless asserted the original unity of II–Va. 'Chantecler', 'Mésange', 'Tibert', and 'Tiécelin' contain important structural and thematic similarities; 'Isengrin's Complaints' is a logical continuation of 'Renart and Hersent'; there are back-references in 'Isengrin's Complaints' not only to 'Renart and Hersent', but also to 'Mésange', 'Tibert', and 'Tiécelin' (though strangely not to 'Chantecler'). However, does that mean that they were all composed *tout d'une pièce* by one author? We have expressed our doubts about the unity of II–Va elsewhere (Lodge and Varty, 1981): it is possible to point to sizeable differences of theme and structure between the various episodes in II–Va; back-references could be to pre-existing stories composed by other authors; 'Isengrin's Complaints' is a logical continuation of 'Renart and Hersent', but is it a necessary one? Foulet himself notes that 'Renart and Hersent' has a self-standing antecedent in the *Ysengrimus* (Mann, 1987), that is, a rape without a trial. The object of the present essay is to spread further doubt by consideration of linguistic evidence gleaned from a close study of MS M (Turin varia 151, late thirteenth century).

The Experiment

We chose MS M as the base for our edition of II–Va (and hence for the present exercise) because it had never been edited, and because before the work of Fukumoto, Harano and Susuki (1983) the γ family was known only very imprecisely. Fukumoto *et al.* selected MS C to represent the γ family, whereas we preferred MS M for reasons of mechanical accuracy (Lodge and Varty, 1981). Was any manuscript from the γ family a safe choice for the purposes of the present experiment?

In certain respects, the γ family is idiosyncratic compared with a and β. This we have seen in the compiler's readiness to re-order the branches and episodes in the anthology; it appears, too, in the compiler's desire to be encyclopaedic — for example, where two dénouements to 'Isengrin's Complaints' are available, he does not select one in preference to the other, he puts both in. At a more literal level, however, the scribes of γ are much more cautious. It is the scribe of MS A who emerges as the most innovative in the principal MSS at the level of individual word-forms and lexical choices. The scribe of M in contrast rarely strays from the well-worn path of readings widely attested in the other MSS. Thus, at the higher level M (following γ) is quite innovative, while at the lower level it stays in the mainstream of the *Renart* manuscript tradition. The chances are, therefore, that the language of this MS is neither closer to nor further from the language of the author(s) than that of the rest.

It was decided to examine individually and in detail the eight sections of II–Va (as transmitted in MS M) with a view to quantifying as far as was possible the linguistic homogeneity/heterogeneity of the episodes attributed to Pierre de Saint Cloud. These are:

(1) Chantecler (448 lines)
(2) Mésange (204 lines)
(3) Tibert (168 lines)
(4) Tiécelin (162 lines)
(5) Renart and Hersent (414 lines)
(6) Isengrin's Complaints (887 lines)
(7) Dénouement (1) (317 lines)
(8) Dénouement (2) (202 lines)

Following a long established tradition I looked first of all at the rhymes and spellings of the text. However, a phonological/graphemic analysis of II–Va reveals nothing which supports strongly or negates single authorship. The spellings of the Turin manuscript are not marked by strong regional characteristics. The spelling alternations present were current in the appropriate proportions in the Ile de France in the thirteenth century (Dees, 1980) and show no significant variation across the various episodes of II–Va. The provenance of the manuscript seems to be Paris or the surrounding region, i.e. the same area where an examination of the place-names occurring in the text suggests that most of the *Roman de Renart* was composed. The phonological system which can be inferred from the rhymes likewise shows no significant variation across the different episodes in the text. Prima facie this suggests unity of authorship, but the argument is not a strong one since the authors of most of the branches of the *Renart* used similar rhyming-vowels.

However, while the rhyming-vowels of the text do not vary significantly, the rhyme-schemes employed do appear to do so. Could this variation be measured? The rhymes used were classified into three broad types:

(*a*) *Minimum rhyme (V⟶)* = the last stressed vowel and any subsequent phonemes,

  e.g. masculine *Renart: d'art*
     feminine *guile: vile*

(*b*) *Rich rhyme (CV⟶)* = as (*a*) plus the preceding consonant or consonant group,

  e.g. masculine *d'os: dos*
     feminine *forteresce: adresce*

(*c*) *Leonine rhyme (VCV⟶)* = as (*b*) plus the preceding vowel,

  e.g. masculine *bessié: plessié*
     feminine *apelee: celee.*

Each of the above rhyme-schemes can be regarded as a variable with a particular proportion of tokens in each episode of the text. The totals for each episode are as in Table 2.

A simple statistical operation was carried out on each of the totals to calculate the extent to which that number deviates from the mean for the text as a whole. This is the score quoted in brackets. A figure with a high bracketed score, e.g. those in 'Chantecler' and 'Dénouement (1)', implies relative idiosyncrasy in the handling of the variable in question. A chi-square test was then applied to the results to evaluate the discriminatory power of the rhyme-scheme variable as a whole. The chi-square test is a procedure which is used to measure whether a particular distribution of observed frequencies is sufficiently different from an

TABLE 2

	Minimum F M	Rich F M	Leonine F M
Chantecler	59 92 151 (7.33)	15 15 30 (0.64)	9 34 43 (9.25)
Mésange	32 . 27 59 (0.26)	5 9 14 (0.21)	3 26 29 (0.13)
Tibert	29 22 51 (0.68)	4 6 10 (0.70)	3 20 23 (0.25)
Tiécelin	30 17 47 (0.23)	4 4 8 (1.65)	3 23 26 (0.08)
Renart and Hersent	80 29 109 (0.11)	11 17 28 (0.55)	12 59 71 (0.95)
Isengrin's Complaints	136 66 202 (4.04)	24 42 66 (0.01)	20 142 162 (7.48)
Dénouement (1)	45 38 83 (0.01)	9 32 41 (10.88)	5 28 33 (4.87)
Dénouement (2)	21 26 47 (0.93)	6 12 18 (0.41)	2 33 35 (0.69)

expected distribution to indicate that it cannot be explained as a chance occurrence (see Butler, 1985, p.112 ff.). A low chi-square total (i.e. below 10.0) indicates that variation between the episodes is not wide enough to be significant, i.e. that one author could have been responsible for them all. A high chi-square total (i.e. above 10.0) suggests that variation between the different episodes is too wide to be purely fortuitous, i.e. that multiple authorship cannot be ruled out. In the case of the rhyme-schemes the overall total of the chi-square test is 52.33, i.e. a high score suggestive of multiple authorship. As we have seen, 'Chantecler' and 'Dénouement (1)' are particularly idiosyncratic with regard to this variable.

Clearly, the text's performance on a single variable could not be conclusive. It was decided to look for other variables attributable to the author(s) which could be similarly quantified. The statistical analysis of morphological variables in Medieval French was admirably utilised by G. A. Runnalls (1971) to help with dating the composition of fourteenth- and fifteenth-century plays. He isolated three morphological variables affecting versification — subject case (e.g. *nommés: avez*), etymological feminine adjectives (e.g. *grant: grande*), and first person singular present tense etymological (e.g. *suy: ennuy*). By comparing the incidence of such 'old forms' in a variety of dated texts with their proportion in an undated text, he was able to edge towards a date of composition for the latter. Use of these particular variables in an examination of our II–Va would not have been productive, since language variation on these points was not particularly significant during the twelfth century. However, the principles underlying Runnalls's work were clearly useful, provided suitable variables with discriminatory power could be found. It was decided to look at syntactic features which varied freely or stylistically within twelfth-century French texts, and the following were isolated:

(*i*)   position of the subject
(*ii*)   the narrative tenses
(*iii*)   negation.

We will consider each of these in turn, but it needs to be stated at the outset that the value of the statistics quoted is by no means absolute, for the volume of data analysed is extremely small (2800 lines) and the eight episodes compared are of very uneven length.

(*i*) *Subject position*

The morphology of noun and verb phrases in Old French allowed a wide range of variation of the order in which the principal ingredients in the sentence could occur. The ingredients which concern us here are Subjects (nouns or pronouns, abbreviated here to Sn and Sp), Verbs (abbreviated here to V), and Complements (direct and indirect objects, adverbials, adjectives, etc., abbreviated here to C (Price, 1971, pp.258–61)). Since the situation with Noun Subjects (Sn) is different from that with Pronoun Subjects (Sp), let us look at them separately. In order to limit our analysis, only the main clauses of declarative sentences were considered.

(*a*) *Noun subject position*. Four orders occur:
Sn V C, e.g. *La vile sëoit en. i. bos.*
C V Sn, e.g. *Plenteïve estoit sa mesons.*

Sn C V, e.g. *Chantecler lors s'aseüra.*

C Sn V, e.g. *Onques nus cos si ne chanta.*

Of these, the first two (Verb second) are by far the most frequent. Indeed, the numbers in the Sn C V and C Sn V categories were so small that it was preferable to leave them out of the calculations (Table 3).

The overall total of the chi-square test (18.62) shows these figures to be significant in indicating multiple rather than single authorship. As with the rhyme-schemes, we note that 'Chantecler' is linguistically idiosyncratic, with its particular preference for CVS order, as is 'Dénouement (2)'.

TABLE 3

	SVC	*CVS*	*SCV*	*CSV*
Chantecler	28 (1.76)	22 (4.49)	3	1
Mésange	11 (0.65)	1 (1.67)	2	0
Tibert	20 (0.03)	9 (0.09)	4	0
Tiécelin	17 (0.24)	4 (0.61)	2	1
Rape	31 (0.08)	10 (0.20)	1	2
Trial	75 (0.66)	20 (0.69)	1	2
Dénouement (1)	28 (0.17)	8 (0.44)	2	3
Dénouement (2)	15 (1.64)	14 (4.19)	0	1

(*b*) *Pronoun subject position.* Given the capacity of verb-endings to mark the person of the verb in Old French, the incidence of the Sp was greatly reduced compared to modern French. The prime function of Sp (when it did appear) seems to have been to ensure that the V came second in the sentence (Price, 1971, pp.145–9), e.g. *Il avint chose . . .* When the initial position *was* occupied by a C, the Sp was normally omitted (= Sp°), e.g. *hordez estoit d'aubes espines . . .* However, this pattern was not absolute, e.g. *ce ne devriez-vos pas dire.* The position and incidence of Sp in this text are indicated in Table 4. The overall total of the chi-square test on these figures (16.98) shows 'Chantecler' and 'Dénouement (1)' to be idiosyncratic.

TABLE 4

	$C\,V\,Sp^{\circ}$	$C\,V\,Sp$	$Sp\,V\,(C)$
Chantecler	94 (0.73)	4 (3.20)	32 (0.17)
Mésange	24 (0.52)	6 (2.78)	12 (0.07)
Tibert	26 (0.59)	1 (0.89)	7 (0.45)
Tiécelin	30 (0.01)	2 (0.56)	14 (0.27)
Rape	72 (0.05)	8 (0.01)	26 (0.15)
Trial	107 (0.02)	16 (1.33)	41 (0.14)
Dénouement (1)	48 (1.40)	7 (0.08)	31 (2.97)
Dénouement (2)	27 (0.10)	3 (0.10)	8 (0.45)

(ii) Narrative tenses

Old French verse narratives use four principal tenses to recount events in the past: past historic (*fist*), perfect (*a fet*), imperfect (*fesoit*), 'historic' present (*fait*). While each of these had quite distinct temporal values, different authors used them in different proportions according to their personal storytelling style (Foulet 1961, § 320–6). The way each episode of II–Va used the different tenses was analysed, and the results are shown in Table 5.

The overall total of the chi-square test (104.42) is extremely significant (statistically speaking) and points to a very strong likelihood of multiple authorship. 'Chantecler' is again very idiosyncratic, this time in its frequent use of the imperfect.

TABLE 5

	Past historic	Perfect	Imperfect	Present
Chantecler	58 (1.21)	25 (2.24)	44 (36.89)	111 (0.56)
Mésange	15 (7.18)	16 (0.09)	0 (8.00)	74 (8.73)
Tibert	35 (0.02)	29 (6.77)	2 (6.09)	61 (0.11)
Tiécelin	39 (2.61)	12 (0.65)	6 (0.57)	50 (0.24)
Rape	57 (0.12)	34 (0.53)	13 (0.62)	108 (0.03)
Trial	111 (7.93)	39 (0.33)	19 (0.70)	133 (2.20)
Dénouement (1)	46 (1.53)	19 (2.75)	16 (0.08)	115 (2.90)
Dénouement (2)	27 (0.07)	21 (5.12)	5 (0.54)	38 (1.26)

(*iii*) Negation

Old French negatived finite verbs sometimes with *ne* alone, e.g. *Je ne sai quel beste*, sometimes with *ne* + *pas, point, mie,* etc. There were regional and syntactic differences between the three particles just listed (Price, 1971, pp.252–4), but for the purpose of the exercise, the only comparison made was between the incidence of *ne* alone and that of *ne* + particle (taking *pas, point,* and *mie* together). The results are given in Table 6, where we note that the overall chi-square total is 7.76, which is statistically not significant. In other words, negation is either a poor measure of authorship, or points to one author for the whole text.

TABLE 6

	ne alone	*ne* + particle
Chantecler	39 (0.51)	7 (1.58)
Mésange	17 (0.01)	6 (0.03)
Tibert	7 (0.82)	6 (2.53)
Tiécelin	7 (0.15)	1 (0.46)
Rape	36 (0.01)	11 (0.02)
Trial	48 (0.00)	16 (0.01)
Dénouement (1)	17 (0.01)	5 (0.27)
Dénouement (2)	12 (0.39)	7 (1.21)

Conclusions

No reader of Old French texts as experienced and perceptive as the dedicatee of the present volume will give enormous weight to the statistical data we have looked at here. The size of the corpus of data is not large and no control analyses of comparable Old French texts have been undertaken. However, the evidence is not entirely valueless and, such as it is, points us in the direction of multiple rather than single authorship, the situation of 'Chantecler' being particularly striking. This episode behaves idiosyncratically on Noun Subject Position, Pronoun Subject Position and Narrative Tenses, as well as in Rhyme Scheme, and it seems quite possible that it was not composed by the same author as the rest of the text. Internal evidence corroborates this: we saw earlier how 'Isengrin's Complaints' contains back-references to 'Renart and Hersent', 'Mésange', and 'Tiécelin'. The fact that it contains no back-references to 'Chantecler' suggests a distance between this episode and the others. The statistics also show up the idiosyncratic nature of the 'Dénouements' — but this is not at all surprising, given the obviously makeshift character of these parts of the text, particularly in MS M.

Foulet's 'unity hypothesis' is not totally exploded by our efforts, however. While it appears likely that 'Chantecler' should be detached from the rest, Foulet's first priority was to forge a link between 'Renart and Hersent' and 'Isengrin's Complaints'. Our statistical data do not point unambiguously to multiple authorship in *this* crucial part of II–Va.

References

Butler, C. (1985) *Statistics in linguistics*, Oxford: Blackwell.

Dees, A. (1980) *Atlas des formes et des constructions des chartes françaises du 13e siècle*, Tübingen: Max Niemeyer.

Foulet, L. (1914) *Le Roman de Renard*, Paris: Champion.

—— (1961) *Petite Syntaxe de l'ancien français*, Paris: CFMA.

Fukumoto, N., Harano, N. and Susuki, S. (1983–5) *Le Roman de Renart*, Tokyo: France Tosho, t.I 1983, t.II 1985.

Lodge, R. A. and Varty, K. (1976) 'Towards a new edition of the *Roman de Renart*', Nottingham Medieval Studies, 20, pp.41–63.

—— (1981) 'Pierre de Saint Cloud's *Roman de Renart*: Foulet's thesis re-examined', in J. Goossens and T. Sodmann (eds), *Third International Beast. Epic, Fable and Fabliau Colloquium*, Munster, 1979, Böhlau, Köln, Wien, 1981, pp.189–195.

Mann, J. (1987) *Ysengrimus. Text with Translation, Commentary and Introduction*, Leiden.

Martin, E. (1882–7) *Le Roman de Renart*, Strasbourg, t.I 1882, t.II 1885, t.III 1887.

Price, G. (1971) *The French Language: Present and Past*, London: Edward Arnold.

Roques, M. (1948–63) *Le Roman de Renart*, Paris: CFMA, t.I 1948, t.II 1951, t.III 1954, t.IV 1958, t.V 1960, t.VI 1963.

Runnalls, G. A. (1971) 'A Newly-Discovered Fourteenth Century French Play? *Le Mystère de Saint Christofle*', Romance Philology, 24, pp.464–77.

Sudre, L. (1892) *Les Sources du Roman de Renart*, Paris.

Wolfgang van Emden

6. SOME REMARKS ON THE CAMBRIDGE
MANUSCRIPT OF THE *RHYMED ROLAND*

It is gratifying to be asked to contribute to a volume of essays in honour
of Professor Holden, who gave a very new Temporary Lecturer billeted
on him in his office in 1957–8 much valuable advice and friendly
support. The memory of those Edinburgh days in Minto House, with
the fine dust produced by the neighbouring brewery quickly colouring
any exposed surface a delicate speckled brown, remains as clear as the
scholarship generously shared with a new colleague. This chapter seeks
to offer one of our foremost editors of mediaeval French texts something
of a progress report on that colleague's work on MS Trinity College,
Cambridge, R 3.32, otherwise known as MS *T* of the *Rhymed Roland*,
and on some cases where it may help us throw light on the nature of this
remaniement of the assonanced *Roland* text.

This work is part of the collaboration between a number of American
and British scholars, co-ordinated by Professor Joseph Duggan, to
produce the 'New Mortier'. It is perhaps worth stating here that this
collaboration has disclosed a worrying state of affairs touching both the
Foerster and Mortier editions of the *Roland* texts. The former, when
compared with the manuscripts, proves remarkably variable in quality:
it looks as though Foerster used amanuenses (without, as far as I know,
acknowledging their contribution), some of whom were much abler
than others. From correspondence with Professor Duggan (CV^7) and
Dr Annalee Rejhon (*P*), who reported also on the findings of Professor
William Kibler (*L*), I gather that those copying MSS *P* and *L* are
relatively weak (an error on a rough average every forty-nine and thirty
lines respectively), while V^7 errs only in about 1 per cent of the lines; I
have not systematically noted the errors in *T*, but they are few and far
between, probably not more than 1 per cent, and Duggan has not
counted *C* yet.

Worse, from the point of view of scholars relying on Foerster and
Mortier, is to follow. I have found that, practically without exception
(and then probably coincidentally), Mortier simply reproduces Foerster's
errors in *T*, while adding a number of his own. It is clear that he used
Foerster, and not the Cambridge manuscript, as his base text. Given the
circumstances of the production of his edition, this is not surprising,

but he has misled scholars by not admitting it. A nice proof of this occurs as a result of Foerster's accidental failure to indicate the foliotation at the point where folio 18 recto begins (1.980 in my edition, T 61, 1.7 in his). Mortier miscalculates, and puts '[18r]' beside his 1.995 (= 985 in my edition): five lines out. In the case of the other manuscripts, the situation appears more complex: Kibler has found in Mortier some fifty extra errors on top of the hundred or so reproduced by the French editor from Foerster's L; the manuscript does not appear to have been consulted. Rejhon has evidence, which I will not anticipate here, that, for P, Mortier did consult the manuscript and may also have had a probably poor microfilm of it for routine use. He does correct some of Foerster's errors in P.

It seems clear, therefore, that Mortier's reliability is linked to the variable accuracy of Foerster, and that he often adds errors of his own, among which are errors in numbering the lines. The French edition cannot, therefore, be said to be any real advance on the old German one. In view of the number of scholars who have relied on Mortier since the war, this is a point very much worth making in advance of the publication of the collaborative editions now in progress.

In this essay I shall quote MS T from the typescript of my edition; it should be noted that Mortier numbers 1.235 as '240', hence a disparity of five between my numbers and his up to 1.260 in my edition, numbered 270 by Mortier, giving him a lead of ten; this lead increases to fifteen at van Emden 2045, numbered 2060 by Mortier, and the difference should be kept in mind in what follows.[1] For different reasons, my *laisse* numbers are two ahead of Foerster's, but agree with Mortier's, in the part of the poem on which this essay mainly concentrates. Despite his weaknesses, I have nevertheless decided to use Mortier except for T (and to show his line and *laisse* numbers, where these differ), for V^4 and all the rhymed manuscripts except V^7, of which the French editor offers only a photographic reproduction. For O, the Whitehead edition (1942, 1946) will be quoted, although I have also consulted others, particularly Segre (1971).

MS T is, of course, the youngest, by a considerable margin, of the copies of the *Roland* corpus in French (Segre, 1971, P XLI; Horrent, 1951, pp.57–60). 'C'est dans l'Ouest de la France septentrionale qu'un remanieur s'est chargé, à l'époque de François Villon, sinon à celle de Marot, de recopier et de retoucher l'antique récit de Roncevaux.' (Horrent, 1951, p.60). Since these words were written, Dr Fanni Bogdanow (1960) has, of course, published a single folio of the much earlier, but closely related, manuscript B; the existence of clear common

innovations is amply demonstrated in Dr Bogdanow's article (pp. 503–4).
This publication allows us to examine the implications of the word
retoucher more precisely in relation to the detail of the text.

Perhaps the most remarkable example of retouching, but also the
least significant for the criticism of the Oxford or indeed the *Rhymed
Roland* text, is the adjunction of a *petit vers* at the end of each *laisse* of
B (except the first, of which the final, partly illegible, line, though
peculiar to *B*, seems too long for an *hexasyllabe*). This is a feature
otherwise unknown in the *Roland* tradition, apart from the interpolated
and unrelated *Prise de Narbonne* in V^4 (Mortier, ll.3847–4417).
The *petit vers* appears only sporadically in this episode, evidently taken
from a version of *Aymeri de Narbonne* different from the extant one.
The *petit vers* and its relationship with the poems of the *Petit Cycle de
Narbonne* are dealt with by Roncaglia (1959, pp.141–59) and Tyssens
(1959, pp.429–56).

There is no *vers orphelin* in *T*, and Bogdanow (1960, pp.504–5)
argues that the decision to follow this fashion was restricted to *B*, on the
grounds that, in its *laisse* 154, corresponding to *B*'s *laisse* III, *T*
preserves more or less textually l.2826 from *O* ('Sus en la chambre ad
doel en sunt venut'), which is replaced by the *petit vers* in *B*. It is true
that in *T*, as well as in $V^4 PCV^7$ (MS *L*, of course, lacks the entire
context, along with the rest of the Baligant Episode), the line in
question is present (at the end of the *laisse* in all but *P*); but *BT* are also
the only two manuscripts to introduce the idea of Baligant's pity for
'Barimonde' ('Binamonde' in *T*; *B* 68, *T* 2372 = Mortier 2387), which
appears to motivate the curse in *B*'s *petit vers*: 'Damedieu le maudie!' It
seems equally possible that *B* simply omitted a line corresponding to *O*
2826, which may have been followed by 'Damedieu le[s (?)] maudie' in
a common ancestor of *BT*.

This is mere speculation, of course, but it is motivated by the fact
that *B*'s *laisse* II and *T*'s *laisse* 153 have a common development of the
motif of vengeance for the loss of Marsilion's hand, which closes the
corresponding *laisses* in all the other relevant manuscripts (CV^7 have a
somewhat different reading), a development which seems to lead
naturally to *B*'s *vers orphelin*:

B28   '. . . Pour son poing destre li rendrai prisonier;
                  Li empereres sera pris et liez.
                  Les ieulz *li fase* de la teste sachier
                  Ou desmembrer por soi esbanoier;
                  A son plesir le face traveillier,
                  Seue en ert la justice.'

T 2350   '. . . pour le poign destre qu'i[l] s'est lessié couper
(Mortier 2365)   ly emperiere li mesray prisonnier.
                           Les yeux li traie, ou le face escorcher:
                           a son plaisir le face travailler.'
                           Paiens s'escrïent: 'Bien fait a ottroier!'

T's final line has no parallel in any other manuscript, and is a very banal
one; it could well be a substitute for the logical *petit vers* which closes
the *laisse* in *B*, and which seems to justify the previous development.
The latter should be seen as a common innovation in the context of *O*'s
vers de conclusion, 2809: 'Pur sun poign destre l'en liverai le chef',
with its antithesis (repeated in V^4 and palely reflected by the equivalent
in *P*). A similar analysis could be made of *BT*'s idiosyncratic reference
to Charlemagne's sleep at the end of *laisses* IV and 155 respectively,
which again leads naturally to *B*'s line 97 'Qu'il ne s'esveilla mie'; this
line may at least as easily be omitted in *T* as added in *B*. The two
manuscripts share a different rhyme from the others in the next *laisse*,
and *B*'s *petit vers* cannot here be shown to be more organic than the
version lacking it in *T*; but in the next, *B* VI, *T* 157, the ending in the
latter:

T 2422   Nostre emperiere se print a regarder;
(Mortier 2437)   devant les autrez comm[en]ça a aler.

seems abrupt without the *vers orphelin* in *B* 134 'Que nus n'i volt
atendre', though the effect is increased by *T*'s lack of *B* 132 'Plus que ne
puet un bastoncel geter', a line shared with OV^4. The next stanza (*B*
VII, *T* 158) in -*on*, is the last complete *laisse* in *B* and is unique to *BT*;
its end is certainly more satisfactory in the former:

B 150   '. . . Lessiez le duel, car mener nu devon;
                           La sorde oreille n'i vaut pas un bouton.
                           Vez com grant gent ja n'avront raançon.
                           Se il nos prenent, n'i avra achoison
                           Ne vos ocient a grant destrucion.
                           De ce ne dout je mie.'

T 2436   '. . . lesson cest deul, car mener nel devon,
(Mortier 2451)   se vous mourez, ditez que nous feron?'

The reference by Naimon to the possibility of Charlemagne's death in *T*
seems abrupt and unmotivated by his swoon, but we may understand it
as a summary of the more detailed representations he makes in *B*. The
unsatisfactory ending of *T*'s *laisse* may well be the result of the excision

of a *petit vers*, either in our manuscript or in one of its ancestors.

It would seem, then, that there is a good chance that it was the *BT* sub-family which injected the *petit vers* into the tradition, contrary to the opinion of Bogdanow, though there is no certainty to be had. Obviously, on this hypothesis, *T* or one of its ancestors regularised the situation by excising the stylistic anomaly.

The existence of the *B* fragment allows us also to assess the nature and extent of the irregularities of prosody which are a striking feature of MS *T*. This remark clearly applies less to the rhymes than to the metre. In general, rhyme is fairly well respected, though no better than in MS *P*. In view of its date, it is not surprising that *T* does not respect the distinction between the rhymes *-er* and *-ier*. There are also tolerances, for example, on *-z* and *-s*, *-ent* and *-ant*; and there are frank assonances in places (*laisses* 22, 68, 105, 123, 132, 140, and 141 are relatively striking cases, but none contains many; perhaps 20 per cent of *laisses* contain one or more imperfect rhymes in the portion I have edited so far).

The most interesting aspect here is what happens in those passages where there is recourse by a common ancestor of *PT(L)* to an assonanced version, a phenomenon discussed by Segre (1974, Chap. 7; see the Tables, pp. 164–5, for the three passages involved, and pp. 152–7). It is not my intention to discuss the nature of these borrowings in detail, as Segre has done so very persuasively; but the fact that fragment *B* covers part of one of the passages concerned (Segre, Table V) allows some conclusions as to the attitude of the various scribes to the prosodic anomaly involved in the adoption, in the rhymed *remaniement*, of parts of an assonanced version.

Comparison of *T* with *P* (and, where it is available, with *L*) in the assonanced passages generally shows that *P* remains quite close to the assonances, while *L* (to a limited extent) and *T* (very clearly) strive in their own ways to reduce them to rhyme. There are exceptions, however, such as *T* 140 and 141, the former of which lies just outside the assonanced borrowing identified by Segre (1974, Table V). Nevertheless, *T* is very close to *O laisse* CLXXXVI, *V⁴ laisse* 204, while *P* 156, *L* 110, and *C* 258, *V⁷* form two groups working independently on a rhymed version, one or two lines of which are found in both versions. Here, *T* seems to preserve the assonanced text better than the other rhymed manuscripts, and it is not clear why the *laisse* has been left out of Segre's discussion. In the case of *T* the adoption of rhyme extends to changing the final tonic vowel to something easier where necessary, particularly substituting a masculine for a feminine ending (e.g., in

Segre's Table IV, *P laisses* 237–9 and *T* 212–14, *P* 242–3 and *T* 218–19). What the availability of *B* for part of Segre's Table V shows is that this technique is not some late medieval initiative from the scribe of *T*, but goes back to at least the time of the common ancestor of *B* and *T*: it is applied to the difficult feminine assonance of *P laisse* 175 (*-able*, *-arle*, *-aille*, etc. cf. *O* CCIV, *V*⁴ 221) in *laisse B* V, *T* 156, which is in *-a*. In addition, the two related manuscripts show the same effort to produce acceptable rhymes throughout. In the next *laisse*, for example, the assonanced mixture of *-er*, *-ez*, *-ét*, etc., still largely preserved in *P*, is regularised as *-er* in *BT*.

But *T* does represent a further step in this direction: in the few places where *B* has, say, *-er* in a *laisse* in *-é*, like its first, *T* generally turns the second hemistich to produce a better rhyme: thus at *B* 1.7 'que tant soloit amer', *T* 2325 (Mortier 2340) offers 'que tant avoit amé'. Even *T* is not wholly consistent in this direction (the first two lines of the *laisse* are in *-er*), but the pattern is fairly clear: see the variants given for *T* by Dr Bogdanow (1960) in relation to *B* ll.1, 5, 9, 14, 16, 39, 55, of which ll.1, 9, and 55 are lines lacking in *T*; at l.8, syntactically correct *menez* is replaced by *mené* in *T*.

This apparent effort is in line with earlier deformations (within the assonanced passage, but before *B* becomes available) for the sake of 'better' rhymes. Infinitives are so affected at ll.2250 *plaidiers*, 2251 *essauciers*, 2254 *entargiers* (Mortier 2265, 2266, 2269) etc., in *T laisse* 147 which the scribe tries to standardise in *-iers* (cf. *O* CXCIII, *V*⁴ (Mortier) *laisse* 211). In spite of *T*'s efforts, ll.2249, 2260, and 2261 (Mortier 2264, 2275, 2276) defeat him. Similar deformations are to be found also at e.g. ll.2157–60, 2162, and 2225 (Mortier 2172–5, 2177, 2240), in earlier *laisses*. The embarrassment of the *T* scribe, who is certainly not personally responsible for the editing-in from the assonanced tradition demonstrated by Segre, can be examined in the *laisses* listed in Segre's Table V, by comparison with MSS *O*, *V*⁴ and *P*. On his rhyming technique, see Segre (1974, pp.155–6). Certainly, the comparison with *B* and *P* shows that the Italian scholar is right in seeing the rhyming efforts of *P* and *T* as independent from each other; the starting-point for *T* can be seen in *B*, which is closer than *T* to the assonanced text, though it and the assonanced ancestor of *P* may already have diverged significantly from the source and from each other. It becomes clear from many of the *T* scribe's graphies that final consonants are largely silent for him.

But there is no reason why a text from around 1500 should not show an accurate syllable-count, and the metrical irregularities which litter *T* are all the more surprising in the context of the care given to rhymes in many places. This irregularity is such that, for one thing, the editor has seriously to consider the possibility that the *césure lyrique* may apply in places, such as ll.229 (*et Europe a il en sa baillie*) or 2903 = Mortier 2918 (*Devers Charles a s'ensaigne tournee*; or does one correct *Charlon* with other manuscripts?); and where does the caesura come in a line like 2997 (Mortier 3012), though it does consist of ten syllables: *l'erbe verte du prey en est mouillie?* But the commonest manifestations of metrical irregularity are the many hypermetrical and hypometrical lines present in the manuscript (apart from a certain small incidence of regular *alexandrins*, which it is the policy of the collaborating editors to preserve in all manuscripts). There are so many examples of grossly wrong syllable-count that the possible solution of using lyric caesuras is put in question by the relative insignificance of the number of lines which could be 'corrected' in this way. Some others can stand if one assumes that hiatus is preserved here but effaced there, on a random basis. As examples, here are a few lines drawn from the portion of *T* which corresponds with *B*: *T* 2358 (Mortier 2373) 'ly admirant pour qui se sont esmeu' (= *B* 49, except that *B* lacks *se*); *T* 2411 (Mortier 2426) 'mon corps me[ï]smez lessiez avant aler' (= *B* 120); *T* 2431 (Mortier 2446) 'le corps enbrasse par grant aïroison' (= *B* 145). *T* 2427 (Mortier 2442) 'ensanglanté de sanc a veü maint baron' is an alexandrine if hiatus is maintained in *veü*, though *B* has a different, decasyllabic, version: *B* 138 'Ensanglantee de maint riche baron' (cf. *O* 2872 'Ki sunt vermeilz del sanc de noz barons', *V*[4] 3056 'Chi e vermie del sangue di nostri mio'). But, apart from such marginal lines, there are, in the first 3000 lines of text (for which I have figures available at the moment), about 13 per cent of hypometrical and hypermetrical lines, some as much as three or even four syllables out; significantly, they tend to be particularly common where the manuscript has a passage peculiar to it (e.g. ll.1568–84), while famous passages, reproduced relatively faithfully to the rhymed tradition (such as ll.1199–1250 (Mortier 1209–60), Second Horn Scene), tend to greater regularity.

The comparison with *B*, even more than that which can be made with the manuscript tradition as a whole, permits some tentative conclusions on the graphical habits of the *T* scribe (or possibly his immediate model), conclusions which can help in the correction of metrical eccentricities throughout. In the first place, there is a general, though not wholly consistent, tendency to avoid features which were archaic by *c*.1500, even at the price of metrical inaccuracy in many cases:

(*a*) *B* 7   Son filz est [mort], que tant *soloit* amer, (cf. *O* 2782, *V*⁴ 2971)

T 2325 (Mortier 2340)   et son filz mort, que tant *avoit* amé, (the change in this line may, of course, also be motivated, as I said above, by the desire for a purer rhyme).

(*b*) *B* 12   Quite vous *claime* d'Espaigne le regné. (= *O* 2787, *V*⁴ 2975, *P* 3210)

T 2330 (Mortier 2345)   vous *quite* tout d'Espagne le regné.

(*c*) *T* 2345 (Mortier 2360)   Se vous voulez, tart *est* son reperier! Compare (*i*)*ert* in *OBPCV*⁷; *V*⁴ 2987 has a considerably different line and *L* lacks the entire context).

B 53   Et il respont: 'Volentiers *iert* tenu'.

T 2362 (Mortier 2377)   Et il respont: 'Vostre commant *sera* tenu'. (No real equivalents in other manuscripts.)

There is, indeed, a general tendency in *T* to avoid the etymological future of *estre*, with the normal consequence of hypermetricity; but it must be admitted that at l.2416 (Mortier 2431) *T* has 'La y erent (yerent?) logiez ycil bacheler' for *B* 124 'La se [va]ntoient cil legier b.' (cf. *O* 2861, *V*⁴ 3044; no other corresponding reading), showing the inconsistency referred to earlier.

(*d*) *B* 35   'Frans Sar*asins*, pensez du chevauchier! . . .'

T 2348 (Mortier 2363)   'Frans Sarrasins, pensez d'explaitier!'

BT are the only manuscripts to use this construction, though the use of the verb *chevauchier* is clearly primitive, since it figures in the corresponding lines of *O* and *V*⁴ (2806 and 2992 respectively) in different ways. What the *T* scribe does not seem to recognise is the use of the definite article in this construction and, having changed the verb to one beginning with a vowel, he produces a hypometric line.

(*e*) *T* 2373 (Mortier 2388)   dedens la chambre sont eulx .ii. venu. The apparent rejection, in favour of a more modern expression, of the probable β reading *ambedui* (*V*⁴ 3010, *P* 3247; *OCV*⁷ have different readings and *B* lacks the line, as of course does *L*) again results in hypometricity in *T*.

(*f*) *T* 2414 (Mortier 2429)   Aise estoie, ne le vous quier celer, (cf. *O* 2860 'A Eis esteie a une feste anoel', *V*⁴ 3043 'Ad Asia stet ad una festa Nael'; lacking in *BPLCV*⁷): this line well illustrates a not uncommon ignorance in T about some of the place-names (and personal names) which are commonplace in earlier versions.

The comparison with B, and, where appropriate of course, other manuscripts, highlights certain characteristics of T which are almost certainly a function of its relative youth. At the same time, T (and B, in spite of its omission of the line just discussed) are the only rhymed manuscripts to have the story about Roland's prophecy that he will die ahead of his men; their sharing it with the assonanced manuscripts guarantees the presence of this significant element in the borrowing from the assonanced tradition which Segre posits for the common ancestor of $PLTB$, even though it has been omitted again in P and is lacking as part of the omission of the Baligant Episode in L.

This is also typical of our version: there are, as has been said by Edward Heinemann (1974; T is considered to be contaminated occasionally by an assonanced version in the a tradition, from which O itself descends), a good many places where T shows an archaic reading on its own. I will finish with a few examples from the first 3000 lines of the manuscript, which is what I have edited so far. My provisional impression is that the conservative lines occur in batches, rather than being spread evenly; but account must be taken of the existence of assonanced insertions in the rhymed version and also of the change of perspective which the availability or non-availability of one or more other manuscripts at a given point may produce.

(a) T 1011 (Mortier 1021) 'fierent Franceys de leur espees fourbies' alone preserves O 1662, V^4 1635 (in a form close to the latter) at the original point in the *laisse*. P 1402, L 660, C 2797, and V^7 postpone the line, in what appears to be a common innovation.

(b) The rhymed versions all agree with V^4 in having two *laisses*, separated by four others (except in the case of L), in place of O CXXVII: V^4 132, 137; C 178, 183 agreeing with V^7; T 71, 76; P 84, 89; L 47, 49. At the end of *laisse* 76, T agrees with O, V^4 and CV^7 in lacking a clear common addition in PL (P 1631–7, L 797–803), dealing with the appearance of one Estorgant d'Ali(j)er, who plays no further part in the action. In addition, PL use the equivalent of O 1678 to start the second *laisse*; V^4, CV^7, and T use the equivalent of O 1680. (See, on the general question of the division of the *laisse*, Segre, 1971, note to l.1679, with references to previous scholarship; nothing is said about the apparent innovations in PL.)

(c) In *laisse* 87, T 1326 (Mortier 1336): 'tout le plus (grant) mestre en apella par nom' preserves alone (at this point) the first hemistich of O 1818; contrast V^4 1922, 'Tut *in* primera si apella Begon' and C 3137

V^7, 'Maistre cons fu, si l'apelent Bovon'; the line is lacking in *P laisse* 99, *L laisse* 57. The whole tradition of this *laisse* is significant. The passage leads into one of the assonanced insertions (Segre 1974, Table II and pp.151–2) but is still part of the δ tradition; in it, CV^7 are closest to the assonanced tradition (in which V^4 and *O* are close together, though the former has two *laisses* corresponding to *O* CXXXVII); *P laisse* 99 and *L laisse* 57 are very close to each other and furthest from the assonanced version, with which they share only half a dozen lines (fewer in *P*), one of which (= *O* 1812) is repeated (twice in the case of *P*). *T*, while having some features of its own, is clearly closer to CV^7 than to *PL*, which once more appear to have a common innovation extending over several lines, especially at the end of the *laisse*. The fact that, as Segre points out, *C* (without V^7) goes over the same ground again, the last four lines of *laisse* 198 (Mortier), *laisses* 199 and 200 being an assonanced version of the same material based on a β or a γ manuscript, is not relevant to our argument: there is no evidence of *C*'s having edited from the second of its versions to the first, which is in any case, unlike the second, shared by V^7.

(*d*) *T laisse* 91 is lacking in *O* (after *O* CXL) and (like 94, see Segre, 1971, p.365) appears to be a feature common to the β tradition. Its manuscript tradition is complex and I do not wish to tackle the problem in detail here (see Segre, 1974, pp.151–2, though it seems to me that *P*'s key version is not taken sufficiently into account); but it is relevant to our purposes that there is an assonanced version, represented by V^4, *laisse* 153 (ll.1977–85 only), by *C laisse* 203 and by *P*; the latter includes it in *laisse* 102, ll.1855–67, but the *laisse* ALSO has the rhymed version (ll.1836–49). The rhymed text is found also in *L*, *laisse* 60, with an identical development in which Justin de Valfondee is killed; the first part of this rhymed version is, as has been said, also in *T*, but here the Saracen's death is not reported; instead the last two lines of the *laisse* rejoin the assonanced version:

T 1399	le cheval broche tout une randonnee,
(Mortier 1409)	si va ferir de la tranchant espee.
	[cf. V^4, 1984–5; *C* 3244–5; *P* 1866–7].

Whatever the reason for the duplication of texts in *P*, it seems that a scribe somewhere in the *T* tradition had access either to a manuscript related to *P*, with its double account, or to both the rhymed text and the β branch of the assonanced text. He would, on either supposition, have done some editing.

(*e*) At the head of *laisse* 93, *T* agrees with *O laisse* CXLII, V^4 154, *C*

205, V^7 against P 104, L 62, where PL have an extra and banal first line: 'Seignor, oiez [o.s. L], franc chevalier baron', which appears to be a common innovation.

(*f*) T 1744 (Mortier 1754) confirms O 2161 'desuz le cunte', or at least the preposition and its place in the first hemistich; P 2456, L 1359 have 'entre ses cuisses'; C 3671, V^7 'ses chevaus fu desoz lui decoupez (decolé V^7); V^4 2304 'e desoto lui pois l'ont mort jeté'; all except CV^7 incidentally support Segre's emendation *getét* for O's *laissét*.

(*g*) Without wasting space on a detailed discussion, one may point to T *laisses* 114 and 116 as being much closer to the assonanced version (O *laisses* CLXI, CLXIII, V^4 176, 178) than any of the other rhymed manuscripts which have equivalents (C 229, V^7 for T 114, where PL lack; C 232, V^7, P 132, L 87 for T 116). Some details suggest that T, as usual, belongs to the β tradition. There are considerable common innovations in CV^7 and, separately, in PL (the most obvious being ll. 3819 and 3821–9 in CV^7 and 2505–11 in P, 1400–3 in L).

(*h*) At ll. 2026–7 (Mortier 2036–7), T is the only rhymed manuscript to preserve in fairly similar form two out of four lines which V^4 adds, as compared with O 2384–8, to the *crédo épique embryonnaire* from Roland's last speech. They concern St Mary Magdalene and the Crucifixion; C 4158–73 have a very different text on a different rhyme (though V^7 alone does refer to the Magdalene, in a totally different line, after C 4164), while P 2703–8, L 1567–71 restrict themselves to O's two references: Lazarus and Daniel (whether by contamination or by chance is uncertain). A collation of all the β manuscripts allows the fairly certain conclusion, based mainly on T's account, that the Credo in β originally quoted Lazarus, Daniel (omitted in V^4), the 'Trois Enfants', Mary Magdalene, Crucifixion, Sepulchre (? present in T 2028 alone), and Resurrection.

Two points arise from the cases examined above. T is often closer than other rhymed manuscripts to the assonanced version, as Heinemann has also said. Where the passages concerned lie outside the assonanced insertions, this argues that the original *Rhymed Roland* was perhaps not as far from the assonanced version as the perusal of manuscripts like Châteauroux and Paris often suggests. For all its youth, the Cambridge manuscript (with fragment B) points to a somewhat simpler rhymed *remaniement*, at least over the part we have been examining. I have not, on the other hand, found any evidence to support Heinemann's suspicion that T may have been contaminated at times from the a side of the stemma; where it is close to the assonanced version, it seems to be resolutely of the β camp, at any rate in my investigations to date.

The other main indication to arise from the sampling carried out in this article is that P and L regularly have common innovations which exclude T. That being so, at least for these parts of the poem, I find it hard to see how one can make P, T, and L all derive from one common ancestor, δ '', as does Segre in his well-known stemma (see, e.g. 1974, p.ix). The complexities of the various possibilities set out by Heinemann (1974), in which T derives from a source higher up the β side, seem to me to account better for the relationships discussed in this chapter.

All in all, there is some reason to enter a caveat about the contemporary of Villon who 'retouched' the old legend, in the words of Horrent quoted at the outset; he certainly did, much of the time, but he also left some significant material untouched, and this gives T a critical value which has not always been recognised.

Note

1. Dr Rejhon draws attention, in her letter to me, to a similar numbering error in Mortier's edition of MS P, where he skips from l.3544 to l.3550.

References

Bogdanow, Fanni (1960) 'Un fragment méconnu de la *Chanson de Roland* (version rimée)', *Romania*, 81, pp.500-20.

Foerster, Wendelin (1883, 1967) *Das altfranzösische Rolandslied: Text von Châteauroux und Venedig VII*, Heilbronn: Henniger; repr. Amsterdam: Rodopi.

—— (1886, 1967) *Das altfranzösische Rolandslied: Text von Paris, Cambridge, Lyon und den sog. lothringischen Fragmenten*, Heilbronn: Henniger, repr. Amsterdam: Rodopi.

Heinemann, E. A. (1974) 'Sur la valeur des manuscrits rimés pour l'étude de la tradition rolandienne: tentative pour trouver les filiations des manuscrits *TLP*', *Le Moyen Age*, 80, pp.71-87.

Horrent, Jules (1951) *La Chanson de Roland dans les littératures française et espagnole au moyen âge*, Paris: Belles Lettres.

Mortier, Raoul (1940-44) *Les Textes de la Chanson de Roland*, 10 Vols, Paris: Editions de la Geste Francor (*T* = Vol. 7).

Roncaglia, Aurelio (1959) 'Petit vers et refrain dans les chansons de geste', in *La Technique littéraire des chansons de geste. Actes du colloque de Liège (septembre 1957)*, Paris: Belles lettres, pp.141-59.

Segre, Cesare (1971) *La Chanson de Roland. Edizione critica*, Milan and Naples: Riccardo Ricciardi.

—— (1974) *'La Tradizione della Chanson de Roland'*, Milan and Naples: Riccardo Ricciardi.

Tyssens, Madeleine (1959) 'Le problème du vers orphelin dans le "cycle d'Aliscans" et les deux versions du *Moniage Guillaume*', in *La Technique littéraire des chansons de geste. Actes du colloque de Liège (septembre 1957)*, Paris: Belles Lettres, pp.429-56.

Whitehead, Frederick (ed.) (1942, 1946) *La Chanson de Roland*, 2nd ed., Oxford: Blackwell.

Angus J. Kennedy

7. EDITING CHRISTINE DE PIZAN'S
EPISTRE A LA REINE

Christine de Pizan's *Epistre à la reine* of 1405 represents the first of a
number of prose epistles written to reflect her concern at the
deteriorating political situation in France and her determination to
comment on and, if possible, influence contemporary affairs. Addressed
to Isabeau de Bavière, wife of the unfortunate Charles VI, whose
intermittent mental illness had made his court the inevitable focal point
of a relentless power struggle between various rival factions, it urged
her to act as mediator in a particular episode in the rivalry between the
houses of Orléans and Burgundy which had brought France to the brink
of civil war in 1405. In the summer of that year Jean sans Peur, duc de
Bourgogne, had foiled an attempt by the Queen and Louis, duc d'Orléans,
to remove the Dauphin from Paris to Melun. Although the Dauphin
was safely escorted back to Paris, deadlock ensued, since the rival forces
refused to disband, Jean sans Peur being based in Paris, and Louis and
the Queen in Melun. The terms of a reconciliation were, indeed, not
worked out until 16 October 1405, eleven days after the date of
composition of Christine's letter. Whether Christine's appeal to the
Queen played a part in bringing about peace is impossible to say (for
differing assessments, see Thomassy, 1838, p.xxiii; Mirot, 1914, p.384);
what is certain is that the peace that was negotiated (the Paix de
Vincennes) was simply one of a long series of fragile, illusory truces
that were to punctuate the next decade and a half without ever solving
the problem of civil war (Louis was to be assassinated in 1407, Jean
sans Peur in 1419). The purpose of the present essay will be to
examine and illustrate some of the problems that confront the editor of
the *Epistre à la reine*. It will look in particular at (*i*) editorial problems
involved in the establishment of the text, including the relevance of
textual data to the claim that B.N.f.fr.580 is an autograph manuscript
(on this claim, see Willard 1965; Ouy and Reno 1980, pp.223–4; de
Winter 1982, pp.336–337, n.4); (*ii*) the interrelationship (if any) of the
text and the sole miniature, in B.N.f.fr.580; and (*iii*) two still unsolved
problems in the manuscript tradition. A proper context for a discussion
of these issues will be provided by a brief description of manuscripts and
editions.

Manuscripts and Editions

The text survives in six manuscripts, all fifteenth century, four being complete (B.N.f.fr.580, ff.53^r–54^v, 605, ff.1–2^v Chantilly, Musée Condé 493, ff.427^v–429^v, Oxford, All Souls 182, ff.230^d–232^d) and two incomplete (B.N.f.fr.604, f.314^r–314^v and Brussels, Bibliothèque Royale, IV 1176, 8ff.). B. L. Harley 4431 contains an erased section of the text (the second half of the letter) on f.255^r–255^v col. a. Although any of three of the complete manuscripts (B.N.f.fr.580, 605, and Condé 493) would provide a reasonable base text (they are all early fifteenth century), B.N.f.fr.580 emerges as the natural choice, since it has a number of features that make it unique (it alone contains the miniature at the beginning of the text and the rondeau at the end, and it has claims to being an autograph manuscript). There are five editions of the text available, only the most recent being based on all six manuscripts. The first edition was printed in 1838 by R. Thomassy in his pioneering study of Christine's political writings, the *Essai sur les écrits politiques de Christine de Pisan*, pp.133–40. Despite its inaccuracies, Thomassy's transcription of this and other texts was extremely important, in that it opened up discussion of Christine's reactions to contemporary affairs and made available to scholars an anthology of hitherto unpublished material. Thomassy consulted only two manuscripts, choosing Paris, Bibliothèque Royale 7073-2 (now B.N.f.fr.580) as his base text, and using (without identifying where) a few variants from Paris, Bibliothèque Royale 7088 (now B.N.f.fr.605) to rectify what he considered to be errors. L. Mirot's edition of 1914, based solely on B.N.f.fr.580 is also inaccurate, containing as it does a good number of minor slips and some important misinterpretations (e.g. *basses demeres* for *lasses de meres* l.111; *si lait diffamé nom accoustumé* for *si lait diffame non accoustumé* l.119). In her invaluable edition of Anglo-Norman letters and petitions in Oxford, All Souls 182 of 1941 (pp.144–50), the late Professor Dominica Legge included a transcription of the *Epistre* from this manuscript, variants being provided from B.N.f.fr.580, 604, and 605. Though this text has been rightly and widely used as the most accessible scholarly edition, it does, however, present a number of significant drawbacks. First, All Souls 182 is not the most suitable base manuscript for an edition of the *Epistre* — the orthography is somewhat idiosyncratic, earlier manuscripts are available. Secondly, the restrictions of the war years meant that the manuscript was not accessible to Professor Legge when her volume was in proof (this may explain some of the slips, e.g. the editor has read *n* with a backwards flourish as a *u* accompanied by the usual sign indicating a missing *m* or *n* — hence the misreadings *affecioun* l.7, *guerisoun* l.13, *afflicioun* l.28, *restauracioun* l.55, *tribulacioun* l.171 of Legge's edition; in the prologue transcribed from B.N.f.fr.604 at the end of her text, *le roy de Scale* should read *le roy de Secile*, and the *duc de Lembourde, duc de Lembourch*). In 1984 Josette A. Wisman published her edition of the *Epistre*, but instead of basing herself on the manuscripts, relied on Thomassy's transcription and the variants and critical apparatus provided by Legge. Thus, the inaccuracies of both Thomassy and Legge have been retained in Wisman's text and variants. The most recent edition, that of Kennedy in 1988, attempts to produce a critical text based on B.N.f.fr.580, with variants from all the surviving manuscripts apart from the deleted text in B. L. Harley 4431, f.255. A number of corrections require to be made to this text ('on est toujours un peu fautif', as Camus once said): l.21, read *besoingnes*; l.66, read *faicte*; the line numbering on p.257 should read 120, 124, 128; l.158, read *cest*; *variants*: l.4 read *veulle* BC and *ou (despris)* F; l.21, *besongnes* E; l.38, add *ung* D; l.51, *ffrance* F; l.88, replace *om. et (bonne)* by *querir before*; l.92, add *royne faictes* F; l.103, *ennnemys (sic)* F. A more acceptable punctuation for ll.8–17 (despite the clear pause indicated in the manuscript after *remede* l.11) would be: full stop after *choses* l.8, replace full stop after *remede* l.11 by comma, ll.8–17 now to be read as one single sentence with no change of paragraph.

Editorial Problems in the Establishment of the Text

B.N.f.fr.580 contains a number of scribal errors and corrections of the kind one would expect to find in any manuscript, irrespective of the status of the scribe: *criant* for *crient*, l.25; *appellee* for *appelle*, l.39; *nom* for *non*, l.119; *les* for *des*, l.141; *come* inserted in right hand margin, l.38; *ne* scored out after *gouvernerent*, l.61; *condampne* has an extra *e* which has been scored out, l.77; *royne* is scored out after *dure*, l.99; *noble* inserted above line after *ce*, l.119; *fertilite* is scored out after *de* and before *tribulacion*, ll.148–9. There are other errors or textual problems, however, that deserve closer investigation either in their own right (ll.124–8) or for the light they may shed on the claim that B.N.f.fr.580 should be seen as an autograph manuscript (ll.53–6 and l.24).

(*a*) ll.53–6 and 24. B.N.f.fr.580, f.53 verso a, ll.24–31 (corresponding to ll.53–6 of Kennedy, 1988) raise a number of problems for the establishment of the text which, rather surprisingly, are not discussed at all in Wisman's recent edition (1984). After listing three benefits that Isabeau will obtain if she will devote her energies to securing peace (she will avoid further bloodshed, she will be seen publicly as a peacemaker, she will be remembered for her role as mediator in the chronicles of France), Christine goes on to counter reasons which the Queen might advance for not intervening — one being that the Queen might feel that she has been injured by one of the parties and might therefore be rather reluctant to become involved. The reading in B.N.f.fr.580 at this point, retained by Thomassy, Mirot, and Wisman, is as follows (accents and punctuations have been added): 'Et ma redoubtée dame, à regarder aux raisons de vostre droit, posons qu'il soit ou feust ainsi que la dignité de vostre haultesse se tenist de l'une des partiez avoir aucunement blecée, par quoy vostre hault cuer feust mains evolu que par ceste paix feust traictiée.' The readings in the five other manuscripts (the fragment in Harley 4431, f.255 does not contain this part of the letter) all correct three main errors in the base manuscript: the omission of *esté* after *avoir*; *evolu* for *enclin*; the omission of *vous* after *par* and before *ceste paix*. Each of these represents of course a perfectly understandable scribal error (the omission of *esté* and *vous* could be explained by momentary inattention, whilst *enclin* could very easily be misread as *evolu*). What is more difficult to accept, however, is that these three errors in one short sentence could have been made by a copyist who was also the author of the text. Is it conceivable that Christine, author and scribe, could have left uncorrected such an obviously incorrect and (as it stands) not very meaningful sentence? Similar doubts are raised by the fact that *tretresse* (for *tristesse*) is left uncorrected in l.24. The textual evidence at these points, which admittedly is only one of the factors to be reckoned with in the identification of Christine's autograph manuscripts, could be seen to argue against the view that B.N.f.fr.580 was copied by Christine herself.

(*b*) ll.124-8. After evoking the calamities that civil strife between the princes of the realm would inflict on the 'pouvre pueple', Christine forcefully warns the great of the land that, should they persist in their irresponsible and sinful disregard of the sufferings they may cause, they too could fall victim to the fickle goddess Fortuna: 'Et oultre seroit-ce encores à notter à cellui prince ou princesse qui le cuer aroit tant ostiné en pechié, qu'il n'acompteroit nulle chose à Dieu ne à si faictes douleurs, s'il n'estoit du tout fol ou folle, les tres variables tours de Fortune, qui en un tout seul moment se puet changier et muer (ll.124-8). This sentence raises a number of problems, some editorial, some of interpretation. The word before *douleurs* in B.N.f.fr.580 is abbreviated to four letters (*fces*) which are accompanied by a standard sign indicating an abbreviation, thus, *fc̄es*. Thomassy (p.139) resolved this abbreviation as *fortes*, a reading retained in the 1984 text edited by Wisman (p.80, l.7), who misleadingly states in the notes that the variant *saintes* is provided by B.N.f.fr.604, 605, and Oxford, All Souls 182. The reading *saintes* does not occur in any of the manuscripts but represents in fact a correction proposed by Dominica Legge to replace *faittes* (not *faites* as stated by Legge) in her transcription of All Souls 182 (p.148). The variants in Condé 493 and Brussels IV 1176 (*faictes*), B.N.f.fr.605 and All Souls 182 (*faittes*), and Harley 4431 (*faites*, just visible on f.255 col. b, l.23) all point to the fact that *fc̄es* should be resolved as *faictes* (B.N.f.fr.604 does not contain this section). Further confirmation of this is provided from within B.N.f.fr.580 itself: on f.53 verso b, l.10 virtually the same abbreviation occurs, although on this occasion it points to a singular not a plural form: 'la vaillant dame, non obstant la villeinie faicte, ne vint-elle au devant de son filz et tant fist qu'elle appaisa son yre et le pacefia aux Rommains" (ll.65–7). Clearly, in this sentence, the only appropriate resolution of the abbreviation would be *faicte*. With regard to l.126, therefore, there are no grounds for retaining *fortes* (Thomassy, Wisman), or for rejecting *faictes* and replacing it by *saintes* (Legge): all the manuscript evidence points rather to *faictes* as the correct reading (Mirot, Kennedy). The meaning of 'si faictes douleurs' would be 'sorrows of this kind', the construction 'si fait' here being exactly in line with its widely attested usage and meaning (for some examples in Christine, see Roy, 1885–96, I, p.37, ll.17–18: 'si ne pourroit jamais estre arrachée/ si faitte amour'; Roy, I, pp.113–14, ll.11–12: 'ains deust on rudement/ d'entre les bons si faitte gent sortir'; Roy, II, p.25, l.792: 'sanz plus souffrir nulle injure si faitte'; Roy, II, p.276, ll.1704–6: 'Mais, pour voir, sus sains vous jure/ Que jamais si faitte injure/ Ne feray a mon honneur'; Roy, II, p.179, l.675: 'N'oyent parler fors de si faittes proses'). But sorrows of which kind? In proposing *saintes* for *faittes* Dominica Legge was clearly relating the sorrows to the sacred sorrows suffered by Christ on the cross. In context, this interpretation seems unlikely: 'sorrows of this kind' must refer to the sorrows and sufferings referred to in the immediately preceding section i.e. those endured by the ordinary people as a result of civil strife dividing the princes of the realm (ll.104–24).

There remains now the problem of interpreting the grammar, syntax, and sense of the sentence as a whole. The clause 'qu'il n'acompteroit nulle chose à Dieu ne à si faictes douleurs' should be seen as dependent on 'cellui prince ou princesse qui le cuer aroit tant ostiné en pechié' i.e. the basic construction here is *tant* followed by *que* introducing a result clause. One would then have to assume that the *ce* in *seroit-ce* is designed (despite the singular verb) to anticipate the plural subject 'les tres variables tours de Fortune'. The general sense would then be as follows: 'And in addition, the very capricious tricks/turns of Fortune, which can change and transform itself in one single moment, should be noted by a prince or princess (assuming that he/she was not completely mad) whose heart is so set on sin that he/she would give no thought to God or to sorrows of this kind'. In other words, Christine is warning that a person of rank cannot with impunity turn his or her back on God and the sufferings which selfish, irresponsible conduct may inflict on ordinary people.

Text and Miniature

The miniature in *grisaille* at the head of column a on f.53 recto of B.N.f.fr.580 depicts a lover and his lady sitting on a long wooden seat, beneath a canopy that forms part of the architectural setting; the man is holding out a scroll bearing the motto 'mort ou merci', words which clearly constitute his appeal to the lady to make up her mind either to bring about his death by rejecting him or to ensure his happiness by adopting a more compassionate, conciliatory attitude towards him. When one looks in detail at the thrust of Christine's appeal to the Queen, it soon becomes clear that the terms of this alternative (death, clemency), though formulated in the specific terminology of courtly love, are applicable to the wider, political choices with which Christine confronts Isabeau. The following brief analysis will confirm that, despite Paulin Paris's doubts (p.73) and those more recently expressed by de Winter (pp.336–7, n.4), Thomassy, the first editor of the *Epistre*, was right to suggest a link between text and illustration. In a brief note (p.140, n.1) he interpreted the words 'mort ou merci' as a 'cri de désespoir dans la bouche de Christine', i.e. as Christine's despairing response to the continuing threat of civil strife.

In order to secure Isabeau's involvement as mediator, Christine simultaneously develops two contrasting themes in her letter: she evokes, on the one hand, the inevitably disastrous consequences that France would have to endure if the Queen failed to take action; and, on the other, the benefits that would accrue to France (and the Queen personally) if she were to succeed in reconciling the Dukes of Orléans and Burgundy. Death and destruction threaten to engulf the kingdom of France, which is divided against itself, 'playé et navré piteusement et en peril de piz' (ll.14–15); its people are 'reampliz d'affliccion et tristesse' (l.24); the princes of the realm who should constitute 'un

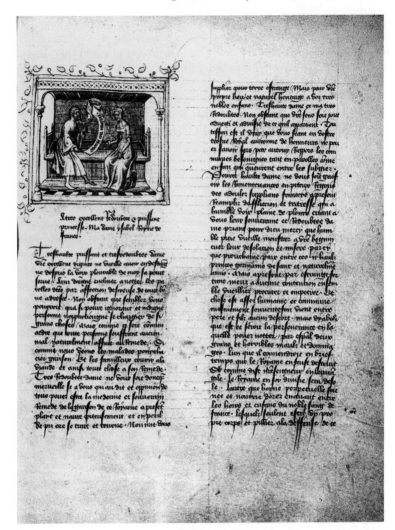

Bibliothèque Nationale, f.fr. 580, f. 53 recto

propre corps et pillier à la deffense de cestui dit royame' (ll.38-9) risk being caught up in internecine strife and divided forever by 'hayne perpetuelle' (l.36); if civil strife continues, the result will be further bloodshed and the fragmentation of the corporate body: 'si honteuse effusion de sang ou tres crestien et de Dieu establi royame de France' (ll.45-6) . . . Helas doncques qui seroit si dure mere qui peust souffrir, se elle n'avoit le cuer de pierre, veoir ses enfans entreoccire et espendre le sang l'un à l'autre et leurs povres membres destruire et disperser' (ll.99-102); and the innocent ordinary people ('le pouvre pueple', l.109) will be forced to pay for the sins of those who should have been their protectors ('ceulz qui garder les devoient', l.118). To demonstrate the urgency of the situation, Christine makes clear to the Queen that these dreadful possibilities are already being realised: 'Et certes, noble dame, nous veons à present les apprestes de ces mortelz inconveniens qui ja sont si avanciez que tres maintenant en y a de destruiz et desers de leurs biens, en destruit-on touz les jours de piz en piz, tant que qui est crestien en doit avoir pitié' (ll.120-4). Counterbalancing, however, this scenario of death and destruction is the prospect of peace and reconciliation that only Isabeau can open up through her direct intervention in the quarrel. She will constitute the only effective remedy to her country's continuing sickness, as she is 'la medecine et souverain remede de la garison de ce royame' (ll.13-14); she alone can prevent the anticipated shedding of blood: 'par vous seroit eschevée si grant et si honteuse effusion de sang' (ll.44-5); she will be regarded as the 'pourchacerresse de paix et cause de la restitucion du bien de vostre noble porteure et de leurs loyaulx subgiez' (ll.47-9); her achievements will be crowned with honour in the 'croniques et nobles gestes de France' (ll.50-1); as a woman and as a queen, she is the natural repository of the virtues of compassion, charity, clemency, and goodwill and ought to use these qualities to bring about peace: 'Helas, honnourée dame, doncques quant il avendra que pitié, charité, clemence et benignité ne sera trouvée en haute princesse, ou sera-elle doncques quise? Car, comme naturelment en femenines condicions soient les dictes vertus, plus par rayson doivent habonder et estre en noble dame, de tant comme elle reçoit plus de dons de Dieu' (ll.67-72). It is up to Isabeau herself to choose whether she wishes to follow in the footsteps of the great women whose role as mediator is recorded in scripture or history (e.g. the Virgin, Veturia, Esther, Bathsheba, Blanche de Castille) or to behave like a Jezabel or Olimpias and bequeath to posterity an unenviable reputation for excessive violence and cruelty.

It is clear, then, that the terms of the alternative put by the lover to his lady in the miniature are applicable to the choices with which Christine confronts Isabeau in the text of her letter. Like the lady in the miniature, Isabeau has it within her power to bring about either death and destruction, on the one hand, or, on the other, joy and reconciliation; and the fact that in the miniature it is a man who formulates Christine's 'cri de désespoir' is fully appropriate in the context, given that B.N.f.fr.580, the only manuscript of the text to contain an illustration, is also the only one to contain the rondeau addressed to the 'noble seigneur' (l.160) who may have commissioned the letter. Encapsulating as it does in visual form the central choice formulated in the text of the letter, the miniature in B.N.f.fr.580 clearly constitutes an indispensable part of the manuscript evidence available to an editor. Image, as well as text, deserves to figure in any edition of the *Epistre*

Two unsolved problems in the manuscript tradition

(a) B. L. Harley 4431, f.255 (recto a and b, verso a) contains an erased section of the *Epistre*, visible under ultra-violet light and corresponding to ll.91–157 of Kennedy, beginning 'entre ses bras le tenoit'. Given that forty-six lines of the printed text correspond to two columns each of thirty-nine lines on f.255 recto, one can estimate that the missing preceding lines (1–90) would have required about 3.9 columns in the manuscript, i.e. almost a complete folio, recto and verso. As Hindman has demonstrated (p.109), the original folio 254, which would have contained the end of the *Epistres sur le roman de la rose* and ll.91–136 of the letter to the Queen, was replaced by a new leaf, on which were copied only the concluding lines of the *Epistres sur le roman de la rose* (thirteen lines plus Christine's name). Running titles for the *Epistre à la reine*, which would normally have been written in at a fairly late stage of the copying process are just visible on f.255. The codicological evidence here points clearly to two incontrovertible facts: one, that it was originally planned to include the *Epistre à la reine* in the Queen's manuscript; and two, that shortly before the volume was presented to the Queen, a decision was taken to remove/erase the text of the letter. Various reasons have been put forward to explain these alterations: fear of offending Isabeau in a volume commissioned by the Queen herself (Mombello, 1967, p.203 and Hindman, 1983, pp.109–11); a request from Isabeau that a letter critical of herself be omitted (Hindman, p.111); the possibility that a scribe may have copied out the letter, not realising that it was inappropriate to include it since the Queen had already received her copy some years before (Laidlaw, 1987, p.65). To these various possibilities, each one plausible in its own right, one could add yet another. Assuming that Christine intervened to order the deletion of a text copied out by a scribe unaware of the implications of including this particular work, would it not be reasonable to conclude that Christine simply thought it inappropriate in 1410 (the date of Harley 4431) to include the 1405 letter urging Isabeau to reconcile two warring princes, one of whom (Louis d'Orléans) was by now dead, assassinated on the orders of the other (Jean sans Peur) in 1407? Both Christine and Isabeau must have found themselves overtaken by events, and it may have seemed pointless to include a letter so closely tied to particular historical circumstances. A sense of inappropriateness, therefore, rather than fear or deference, may explain the deletion of the letter. It goes without saying, however, that all the reasons adduced must remain speculative: only the discovery of new evidence, either internal or external, is likely to solve this particular enigma.

(*b*) A second problem in the manuscript tradition is one that, to my knowledge, has not been noted or discussed. A systematic survey of nineteenth-century periodicals for references to Christine has brought to light some contributions to the *Revue des Sociétés Savantes des Départements* that mention a then privately owned manuscript containing the *Epistre à la reine* (5e série, vol. 6 (1873), pp.6–7; vol. 7 (1874), pp.412–13, 522–5). At a meeting of 9 June 1873 of the Section d'Histoire et de Philologie of the journal, chaired by Léopold Delisle, the secretary, Ch. Hippeau, reported the following:

> M. Victor de Saint-Genis, conservateur des hypothèques à Châtellerault (Vienne), adresse copie d'un mémoire sur un manifeste inédit du parti français en 1405, adressé par Christine de Pisan à la reine Isabeau de Bavière. La pièce originale est tirée d'un magnifique manuscrit existant à Châtellerault. Elle figure à la fin de ce manuscrit, qui a pour titre: 'La viie partie du livre de la mutacion de fortune qui parle de l'histoire des Romains abrégée, celle d'Alexandre et des principaux régnans environ l'âge de la personne qui a composé ledit livre'. (vol. 6, pp.6–7)

The copy of the 'mémoire' was then referred to M. Marty-Laveaux for further consideration, and eventually deposited in the society's archives. Marty-Laveaux's reports are to be found in vol. 7, pp.412 and 523–4. There we discover that the text was taken from a manuscript belonging to M. Arnaudeau, maire de Châtellerault, that M. de Saint-Genis was aware that there existed another copy of the text, with variant readings, at the Bibliothèque Nationale (p.412), and that the aim of the 'document' was to 'développer cette pensée par laquelle il se termine: "Dureté toujours a mené les grans à piteuse fortune, et oncques la honte fut pour les benins"' (p.523). It was decided not to publish the text in the journal, because 'une publication isolée lui ferait perdre de son intérêt, et sa véritable place est dans un choix des oeuvres de Christine de Pisan, ou parmi les pièces justificatives d'un ouvrage historique' (p.524). Further information, however, is given in a second communication from M. de Saint-Genis, this time regarding a satirical paraphrase of the *Pater c.* 1450–80:

> J'ai eu l'honneur d'adresser au Comité un manifeste du parti français en 1405, rédigé dans le dessein de réunir des adhérents et de donner une forme aux doléances des bourgeois et manants des provinces du centre et du nord, pillées par les bandes des princes ennemis. Mais ce manifeste, adressé à la reine Isabeau, qui n'aimait pas les conseils, présenté par le comte de Nevers, qui ne voulait pas *heurter trop rudement à l'huis*, selon ses propres paroles, n'est que l'expression modérée de plaintes atténuées par l'esprit de cour. (pp.524–5)

From all of these details one is tempted to conclude that the manuscript in question must be Condé 492–3, which does contain the *Epistre à la reine* after Book VII of the *Mutacion*; in addition, this manuscript was in private hands at the date in question, since it was not acquired by Chantilly till 1887 (Solente, 1959–66, I, p.cxxix) or 1888 (Mombello, 1967, p.110 and n.4) when it was bought from Morgand et Fatout, who in turn had received it from the Comte de Toustain in 1882 (see Roy, 1886–96, I, p.xix and n.1). Yet some doubts remain. First, the reported rubric of Book VII of the *Mutacion* is not in line with that of 493 as printed by Solente (Vols 1, p.4 and 3, p.171, n.2). Secondly, where does the information come from that the letter was presented to the Queen by the comte de Nevers? Condé 493 does contain a reference to the comte de Nevers in the prologue (see Kennedy, 1988, p.259 — here the reference is to Jean sans Peur's younger brother, Philippe); but there is no indication given that he or anyone else actually presented the letter to Isabeau. Thirdly, and perhaps most importantly of all, the sentence 'Dureté toujours a mené les grans à piteuse fortune, et oncques la honte fut pour les benins' (p.523) does not, to my knowledge, occur in 493 at the end of the letter. The other possibility, therefore, is that reference is being made to another, as yet unidentified manuscript. If this turns out to be the case, the contributions in the *Revue des Sociétés Savantes* will have played a crucial role in at least alerting us to its existence. It should be borne in mind in this context that Christine manuscripts have resurfaced in the recent past, and there is no reason why they should not do so again (the

Brussels *Epistre à la reine* manuscript was not acquired by the Bibliothèque Royale until 1980; a manuscript of the *Mutacion* was sold at Sotheby's on 13 July 1977, and is still privately owned in Germany). If the Châtellerault manuscript cannot be traced, definite answers to all of the questions raised must depend on locating the archives of the *Revue des Sociétés Savantes*, where the original reports were filed. *Hoc opus, hic labor est.*[1]

Note

1. The archives have now been traced and an article on Saint-Genis's report is forthcoming.

References

Hindman, S. (1983) 'The Composition of the Manuscript of Christine de Pizan's Collected Works in the British Library: A Reassessment', *BLJ*, 9, pp.93-123.

Kennedy, A. J. (1988) 'Christine de Pizan's *Epistre à la reine* (1405)', RLR, 92, pp.253-64.

Laidlaw, J. C. (1987) 'Christine de Pizan — A Publisher's Progress', *MLR*, 82, pp.35-75. I wish to record my gratitude to Professor Laidlaw for his comments and advice during the preparation of this essay.

Legge, M. D. (1941) *Anglo-Norman Letters and Petitions from All Souls MS 182*, Oxford: Blackwell (Anglo-Norman Texts Society, III), pp.144-50.

Mirot, L. (1914) 'L'Enlèvement du Dauphin et le premier conflit entre Jean sans Peur et Louis d'Orléans', *RQH*, 95, pp.329-55; 96, pp.47-68 and 369-419.

Mombello, G. (1967) *La tradizione manoscritta dell' 'Epistre Othea' di Christine de Pizan: Prolegomeni all' edizione del testo*, Torino: Accademia delle Scienze.

Ouy, G. and Reno, C. M. (1980) 'Identification des autographes de Christine de Pizan', *Scriptorium*, 34, pp.221-38.

Paris, P. (1842) *Les Manuscrits françois de la Bibliothèque du Roi*, vol. 5, Paris: Techener.

Revue des Sociétés Savantes des Départements, 5e série, 6 (1873), pp.6-7; and 7 (1874), pp.412-13, 522-5.

Roy, M. (1886-96) *Oeuvres complètes de Christine de Pisan*, 3 vols, Paris: Firmin-Didot (SATF).

Solente, S. (1959-66) *Le livre de la mutacion de Fortune*, 4 vols, Paris: Picard (SATF).

Thomassy, R. (1838) *Essai sur les écrits politiques de Christine de Pisan, suivi d'une notice littéraire et de pièces inédites*, Paris: Debécourt.

Willard, C. C. (1965) 'An autograph manuscript of Christine de Pizan?', *Studi francesi*, 27, pp.452-7.

Winter, P. M. de (1982) 'Christine de Pizan, ses enlumineurs et ses rapports avec le milieu bourguignon', *Actes du Congrès national des Sociétés Savantes (Bordeaux, 1979), Archéologie*, Paris: Bibliothèque Nationale, pp.335-76.

Wisman, J. A. (1984) *The Epistle of the Prison of Human Life with An Epistle to the Queen of France and Lament on the Evils of Civil War*, New York: Garland.

J. C. Laidlaw

8. HOW LONG IS THE
LIVRE DU CHEMIN DE LONG ESTUDE?

The composition and publication of the *Livre du chemin de long estude* can be dated with some precision. The poem was begun on 5 or 6 October 1402: overcome by grief as she recalled the death of her husband and disheartened by some adversity to which she makes veiled allusion, Christine de Pizan sought relief among her books. She chose Boethius's *De consolatione philosophiae*, continuing to read until well after midnight when she retired to bed (Püschel, 1887, ll.165–307). The Sibyl of Cumae appeared to her in a dream, offering to conduct her to a more perfect world:

> Je te cuit conduire de fait
> En autre monde plus parfait,
> Ou tu pourras trop plus aprendre
> 652 Que ne pues en cestui comprendre,
> Voire de choses plus notables,
> Plus plaisans et plus prouffitables,
> Et ou n'a vilté ne destrece.

The Sibyl's invitation was accepted with enthusiasm and the journey began.

Five and a half months later, on 20 March 1403 (n.s.), Christine presented a copy of the poem to the Duke of Berry, as is indicated in the ducal inventory:

> Item, un petit livre appellé le *Livre de long estude*, fait et compilé par une femme appellée Cristine, escript de lettre de court, historié de blanc et de noir; couvert de cuir vermeil empraint, à deux fermouers de cuivre et tixus noirs; et au commancement du second fueillet a escript: *de souverain sens*; lequel livre fu donné à Monseigneur en son hostel de Neelle, à Paris, par la dessusdicte Cristine, le xxᵉ jour de mars l'an mil CCCC et deux (Guiffrey, I. no.932, pp.243–4).

That description corresponds exactly with Paris, Bibliothèque Nationale, fonds français 1188 (hereafter Paris fr. 1188), save only that the original binding has not survived (Avril, 1975, p.52, n.23; Solente, 1976, pp.48–51).

(83)

The *Chemin de long estude* was not dedicated to the Duke of Berry alone, as the opening lines of the prologue (ll.1–60) make clear. The king was to receive the first copy:

> A vous, bon roy de France redoubtable,
> Le VIe Charles du nom notable,
> Que Dieux maintiengne en joie et en santé,
> 12   Mon petit dit soit premier presenté . . .

The poem is addressed in addition to the Dukes of Berry, Burgundy, and Orleans, who are asked to arbitrate on the debate which forms the closing section. It is thus entirely appropriate that the opening miniature in Paris fr. 1188 and in other illustrated copies should show Christine presenting the poem to Charles VI, who is flanked by the royal dukes and by other courtiers.

The dedication of the *Chemin de long estude* jointly to the king and to the three royal dukes indicates that four of the earliest copies of the poem must have been prepared for them. It is reasonable to assume that the dukes received their copies soon after the king; to avoid offence and to ensure that the poem was launched successfully, the three presentations must have taken place within a relatively short space of time. Thus, it can be assumed that, when Christine de Pizan presented Paris fr. 1188 to the Duke of Berry on 20 March 1403, at least three other copies of the poem had already been completed. The copy given to Philip the Bold, Duke of Burgundy is probably that described in an inventory drawn up on 20 March 1404: 'Le livre qui parle du *Chemin de Longue Estude*, fermant a deux fermaux de leton' (Doutrepont, 1906, no.131, p.86). Thereafter, Christine may well have prepared additional copies of the poem for other patrons, as she had done with previous works (Laidlaw, 1987, pp.40–2).

Christine had followed a very demanding time-table. The composition of a poem of almost 6400 lines required considerable time, even for an accomplished writer. An analysis of the references to contemporary events in the *Chemin de long estude* led Suzanne Solente to conclude that the poem had been completed before the end of 1402, perhaps as early as November (Solente, 1978).

After the text itself was ready, the presentation copies had to be planned. Before the scribes could begin work, the number of lines per page, the position of miniatures, rubrics, ornamental capitals, and paragraph marks had to be determined. The different operations had to be scheduled: the rubrics and the decoration could be inserted only after the work had been copied. Time had also to be allowed for correcting the text and for binding the finished volume. Not that Christine was a novice in these matters: by 1402 she had gained considerable experience of preparing her works for publication (Laidlaw, 1987, pp.37–49). Nevertheless, it remains a remarkable achievement that in a period of five and a half months Christine both composed the *Chemin de long estude* and supervised the preparation of at least four presentation copies.

The Manuscripts

The aim of this essay is to review the nine surviving manuscripts of the *Chemin de long estude* and to see what light that examination casts on the work's publication and subsequent evolution. The poem was edited by Robert Püschel in 1887 from the seven manuscripts known to him. A new edition, based on all nine extant copies, had been substantially completed by Solente before her death in 1978, but has not yet been published. The line numbers used here are those of Püschel, and his sigla have also been retained and, where necessary, extended to take in the manuscripts of which he was unaware. In quotations from Solente line references and sigla have been appropriately adjusted.

Five of the extant manuscripts contain only the *Chemin de long estude*, and in the other four the poem forms part of a larger collection. Four of the five individual manuscripts, Brussels, Bibliothèque Royale 10982 (A) and 10983 (F), and Paris fr. 1188 (D) and 1643 (B) are copied in early fifteenth-century hands, and they are all laid out and decorated in very similar fashion. The close physical resemblance of ABF to D, the Duke of Berry's copy of March 1403, suggests that these three manuscripts also are presentation copies prepared under Christine's direct supervision.

There is further evidence about ABF which points to the same conclusion. A and F are both included in the catalogue of the library of the Dukes of Burgundy drawn up in 1420 (Doutrepont, 1906, nos 130–1). However, neither manuscript can be identified with certainty as the copy presented to Philip the Bold in 1403. A note by Gilbert Ouy on the front fly-leaf of B identifies the manuscript with the volume described in the catalogues of the Orleans library drawn up in 1417 and 1427 (not 1440 as in the note):

> Le Chemin de long estude, couvert de cuir rouge marqueté;
> Le livre du Chemin de long estude, en lettre courant, en françois, couvert de cuir rouge marqueté, a deux fermouers de cuivre.
> (Champion, 1910, p.32)

The identification rests entirely on the early fifteenth-century binding of stamped brown leather which B retains, and must therefore be treated with caution: bindings in *cuir rouge marqueté* were not uncommon at the time. Even if Ouy's conclusion were accepted, it would not indicate the date when the volume entered the Duke of Orleans's library. To complicate matters further, the back of the binding bears a label in a fifteenth-century hand which reads 'Le chemin de longue estude du duc de Berry'. However, the Duke's inventories contain no reference to a second copy of the *Chemin de long estude*.

B is the only manuscript of the *Chemin de long estude* in which the spaces reserved for the miniatures, five in all, have been left unfilled. That circumstance is not in itself remarkable since there are many medieval manuscripts in which the miniatures originally planned have not been completed. In the case of B, however, the absence of the illustrations has to be considered along with a series of marginal instructions in a second hand, which indicate where a further eleven miniatures should be positioned in a projected copy of the work. A typical instruction reads 'Cy soit laisié espace a faire histoire' (ff.2^r, 27^r). Generally these additional illustrations are to be inserted at a point where B already contains a decorated capital. If there is no such capital, the instruction takes the form, 'Cy soit laissié espace affaire histoire & une grant letre' (fol. 91^v; cf. ff. 51^v, 57^r). Further examples of the same handwriting can be seen elsewhere in B, in the many corrections to the text. Ouy has identified the second hand as that of Christine de Pizan (Ouy, 1985, pp.119–31; see also Ouy and Reno, 1980, pp.221–38). That identification can be confirmed by the presence of corrections in the same hand not only in B but also in each of ACDFLR.

The fifth manuscript in this group, Kraków, Biblioteka Jagiellońska, Gall.Fol.133 (G), formerly in the royal library in Berlin, dates from the middle of the fifteenth century and, unlike all the other copies of the poem, is on paper not on parchment (Dulac, 1986, p.329). Püschel pointed out that G is closely related to F, and also to E (see below). Since it is late and occupies a subordinate place in the textual tradition, G need not be considered further here.

The *Chemin de long estude* is also included in four collections of Christine's works. It is one of four additions to the *Livre de Cristine* which were incorporated in Chantilly, Musée Condé 492–3 (L) between 1403 and 1405. Püschel did not know of that collection, but did have access to Paris fr. 604 (E), a mid fifteenth-century copy of L; E can be excluded from further consideration here for the same reasons as G. The *Chemin de long estude* is included in Paris fr. 836 (C), one of the five parts of the collection which Christine probably intended for the Duke of Orleans and which after his death was acquired by the Duke of Berry in 1408 or 1409. The fourth collected manuscript which contains the poem is London, British Library, Harley 4431 (R), commissioned from Christine by Queen Isabelle and completed in 1410 or 1411 (Laidlaw, 1987, pp.49–59, 60–6). Püschel was unaware of the existence of R.

The miniatures and decoration

Table 1 shows the position of the miniatures, rubrics, decorated capitals with borders, and intermediate capitals in the seven manuscripts which remain to be considered. (The column headed B1 gives details of the instructions added to B.) As can be seen, the decoration is remarkably consistent, the main difference being the number and location of the miniatures. In ABDFL the miniatures are clustered in the first third of the text. Some care has been taken to disperse the additional illustrations in CR and in B1.

It is not surprising that in all the copies the poem opens with a picture of Christine presenting her book to Charles VI, who is flanked by the royal dukes. Two other important passages which are illustrated in all the manuscripts are the beginning of Christine's dream (1.451), and the visit to the Fountain of Wisdom (1.787). At 1.1569 all the copies except L show a figure leaning down from Heaven to address Christine and the Sibyl. Elsewhere, there is consistency only to the extent that, where a line is illustrated in some manuscripts, it is highlighted in the others by an intermediate capital at the very least; however, that is not so at ll.1781 and 6273. Certain lines are marked by an intermediate capital in some copies but not in others, for example ll.147, 315, 635, 3717, 3835, and 6133.

Consistency does not imply uniformity, and that is especially true of the miniatures. Not only have different artists been used but care has also been taken to vary the way in which the subjects are depicted. Each copy of the *Chemin de long estude* has a distinctive character, as was appropriate for a volume destined for a particular patron. The scene in which Christine presents her book to the king is only superficially the same in the different copies: Charles VI and Christine occupy central positions but the grouping of the royal dukes and the courtiers and their relative prominence vary from one manuscript to another. A closer study of the opening miniatures may in due course yield information about the patron for whom a given copy was intended.

If the copies are grouped according to their degree of decorative

J. C. Laidlaw

TABLE 1
Decoration in the Manuscripts of the *Chemin de Long Estude*

Line	A	B	B1	C	D	F	L	R
1	MRD	(M)D		MRD	MRD	MRD	MD	MRD
61	MRD	I	(M)	I	RD	RD	(R)D	I
147	I	I		I	I			I
315	I	I		I	I			I
451	MD	(M)D		MD	MD	MD	MD	MRD
635		I		I	I	I	I	I
659	I	I		I	I	I	I	I
787	MD	(M)D		MRD	MD	M(R)I	M(R)D	MRD
883	I	I		I	(I)	I	I	I
1089	I	I		I	I	I	I	I
1109	I	I		I	I	I	I	I
1171	I	I		I	I	I	I	I
1569	MD	(M)D		MRD	MD	MI	I	MRD
1687	I	I		I	I	I	I	I
1781	I	I	(M)	MRD	I			MRD
2045	MD	(M)D		RI	(R)D	I	MD	I
2253	I	I	(M)	MRD	I	I	I	MRD
2491	I	I		I	I	I	I	RI
2555	I	I		I	I	I	I	I
2595	R	(R)	(M)	R	R	RI	I	(R)
2599	(R)	(R)		(R)	(R)	(R)I	(R)I	RI
2703	I	I		(R)I	I	I	(R)I	RI
2807	I	I	(M)	MRD	MD	I	I	MRD
3005	I	I		I	I	I	I	I
3063	I	I		I	I	I	I	RI
3451	I	I		I	I	I	I	RI
3471			(MI)					
3717	I	I	(M)	I	I			RI
3835	I	I		I	I			RI
3840			(MI)					
4079	I	I	(M)	I	I	I	I	RI
4223	RI	(R)I		RI	RD	RI	(R)I	RI
4581	RI	(R)I		RI	RD	RI	(R)I	RI
4917	RI	(R)I		RI	RD	RI	(R)I	RI
5471	RI	(R)I		RI	RD	RI	(R)I	RI
6103	I	I		I	I	I	I	RI
6133	I	I	(M)	I	I			I
6273			(MI)	MD				MRD

D   Decorated capital with border   M   Miniature
I   Intermediate capital   R   Rubric
( ) Space left for capital, miniature, or rubric

complexity, they divide into five groups, FL, ABD, C, R, and B1, in order of increasing elaboration. D, the only member of that group which can be dated, was completed in 1403, C in 1408 or 1409, and R in 1410 or 1411. Is it possible that the degree of decorative elaboration of a copy may be one indication of where it stands in the textual and artistic tradition? Could FL, therefore, be earlier than ABD?

The textual tradition

Had the second question been put to Püschel or Solente, the answer would have been a definite 'No'. Their views of the manuscript tradition of the *Chemin de long estude* are in close accord, as can be seen from Fig. 1. They both consider that from Christine's original there derived two copies, neither of which survives, and that the existing manuscripts divide into two groups and further sub-groups which trace their descent back to one or other of the lost copies. The places occupied in Püschel's table by F and in Solente's table by FL show that those two manuscripts stand in a less good tradition than ABCD and R. For Solente the choice of base text lay between D and C, and she chose D. Püschel concluded

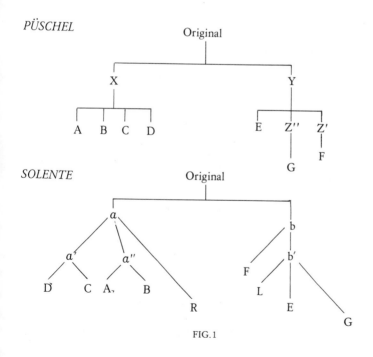

FIG. 1

that A and C contain the most reliable texts, but did not state which manuscript he used as his base.

The two editors based their conclusions on an examination of ten passages, which are included in some copies but not in others, and argue that, where those lines are absent, they have been omitted from the manuscript concerned. However, a re-examination of the lines in question suggests that that is not always the explanation of the differences between the manuscripts of the *Livre du chemin de long estude*. The passages will now be considered in turn.

(*1*) Lines 229–34. As she reads the *De consolatione philosophiae*, Christine reflects that the wrongs which Boethius endured in striving for the common good can be paralleled in other periods of history, including her own:

> Cil (*sc.* Boethius) tout bien leur pourchacoit,
> Merite autre n'y chacoit
> Fors le louier que Dieu(x) donne
> 228 A qui a son vueil s'ordonne.
> Mais mal en fu merité
> D'en estre desherité,
> Et ce fist la fausse envie
> 232 De ceulx qui heent la vie
> Des bons, vrais, non mesdisans,
> A qui mauvais sont nuisans;
> Mais sages est qui se fie
> 236 En Dieu, car philosophie
> Qui l'ot a l'escole apris,
> Ne l'avoit pas en despris . . .

Only FL contain all the lines just quoted; ll.229–34 are not included in ABCDR. Without those six lines, the text makes reasonable sense: trust in God, which rewards and consoles the faithful, forms the subject-matter of ll.227–8 and of ll.235ff. However, *Mais* (235) reads unhappily in a continuing development on that one theme. Püschel considered ll.229–34 to be authentic, the more so since their omission could be readily explained: '229–234 manquent dans ABCD, probablement à cause de *Mais* v. 229 et v. 235' (p.10). Solente came to the same entirely reasonable conclusion.

(*2*) Lines 953–4. The Sibyl describes to Christine the different ways which one takes through the world. The dark and shadowy way which leads to Hell is characterised briefly and rejected. In all the manuscripts except A the passage consists of eight lines (ll.947–52, 955–6). In A ll.953–4 are written in the margin in Christine's own hand. They were probably added to fill out a description which on second thoughts she judged to be too terse.

(3) Lines 1439–42. From the vantage-point to which the Sibyl has taken her, Christine can see the four rivers which issue from the earthly paradise. She names them in turn, Phison, Gion, Tygris, and Euffrates (ll.1432, 1436, 1439, and 1441), and describes the countries through which they flow. ABCDR do not include ll.1439–42 and thus give information about only two rivers, not four. Both Püschel and Solente have recourse to F (and L) to make good the omission in their base texts.

(4) Lines 1778–84. A ladder is lowered from on high to allow Christine and her guide to ascend. On reaching the top, Christine finds herself in the fifth heaven or firmament. The passage describing her arrival and initial reactions is shorter in FL than in ABCDR and, as has already been noted, the decoration does not follow the same plan. Püschel prints the longer text:

> Et la terminoit droitement
> Nostre eschiele qui n'iert de corde
> 1780   Ne de chose qui se destorde.
>
> *Les belles choses que Cristine vit ou*
> *firmament par le conduit de Sebille.*
>
> Quant je me vi en ce hault lieu,
> En merciant de bon cuer Dieu
> J'oz moult grant joie en loiauté,
> 1784   Car oncques ne vi tel biauté.

The rubric is taken from C, the only manuscript known to Püschel which contains a rubric (and a miniature) at this point. (R also contains a miniature and a shorter version of the rubric.) The version in FL is shorter by two lines:

> Et la terminoit droictement
> Nostre eschielle qui n'iert de corde.
> 1780   Quant la me vy, bien m'en recorde,
> J'eus moult grant joye en leauté,
> 1784   Car oncques ne vy tel beauté.

For Püschel and Solente the discrepancy between the two versions resulted from the omission of ll.1780 (*sic*) and 1782 in F (and L). However, when account is taken of the decoration, the explanation turns out to be quite different. In F the significance of l.1780 is indicated by a paragraph mark; there is no decoration at this point in L. In ABD l.1781 is marked by an intermediate capital, and in B1 Christine has added the marginal note, 'Cy soit laisié espace a faire histoire'. As was pointed out above, CR contain a rubric and a miniature at this point.

The differences between the manuscripts represent stages in the development of the poem. Initially, Christine's ascension to the firmament was given no particular emphasis, being unmarked in L and indicated in F simply by a paragraph mark. The passage is given more prominence in ABD where the text has been expanded to thank God for allowing Christine this privilege, the moment of her arrival being marked by an intermediate capital. The third stage of development, foreshadowed in B1, is realised in CR, which include at this point a miniature, rubric, and decorated capital.

(5) Lines 2245–6. Christine concludes her account of the marvels of heaven with a catalogue of the diverse aspects of human life which she had seen there. That long and very general list, which ranges from famine and poverty to freedom and shame, culminates in ll.2245–6, included in ABCDR but not in FL:

> Cupido, Jocus, dieux d'amours,
> 2246   Les filz Venus de franches mours . . .

These mythological figures stand in vivid contrast to the rather lifeless personifications which had preceded them. They may have been omitted in FL or may have been included by Christine in a revised text to make their list end more dramatically. It is impossible to tell.

(6) Lines 2967–8. These two lines pose a similar problem since they, too, are found in ABCDR, but not in FL. The couplet

> Que vault mentir devant Raison?
> 2968   Menconge n'est cy en saison.

has probably been added to provide a more emphatic conclusion to the speech addressed by *Chevalerie* to *Noblece*.

(7) Lines 4007–16. These five couplets, absent from BFL but present in ACDR, form the conclusion to a long speech on wealth. The lines immediately preceding argue with some vigour that the power of wealth is so great that it upsets normal standards, commanding respect and securing advancement where neither is deserved; wealth is portrayed as a corrupting, subversive force. Lines 4007–16 provide a brief corrective to that view, for they point out that, used with prudent discrimination,

wealth can be a force for good. They read as something of an afterthought, inserted to correct an imbalance and to reduce the risk of any possible offence.

(8) Lines 5066–71. The absence of these lines from R is clearly an omission, for the text makes no sense as it stands. There is a ready mechanical explanation: ll.5065–6 and 5071–2 all rhyme in -*aire*, and the scribe has probably combined the first and second lines of separate couplets.

(9) Lines 5213–4. These two lines, included in all the manuscripts except AB, form a significant but not an essential part of a development on knowledge. It is likely that they constitute an omission in AB.

(10) Lines 5264a–b. Püschel printed these lines, found in FL but not elsewhere, among the variants in his edition. Solente is, however, correct in considering them to be an important indication of Christine's source.

Conclusion

Neither Püschel nor Solente represented the manuscript tradition of the *Chemin de long estude* with complete accuracy. Two of the passages just discussed, ll.1439–42, 5264a–b, and probably also ll.229–34, have been shown to be of integral importance, and they are found only in FL. It follows that the other five texts, ABCDR, all derive from a copy of the poem from which those lines were omitted. Further omissions occurred at other points in the transmission of the work, examples being ll.5066–71, omitted in R, and probably ll.5213–4, omitted in AB. The fact that so many copies are defective shows how imperfect were the procedures followed by Christine and her scribes in correcting manuscript text.

The evidence provided by ll.953–4 and 1778–84, and probably by ll.2967–8 and 4007–16 also, indicates that the text of the poem evolved, additions being made to add colour, to underline a point or to modify the emphasis. Associated with these alterations are changes in the decoration which in later collected manuscripts such as C and particularly R is more elaborate and better arranged than in the earlier copies. Whether it is possible to distinguish successive 'editions' of the poem is a question which can only be answered after study of the variants and the many corrections. It is already clear, however, that the textual tradition of the *Chemin de long estude* cannot be satisfactorily represented by means of a stemma of the traditional type, deriving from one original.

The question was asked earlier whether FL are earlier than the other copies. The discussion of the textual tradition has shown that they are, both because of the three passages which they alone contain and because of the absence of the added authorial improvements. Lines 36–7 provide confirmation: in FL we read that Christine has composed her poem *nouvellement*, and not *presentement*, the reading given by the other texts.

How long is the *Chemin de long estude*? As has been seen, the text evolved and grew, additional lines being inserted in later copies. However, the text was also reduced by undetected omissions. And so the answer to the question is paradoxical: longer than any of the extant copies, even though so many of them were copied and corrected under the supervision of Christine de Pizan herself.

Dedication

This essay is dedicated in gratitude and friendship to the scholar and teacher who first introduced me to Middle French in 1955–6.

References

Avril, François (1975) 'La peinture française au temps de Jean de Berry', *Revue de l'Art*, 28, pp.40–52 (p.52, n.23).

Champion, Pierre (1910) *La Librairie de Charles d'Orléans*, Paris: Bibliothèque du XVe Siècle, 11.

Doutrepont, G. (1906) *Inventaire de la 'Librairie' de Philippe le Bon*, Bruxelles.

Dulac, Liliane (1986) 'Review of Angus J. Kennedy, *Christine de Pizan, a bibliographical guide*', *Moyen Age*, 92, pp.325–9.

Guiffrey, Jules (1894) *Inventaires de Jean duc de Berry (1401–1416)*, I, Paris.

Laidlaw, J. C. (1987) 'Christine de Pizan — A Publisher's Progress', *Modern Language Review*, 82, pp.35–75.

Ouy, Gilbert (1985) 'Une énigme codicologique: les signatures des cahiers dans les manuscrits autographes et originaux de Christine de Pizan', *Calames et cahiers: mélanges de codicologie et de paléographie offerts à Léon Gilissen*, Bruxelles, pp.119–31.

Ouy, Gilbert and Reno, Christine M. (1980) 'Identification des autographes de Christine de Pizan', *Scriptorium*, 34, pp.221–38.

Püschel, Robert (ed.) (1887) *Christine de Pisan: Le Livre du chemin de long estude*, Berlin, reprinted Geneva, 1974. For some unexplained reason the text does not include lines 1594a–1594d, which are found in ABCDFLR, and are quoted here from F: 'La figure vers moy se tourne/ Et me regarde et puis s'en tourne,/Disant que voulentiers feroit/Telle eschielle qu'il afferoit'.

Solente, Suzanne (1976) 'Un nouveau manuscrit de présentation du *Livre du chemin de long estude* de Christine de Pisan', *Club français de la médaille*, 50, pp.48–51. The article contains a detailed description of Paris fr. 1188.

—— (1978) Notes and files prepared for a critical edition of the *Livre du chemin de long estude*, which passed to the Library of the Ecole des Chartes in Paris on her death in 1978. I am grateful to the Director, Professor Jacques Monfrin, for his kindness in allowing me access to this unpublished material.

Graham A. Runnalls

9. TOWARDS A TYPOLOGY OF
MEDIEVAL FRENCH PLAY MANUSCRIPTS

The relationship between the theatre and the other literary genres of medieval France has always posed a number of problems. On the one hand, it can be claimed that, during the Middle Ages, the theatre was much closer to the other genres than is the case today; drama was but one extreme of a spectrum of methods of presentation of literary material, and many other genres had dramatic or para-dramatic aspects. Thus the *chansons de geste* were declaimed, lyric poems sung, and romances recited out loud, all before a living audience. *Fabliaux*, dramatic monologues, and *dits*, as well as sermons, clearly had a possible theatrical dimension. On the other hand, one can point out that the theatre, certainly towards the end of the Middle Ages, was able to reach, and to involve actively, a much larger proportion of the general public; the other types of performance mentioned above tended to take place before relatively limited social groups, whereas the performance of a fifteenth-century mystery play could involve a whole community.

Another, less frequently examined, difference between drama and other genres in medieval France relates to the manuscripts that preserve the texts. One important fact that has not always been fully realised is that it is very rare for a medieval play to be preserved in more than one manuscript. Whereas it is quite usual — one could even say that it is the norm — for a romance, or a poem, or a didactic work to have survived in a number of virtually identical manuscript versions, it is exceptional for this to be the case for a play. Thus Chrétien's romances, the Prose *Tristan*, the poems of Adam de la Halle, Guillaume de Diguleville's *Pèlerinage de l'âme humaine* and the narrative *Passion des Jongleurs*, as well as many *fabliaux*, all survive in several, and in some cases scores of, manuscripts; there are, admittedly, often noticeable differences between these various manuscript versions, but there is no doubt that they all preserve versions of 'the same text'. But out of the approximately 230 surviving miracle and mystery plays written in medieval France, only two are preserved by three or more virtually identical manuscript versions. And even these can be shown to be anomalous manuscripts in other respects.

A second point worth making about play manuscripts, apart from their uniqueness, is their diversity; they are at least as diverse as those of the other genres, if not more so. They can be written on large folios or very small narrow ones; they can be of parchment or of paper. They can be richly illuminated, with scores of miniatures, or semi-legible scrawls; they can be copied on one side only of the sheet of paper, or on both sides. The pages can be ruled and text evenly spread out, or the size of writing can vary, as can the number of lines per page. The writing can be in two columns per page or just one. There can be lots of stage directions (either in French or in Latin, either in the margin or in the centre of the page) or there can be none. The manuscript can be roughly contemporary with the play's composition, or much later. It can contain one play, or two, or six, or twelve, or forty, or seventy-three. And there are many more variables that I could add, but which I will spare the reader. This high degree of variability also distinguishes play manuscripts from non play manuscripts.

The specificity of medieval French play manuscripts has remained largely unnoticed, since most play editors do not provide more than a rapid description of the manuscript or compare it with other similar ones. However, in the last couple of years, some types of play manuscripts have been the subject of research; see Runnalls (1988a, 1988b) and Smith and Lalou (1988).

The purpose of the present essay is to discuss play manuscripts as a sub-group of medieval manuscripts in general, to try to account for their uniqueness and for their variability, and to suggest a tentative method of classifying such manuscripts. I shall limit my analysis to historical plays, to use the terminology of Alan Knight (1983), i.e. to plays traditionally labelled miracle plays and mystery plays, dating from the fourteenth, fifteenth, and the first half of the sixteenth centuries.

Why are play manuscripts different from manuscripts of other genres? The answer, I would suggest, lies in the very specific function of a play manuscript. A medieval play was only fully realised, actualised, in a performance; without a performance, the dramatist could not reach his audience. The mere writing out of a text did not permit communication between a playwright and the members of his public, a clearly envisaged group of people, for example, the members of a *confrérie* or inhabitants of a town. With the other genres, however, the writing out of a text, especially in several copies, was all that an author needed or could hope for, towards the end of the Middle Ages, in order to ensure that his work might be read; for reading by one individual, either for his own benefit or for the benefit of several others, was the normal method of transmitting a text other than a play. Play manuscripts were not written in order to be read; they were brought into existence in order to permit a performance of the play. Since virtually all mystery play and miracle play performances were unique, i.e. since it was very rare for several — or even two — performances of exactly the same play to be organised, it is not surprising the play manuscripts tend to be unique as well.

All medieval play manuscripts were in some ways related to a specific performance; but not all such manuscripts served the same purpose. The great variety of play manuscripts is explained by the wide range of functions that manuscripts might have in relation to a given performance. The best way to illustrate this is to imagine how a play is put on nowadays and to see how medieval practice must have been different. Nowadays — and this has presumably been the case for some time — all the participants in the production of a play — playwright, producer, designer, actors, prompter, etc. — simply purchase (or are given) a copy of the printed book, or a photocopy of a typescript; thus every participant has the complete text, i.e. the words for every actor, the stage directions, etc. Clearly, in the Middle Ages, it was not possible for every participant to have a complete copy (manuscript) of the play. The cost and time needed to produce so many copies would prevent this.

Contemporary evidence, including archive information as well as the manuscripts themselves, suggests that, as far as written texts are concerned, the preparation of the performance of a medieval play went through several stages.

(*i*) The dramatist starts composing his play, using several rough drafts.

(*ii*) The dramatist arranges for a fair copy of his final text to be written up; he either does this himself or gets one or several scribes to do the job. This fair copy forms the basis for several other possible manuscripts.

(*iii*) A scribe copies out the roles, referred to variously as the *roole* or *rollet*, or *roullet*, for the actors; each actor was given a manuscript which contained only that actor's lines. But each of his speeches was preceded by the last line spoken by another actor immediately before the speech; these were the cue-lines. The actor used his rôle during rehearsal — and possibly even during the performance.

(*iv*) A special, abbreviated copy might be written up for the producer, the *meneur du jeu*. This would expand greatly the stage directions, but reduce all speeches to two lines, the first and last of each *réplique*.

(*v*) After the performance, a final copy of the text is made, based on the author's fair copy; the purpose of this might simply be to keep a record of the event, or else to present the text as a gift to a patron or person of influence.

Of course, often in the late Middle Ages, a performance was not based on an original, newly created text but on a previously existing one; in other words, somebody else's fair copy was borrowed, either from a neighbouring town or from a much earlier performance. In this case, however, the existing text was usually much revised, and a manuscript with numerous modifications written into it was the basis of the performance. Later, this now rather messy manuscript might be copied up into a new fair copy.

These various stages, not all of which were necessarily gone through for every performance of a mystery play, explain the great variability of play manuscripts. They can also be used as a basis for classifying them. The proposed typology of medieval play manuscripts described below is based on the different functions that a manuscript may have in relation to a specific performance; the types are listed in an order which corresponds to the stage in the preparation of the performance at which the manuscript was used.

Proposed typology
of manuscripts of historical plays (miracles and mysteries)
from the fourteenth to the sixteenth centuries

Type A: the rough work of the author or a scribe

Type B: the fair copy, often referred to as the *original* or the *registre*, used as the basis for the performance

Type C: the actor's role

Type D: a revision of a Type B, with additions, suppressions, and other modifications of the text of the play and/or its stage directions

Type E: the director's copy, with abbreviated text, and large numbers of stage directions and other information related to the actual performance

Type F: a revision of an existing manuscript, but copied up neatly; thus a Type D transformed into a Type B, and often difficult to distinguish from Type B

Type G: a luxury manuscript recording the text of a past performance, belonging to a patron or a guild, and not intended to be used as the basis of a performance; perhaps intended for reading.

Examples of each of these types have survived, though, as one would expect, not in equal numbers; some types are clearly more important than others, and some are subjected to more wear and tear than others. The groupings proposed are only types; they are not always clearly delineated and watertight categories. There are several examples of cross-types, where a manuscript has features of two different types; there are others which are more difficult to classify. But my principal claim is that these types do correspond to the main sorts of different play manuscripts, and, more importantly, that each of these types can be defined by a number of objective criteria relating to the manuscript itself, i.e. to the paper and to the writing on it.

The survey that follows is based on a study of sixty-three surviving manuscripts or fragments of manuscripts that preserve miracle and mystery plays. A numbered list of the play manuscripts consulted, with abbreviated titles and library shelf-marks, is provided in the Appendix. Of these sixty-three, I have seen all but eight myself. I have relied on other sources of information concerning MSS 2, 54, 55, 56, 60, 61, 62, 63. I have not consulted MSS D, F, G, H, I, and J of Gréban's *Passion* (most of these are not complete; see Jodogne, 1983, pp.25–6); seven of the thirteen MSS of Jacques Milet's *Destruction de Troye* (see Jung, 1978); and the Chatsworth MS of Mercadé's *Vengeance*. To the best of my knowledge, this completes the list of surviving manuscripts of medieval French 'historical plays'. The discrepancy between this figure of sixty-three MSS and the 230 surviving miracle and mystery plays, mentioned above, is accounted for by several facts: (*a*) some manuscripts contain many plays, e.g. one contains forty, another seventy-three; (*b*) many late plays survived in early printed editions; and (*c*) several manuscripts of plays that have been edited have subsequently been lost.

In the present chapter, I mention only those features of play manuscripts which seem relevant for my typological purposes; I have therefore omitted several types of information about the manuscripts, e.g. watermarks, division into *cahiers*, catch-words, signatures, etc. In drawing up my initial descriptions of manuscripts, I was greatly helped by the Institut de Recherche et d'Histoire des Textes and its *Guide pour l'Elaboration d'une Notice de Manuscrit* (1977).

A Description of the Various Types of Play Manuscripts

Type A. Since there is only one surviving fragmentary manuscript which can be used to illustrate this group, it might be felt unreasonable to give it the grandiose title of a type; yet it seems to me inevitable that every text has to start with rough drafts. Normally, of course, these do not survive. But MS 5, though consisting of only two small fragments, clearly shows several drafts of the same text. It contains three versions of a prologue to a *Miracle de Saint Nicolas*, to be performed, not for the first time, we are told, by the 'enfans de l'escole du Foys'. One brief attempt at a resounding beginning is abandoned, before another draft of the prologue is squeezed onto both sides and the margins of another piece of paper measuring 12 cm long and 10 cm wide. The final version, almost identical but not quite, is copied up more neatly on another piece of paper measuring 44.5 cm long and 9.5 cm wide. The source of this manuscript is unknown; it probably survived as part of the binding of another book; this would explain the trimming that has caused the loss of the bottom of the fragment containing the draft. The final version, however, is complete.

This manuscript also has features in common with Type C, the actor's roles, which will be discussed in detail shortly. The fragment which contains the final version is made up of two originally separate pieces of paper, each about 22 cm long, which were stitched together. The text is written up from the top of one side of this long narrow strip down to the bottom; but the remaining section is copied, apparently upside down, on the other side of the same strip, starting in the middle of the strip. This curious arrangement is also found in other actor's roles, and is attributable to the fact that the roles were usually wound into scrolls before use, and gradually unwound as the actor read his words; lines that could not be squeezed onto the front of the scroll were sometimes written upside down on the last flap. In this case, it is probable that the author and scribe of the prologue was going to speak the prologue at the performance; he thus copied it up as a role for himself.

Type B. (The fair copy). There are seventeen examples of this type: 4, 7, 10, 11, 12, 14 (second fragment), 19 (*cahiers* 14 and 15), 29, 30, 31, 32, 38, 41, 42, 54, 59, 63). All these manuscripts display almost all of the following features:

    text written on both sides of each folio, one column each side;
    no line ruling;
    no rubrication, no ornamentation, no miniatures;
    no modifications made to text, except very minor;
    no marks of possession;
    no lapse of time between performance and writing of manuscript;
    one play only; and
    stage directions usually in margin.

Although these manuscripts can be of a wide range of dimensions, by far the most frequent is 30 cm × 20 cm (or just under, due to trimming for binding, either contemporary or more recent). Three manuscripts (4, 10, 54) have the *format agenda*, i.e. paper only 10 cm wide (half the most frequent width), which is also associated with many actor's roles.

The name normally given to this type of manuscript was the (*livre*) *original*; they are referred to thus in the *Passion de Mons* (MS 19) and in material relating to the performance of the *Passion de Valenciennes* (MS 23). In other texts the word *registre* is used to describe the fair copy; this is found in material relating to performances of the *Mystère de Saint Martin* (MS 42) and of the *Mystère de Saint Sébastien* (MS 46).

Good examples of complete plays preserved in this type of manuscript are the *Mystère de la Pacience de Job* (MS 11 dating from about 1478) and the *Mystère de Saint Louis* (MS 41 from about 1470), although the latter is exceptional in that it is the only manuscript known to have belonged to the Confrérie de la Passion. Good incomplete examples are the *Passion d'Amboise* (MS 12) and the last two cahiers of the *Passion de Mons* (MS 19), which contain the full text of the prologues and the third *matinée*, of which the *Abregiet* (Type E) has been preserved as well.

Three slightly unusual examples are the *Mystère du Roy Advenir* (MS 29), in which the author, Jehan Du Prier, has not only signed the play, but has also added a small number of last-minute modifications to the stage directions; the *Miracle des Trois Pèlerins*, whose fragments have recently been rediscovered and whose dimensions, 15 cm × 10 cm, are uniquely pocket-sized; and the *Mystères et Moralités Liégeois* (MS 10), which seems to consist of a small repertoire of *originaux*.

Although, in Type B, stage directions are usually found in the margins or to the side of the text proper, it is noticeable that the language of stage directions is never a distinguishing feature between manuscript types. French or Latin, or even both languages, are found in all types of manuscript; one even finds Latin used in the stage directions of actors' roles.

One mysterious feature which is found in some Type B manuscripts (as well as in other types) is 'le petit trait'; see Smith (1986) and Smith and Lalou (1988). This is a small ink mark usually placed horizontally between two lines of text, to the left side of the column. Until Dr Smith noticed the 'petit trait' during his work on the *Mystère de Saint Louis* (MS 41), no one had ever commented on this mark, or included it in an edition. There are grounds, in Dr Smith's opinion, for thinking that this mark is a reference to an unwritten stage direction, perhaps a reminder to the producer that in his copy of the text there is, or should be, further information relating to the staging. Certainly, many of these 'petits traits' appear at points where the text to be spoken by the actors clearly implies some gesture or movement.

Several of the manuscripts listed above as belonging to Type B are in fact what I call cross-types, i.e. manuscripts that, although clearly attached to one type, also have features of another type. Thus the *Mystère de Saint Etienne pape* (MS 38) has all but one of the distinctive features of Type B, and includes some 'petits traits'; but the pages are ruled, and it is written so carefully that it could well have been a gift, i.e. Type G. The Harvard *Passion* (MS 59) has a second set of stage directions and role distribution which suggests re-use; these are features of Type D. One also suspects that the second fragment of the *Passion d'Auvergne* (MS 14), though written up neatly by one scribe with no alterations, is in fact a revision of an earlier text; the first fragment of MS 14 clearly comes in this category. If this is so, then the second fragment is a Type F.

Nevertheless, Type B, the fair copy, the *livre original*, is a clearly distinguishable category of manuscript, of which a large number have survived. It is arguably the most important type of all, since it formed the basis of all the types of manuscript yet to be discussed.

Type C. Actors' roles are arguably the most fascinating and problematic of all. Consisting of just one actor's lines and his cue-words, and copied up by a scribe from the *livre original*, the master-copy, they were of no use once the performance was over and were simply thrown away. Their very survival is a stroke of luck. Often they have come down to us because they have been used as material for a book-binding; they have therefore been cut up and stuck together. It is not surprising therefore that surviving roles are usually extremely fragmentary and in a badly worn condition. The fact that they contain the words of only one actor increases the difficulty of reading, identifying, and making sense of them. In fact, quite a few have survived, though most of them are roles for actors in comic plays, farces, or moralities (see Runnalls, forthcoming). Their distinguishing features are as follows:

text consisting of one actor's lines;

the successive *répliques* are separated by a cue-word (i.e. the last word spoken in the immediately preceding *réplique*);

the cue-word often rhymes with the first line of the actor's speech;

the cue-word is indented half-way across the sheet of paper;

the paper is half the width of a normal folio, i.e. about 10 cm;

the text is written on only one side of the paper;

the narrow strips of paper are often joined together by glue or by stitching or by a pin, to form a long scroll;

any stage directions are at the margin, usually placed in a square;

they are nearly always carelessly written and full of errors; and

there is, of course, no ornamentation, etc.

Three manuscripts of historical plays belong to this type: 2, 33, and 57, though 33 (*Sainte Barbe*) is anomalous in several respects. MSS 2 (*Jeu des Trois Rois*) and 57 (*Passion*) are typical in every respect, and are exactly like the surviving roles made for comic plays. It is thought that the long strips of paper were nailed at the bottom to a stick and rolled up tight to make a scroll, which the actor progressively unrolled as he read his words. Those roles of which the end has survived all have little cuts at the bottom of the paper strip where it was attached to the stick.

Six small fragments have survived in Fribourg of the *Jeu des Trois Rois*; they contain sections of the roles of two characters. The beginning of one of these is entitled *Baltazar*, the name of one of the three kings; the other sections are from the role of Notre Dame. Some of the surviving 170 lines are also found in the *Passion d'Arras*. One notes examples of the 'petit trait', which, as the context clearly shows, are linked to stage action implied in the text.

MS 57, now in Digne, preserves complete the role of Saint Simon in the third day of an unidentified Passion Play. It starts: *Le rôle . . . de sainct Simon per lo ters jort* and concludes with the word *Finis*. The fragment measures 28.5 cm × 10 cm.

We have already observed that MS 5, classed as the only example of Type A, also has many features of an actor's role.

The Sainte Barbe role (MS 33) is different from all other roles (comic as well as serious) in that it consists of a *cahier* of thirteen folios, each measuring 18 cm × 14.5 cm, with writing on both sides of each folio. The writing is unusually careful; otherwise the lay-out of the text is like that of any other role. Although it has not proved possible to identify exactly the play from which this role comes, it does have similarities with one of the two existing Sainte Barbe plays. In both these long plays, Barbe is a major character, with many hundreds of lines to speak. Perhaps the format for the shorter roles described above, i.e. the narrow one-sided scroll, was not used for very long roles.

Type D. These manuscripts are like those of Type B, except that their texts have undergone substantial revisions. Type D manuscripts might appear to suggest a second performance of an existing play; but the revisions were often so far-reaching that the play is no longer the same one. The second performance might take place in a different town, several decades later, with a different stage and a different number of actors. The time available may have been less, the religious views of the producer more conservative, etc. All these factors could lead to a drastically rewritten text. Thus Type D manuscripts have all the features of the Type B manuscript on which they are based (see above), except that there are:

numerous additions to the text, inserted into the margins;

numerous additions to the stage directions, also inserted into the margins, as well as (sometimes) redistribution of minor roles;

passages and stage directions crossed out;

intercalated folios or scraps of paper for long additions;

various signs, symbols, and instructions concerning the exact point at which additions are to be inserted;

many different hands; and

a possible gap between the date of the first writing of the manuscript and the date of the 'second' performance.

There are nine examples of such manuscripts: 6, 14 (fragment 1), 22, 36, 39, 45, 46, 47, 61. Virtually all of these have the same dimensions: 30 cm × 20 cm, or just under if trimmed for binding, although MS 46, a *Mystère de Saint Sébastien*, has the narrow *format agenda*, 29 cm × 10 cm.

A particularly striking example of this type is the *Mystère de Saint Genis* (MS 39), where five or six different hands have introduced a vast number of changes of all sorts to the *original*, including many extra folios, as the first foliotation reveals. The first version (the Type B on which MS 39 was based) would have consisted of about fifty-three or fifty-four folios; a first revision then added another eight folios and cut numerous passages of the original text. Later, a second revision added more folios and cut more original text. One of the most recent hands adds the date 1507 to the text. The date of the first version is not known. Interestingly, it is probable that one of the revisers of *Saint Genis* was also the main scribe of a surviving Type B manuscript, MS 45, a (different) *Mystère de Saint Sébastien*.

In other manuscripts, the amount of change is much less, but nevertheless significant. For example, MS 47, the *Mystère de Saint Vincent*, has only a moderate quantity of alterations. The performance of the *original* is known to have taken place at Angers, before René d'Anjou, in 1471, but the surviving revised manuscript refers to the granting of official permission to perform it in 1476.

Type E. Only one example of a producer's copy survives (MS 19, *cahiers* 1–13), used for the performance of a Passion Play at Mons in 1501. This remarkable manuscript, published by Gustave Cohen (1925, 1957), has provided scholars with a tremendous amount of information about medieval drama. Cohen showed how the inhabitants of Mons, impressed by the performance of a four-day Passion Play in Amiens the year before, decided to emulate their neighbours and to produce their own play, in eight half-day sections. They borrowed the four *originaux* from Amiens, and had them copied to form their own *originaux*; these manuscripts containing the full text were the basis for their new *abregiets*, or producer's copies. The *abregiet*, as the word suggests, was an abbreviated version of the full text; it consisted of the first and last line of each *réplique*, with a number indicating the number of lines in that *réplique*. In this way, a complete text, which must have between 50,000 and 60,000 lines long (it included the whole of Jehan Michel's *Passion*, plus the first and fourth days of Arnoul Gréban's, as well as a considerable amount of additional material), was reduced to less than 10,000 lines. The *abregiet* also included stage directions that were fuller than those in the *livres originaux*, and the names of actors. It seems that two copies were made of each *abregiet*, perhaps because two people were involved in directing the performance. A separate *abregiet* was made for each half-day session, and copied up into a single *cahier* of the usual dimensions, i.e. about 30 cm × 20 cm; the writing was careful, spread out in one column on each side of the folio. The names of the characters were written especially large. The text occupied the centre of the page, leaving plenty of space in the margins for the often very detailed stage directions. It is obvious that all these features were designed to make the work of the *meneur du jeu* as easy as possible. It is assumed that the producer used the *abregiet*, both during rehearsals and perhaps during the performance itself, rather in the way a present-day conductor controls an orchestra. An example of such a producer at work, using his *abregiet* (and a baton) may be seen in Jehan Fouquet's miniature of the *Martyre de Sainte Apolline*.

MS 19 contains fifteen *cahiers*, i.e. one or two copies of the *abregiets* for all eight sessions, together with one cahier containing the full text of all the prologues used in the play. There is also one *cahier* containing the Mons *original* for the *matinée* of day three. It is thus possible to compare the full text contained in this last *cahier*, with the corresponding Mons *abregiet*.

It is uncertain whether every play performance required the use of *abregiets*; the fact that only one example has survived suggests that in most cases the *livre original*, with its complete text and full stage directions, was used by the producer. Perhaps the *abregiet* was necessary only in the case of extremely long plays, which the *Passion de Mons* certainly was.

Type F. In some ways, this is the least satisfactory of my proposed types, since one's knowledge of such a text has to extend beyond what the manuscript and the writing tell us. These are reworkings of earlier plays (thus like Type D) which have been written up neatly by one scribe; they therefore look exactly like examples of Type B. The only way to distinguish a Type F from a Type B is to use archival information or certain types of textual analysis. Physically, Type Fs look exactly like Type Bs (see above).

Two manuscripts at least can be attached to this group, 20 and 21; MS 14 (Fragment 2) is another possible example. The *Passion de Semur* (MS 21) appears to be a standard example of Type B, with the usual page lay-out, dimensions, etc. There are no modifications to the text. Yet critics have always accepted that the play is a compilation, in that some parts are clearly more archaic than others. A recent detailed analysis (Runnalls, 1988b) has confirmed this view, using as evidence internal contradictions and repetitions, faulty rhymes, selection and ordering of source material, and stylistic and linguistic variations. MS 21 is not, therefore, the first version of this play.

Similarly, MS 20 preserves a fragment of a play which is obviously a reworking of the *Passion Sainte-Geneviève*, whose complete text has survived in MS 1. Textual comparison proves that MS 20 is a revision of MS 1, though the manuscript itself shows no visible sign of additions or suppressions. The second fragment of MS 14 has been discussed above, along with Type B manuscripts.

One could also argue that MS 22, the *Passion de Troyes*, classed above as a Type D, belongs to this group. I have classed it as a Type D because it displays all the usual features of a revision, with additions and suppressions. But it is known that the text which has been modified is itself a revision of Arnoul Gréban's *Passion*. MS 22, therefore is a Type F, which has been further revised; it is a good example of a cross-type, linking Types D and F.

Type G. This is by far the largest group of manuscripts, with thirty-two examples: MSS 1, 3, 8, 9, 13, 15, 16, 17, 18, 23, 24, 25, 26, 27, 28, 34, 35, 37, 40, 43, 44, 48, 49, 50, 51, 52, 53, 55, 56, 58, 60, 62. They were written in order to keep a record of a performed text, and were often used as gifts to patrons. They therefore follow a performance, rather than precede it, which is the case with all other manuscript types discussed so far. All of them display most of the following features:

carefully written on both sides of each folio;
the pages are ruled and the text evenly spaced out;
stage directions are often in the centre of the page (not the margin);
the stage directions are often few in number;

no (non-trivial) corrections or modifications to the text;

frequent use of ornamentation and/or rubrics; and

there is often a considerable lapse of time between the date of the performance and the date of the manuscript.

In addition to these regular features, several manuscripts have other distinctive aspects:

miniatures (MSS 3, 13, 15, 16, 17, 18, 23, 24, 35, 50, 52, 55, 60, 62);

parchment not paper (MSS 3, 15, 17, 34, 35, 40, 50, 58, 60, 62);

marks of contemporary possession (MSS 3, 9, 15, 16, 17, 18, 23, 24, 28, 34, 35, 37, 38, 40, 41);

contain more than one play (MSS 1 [six]; 3 [forty]; 9 [twelve]; 13 [two]; 55 [seventy-three]); and

text written in two columns on each side of a folio (MSS 1, 3, 13, 15, 16, 17, 18, 20, 23, 24, 44, 48, 49, 50, 55, 56, 58, 62).

Almost all are written on folios of the usual dimensions, approximately 30 cm × 20 cm or just under, although several are in an even larger format of approximately 35 cm × 27 cm (MSS 15, 16, 23, 55, 56). The best examples to illustrate this type of manuscript are as follows.

(*a*) The *Miracles de Nostre Dame par personnages* (MS 3) — this manuscript contains the text of forty plays performed annually before the Paris Guild of Goldsmiths during the period 1339 to 1382. The manuscript was copied up around 1390, probably as a gift; it is of parchment, with two columns of text on each page. Each play is preceded by a miniature; there are virtually no stage directions; the text is written immaculately, with no corrections.

(*b*) The *Mystères de Lille* (MS 55) — this recently re-discovered manuscript contains the seventy-three plays performed, probably on wagons, in ceremonies at Lille during the middle of the fifteenth century. Though copied a century later than the *Miracles de Nostre Dame*, it is very similar in detail.

(*c*) The *Mystère de la Conception* (MS 8) — though only containing one play and having no miniatures, this manuscript is still clearly an example of Type G. It was copied up after a performance given before a Count of Montpensier, to whom it was probably presented. There is heavy rubrication; the frame of the page is ruled (though the actual lines are not); one scribe has written the text carefully.

None of the manuscripts of this type was destined for use at a performance. Not only is there no sign of wear nor of a producer's handling of the manuscripts but their very nature makes them unpractical for such use.

This is the only category of manuscripts in which one finds examples of two or more 'identical' manuscripts. Manuscripts 15–18 preserve virtually identical versions of Gréban's *Passion*; MSS 48–53 are versions of Jacques Milet's *Destruction de Troye la Grant*; and there are two versions each of the 1547 *Passion de Valenciennes* (MSS 23 and 24), the *Mystère de la Résurrection* (MSS 26 and 27), and the *Mystère de la Vengeance* (MS 13).

We have already seen that, by definition, the manuscripts of Type G were not intended for use at a performance. The existence of one single luxurious copy of a play, kept by the individual or society that commissioned it, needs no explanation or special justification. But why make multiple copies of a play? Surely the reason is the same as the one given in the case of non-dramatic texts, i.e. for reading. I would suggest that the multiple-copy manuscripts, especially those in double-column pages and with miniatures, came into existence solely for the purpose of reading. It is noticeable that one of the plays which has survived in many 'identical' manuscripts, Gréban's *Passion*, was an extremely famous text, although we have no certain knowledge that it was performed more than once or twice. (Of course, reworkings of it were performed more often, e.g. at Troyes and Mons.)

The most striking play in this group is the 27,000-line *Destruction de Troye la Grant*, composed between the years of 1450 and 1452 by Jacques Milet 'estudiant en loys en l'université d'Orleans', as we are told in identical words in almost all the manuscripts. The play is unusual for several reasons. It is the only French mystery play based on classical mythology, and dates from a period when the *menu peuple*, who formed the bulk of the audience of the large scale mystery plays, apparently had no great interest in such material. Moreover, there is no record of any performance of this play. Yet, surprisingly, it has come down to us in thirteen identical manuscripts dating from the 1460s and 1470s and in twelve different early Gothic printed editions published between 1484 and 1544. Although there are ample stage directions (again very similar in all manuscripts), there is no evidence that any of the manuscripts was used for a performance, which is what one would expect with this type of manuscript. All of the surviving manuscripts of the *Destruction de Troye* clearly belong to our Type G; many have large numbers of miniatures (or spaces left for them) and are written in two-column pages; some are on parchment. Given the lack of documentary evidence of a production and the absence of any other type of manuscript, I would conclude, contrary to Jung (1983), that, whether Milet really intended the play to be staged or not (and even this is open to doubt), the

Destruction de Troye was never performed. It remained an 'imaginary' dramatisation of Greek mythology. One could therefore claim that it is not a real play at all!

Any attempt to classify such a large number of different manuscripts is bound to have some degree of arbitrariness about it. But the typology outlined above suggests that there are several distinct sorts of play manuscript, each with a different function, and that each type can be defined by a number of objectively established features relating to the manuscript's paper (or parchment) and writing. The existence of several cross-types demonstrates that some manuscripts have features of more than one type. Moreover, the numbers of examples surviving of each type are very unequal; it is hardly surprising that the most numerous group contains manuscripts intended as permanent records or gifts, whereas there are very few rough drafts and actors' roles. Nevertheless, I believe not only that the proposed typology corresponds to real differences between manuscripts but also that it illustrates the uniqueness and diversity of late Medieval French play manuscripts.

Acknowledgement

I would like to express my thanks to the British Academy, whose generous grant enabled me to visit a number of Libraries in Paris and the French provinces, Belgium, and Switzerland; without its help, I would not have been able to complete this project.

References

Cohen, Gustave (1925) *Le Livre de Conduite du Régisseur et le Compte des Dépenses pour le Mystère de la Passion joué à Mons en 1501*, Paris.
—— (1957) *Le Mystère de la Passion joué à Mons en juillet 1501. Livre des Prologues. Matinée IIIe*, Gembloux, Duculot: Société Belge des Bibliophiles séant à Mons, tiré à 216 exemplaires.
Guide pour l'Elaboration d'une Notice de Manuscrit (1977) Institut de Recherche et d'Histoire des Textes, CNRS.
Jodogne, Omer (1965, 1983) *Le Mystère de la Passion d'Arnoul Gréban*, Bruxelles: Académie Royale de Belgique, vol. I 1965; vol. II 1983.
Jung, Marc-René (1978) 'Jacques Milet et son Epître Epilogative', *Mélanges Rychner, Travaux de Linguistique et Littérature*, Strasbourg, XVI, pp.241–58.
—— (1983) 'La Mise en scène de la *Destruction de Troye*', *Atti del IV Colloquio della Société Internationale pour l'Etude du Théâtre Médiéval*, Viterbo, pp.563–80.
Knight, Alan (1983) *Aspects of Genre in Late Medieval French Drama*, Manchester: Manchester University Press.

Runnalls, Graham (1988a) 'An actor's rôle in a French morality play', *French Studies*, 42, pp.398–402.

—— (1988b) 'The evolution of a passion play: *La Passion de Semur*', *Le Moyen Français*, 19, pp.163–202.

—— (forthcoming) 'The medieval actors' rôles found in the Fribourg Archives', *Pluteus*, 4 (forthcoming).

Smith, Darwin (1986) 'Le Mystère de Saint Louis', unpublished thesis, Paris III.

—— and Lalou, Elisabeth (1988) 'Pour une typologie des manuscrits de théâtre', *Le Théâtre et la Cité: Actes du Ve Colloque de la Société Internationale pour l'Etude du Théâtre Médiéval; Fifteenth Century Studies*, 13, pp.569–79.

Appendix

The Appendix consists of a numbered list of the 63 manuscripts covered in the present survey; an abbreviated title is followed by the name of the Library where the manuscript is located, the shelf-mark of the manuscript, and concise details of published editions (where these exist).

1. *Cycle de Mystères* (and 5 other plays); Paris Bib. Sainte-Geneviève 1131; *Cycle*, ed. G. A. Runnalls, *TLF* Genève, 1976 (q.v. for other eds).
2. *Jeu des Trois Rois*; Fribourg, Archives de l'Etat; fonds Aebischer Litt. I, 16–17; ed. G. A. Runnalls, *Pluteus* IV (forthcoming).
3. *Miracles de Nostre Dame* (40 plays); Paris B.N. fr, 819–820; ed. Paris et Robert, *SATF* Paris, 1876–93.
4. *Miracle de S. Nicolas*; Florence Ashb. 115; ed. Aebischer, *Neuf Etudes*, Genève, 1972.
5. *Miracle de S. Nicolas* (prologues); Paris Arch.Nat. M.877B.15; ed. Samaran, *Romania* (LI), 1925.
6. *Mystère de L'Antéchrist*; Paris B.N. fr. 15063.
7. *Mystère de l'Ascencion de la Vierge*; Rodez, Bib.Mun. 57; ed. B. Lunet, *Mém.Soc.Lettres . . . Aveyron* (IV), 1942–3.
8. *Mystère de la Conception*; Chantilly, Condé 616.
9. *Mystères de Jehan Louvet* (12 plays); Paris B.N. n.a.f. 481.
10. *Mystères et Moralités Liégeois* (2 mystères); Chantilly, Condé 617; ed. Cohen, Bruxelles, 1953.
11. *Mystère de la Pacience de Job*; Paris B.N. fr. 1774; ed. Meiller, Paris, 1971.
12. *Passion d'Amboise*; Paris B.N. n.a.f. 1445; ed. Picot, *Romania* (XIX), 1890.
13. *Passion d'Arras + La Vengeance.*; Arras, Bib.Mun. 697; *Passion*, ed. Richard, Arras, 1893.
14. *Passion d'Auvergne*; Paris B.N. n.a.f. 462; ed. Runnalls, *TLF* Genève, 1982.
15. *Passion de Gréban*; (B) Paris B.N. fr. 815; ed. O. Jodogne, Gembloux 1965, 1983;
16. *Passion de Gréban*; (A) Paris B.N. fr. 816; ed. Paris, Raynaud, *SATF* Paris, 1878;
17. *Passion de Gréban*; (C) Paris Arsenal 6431;
18. *Passion de Gréban*; (E) Chantilly, Condé 614.

112   Graham A. Runnalls

19. *Passion de Mons*; Mons, Bib.Univ. de l'Etat, 535, 1086-8; ed. Cohen, Paris, 1925.
20. *Passion Sainte Geneviève* (Fragment); Troyes, Arch. de l'Aube n.a. 2139; ed. Runnalls, *TLF* Genève, 1974.
21. *Passion de Semur*; Paris B.N. fr. 904; ed. Durbin, Muir, Leeds, 1982.
22. *Passion de Troyes*; Troyes, Bib.Mun. 2282; ed. Bibolet, *TLF* Genève, 1986.
23. *Passion de Valenciennes de 1547*; (A) Paris B.N. Rothschild I-7-3.
24. *Passion de Valenciennes de 1547*; (B) Paris B.N. fr. 12536.
25. *Passion de Valenciennes de 1549*; Valenciennes, Bib.Mun. 449.
26. *Mystère de la Résurrection*; (A) Paris B.N. fr. 972;
27. *Mystère de la Résurrection*; (B) Chantilly, Condé 615.
28. *Mystère de la Résurrection d'Eloy du Mont*; Paris B.N. fr. 2238.
29. *Mystère dy Roy Advenir*; Paris B.N. fr. 1042; ed. Meiller, *TLF* Genève, 1970.
30. *Mystère de S. Adrien*; Chantilly, Condé 620; ed. Picot, Mâcon, 1895.
31. *Mystère de S. Agathe*; Clermont-Ferrand; Arch.Puy-de-Dôme F 0129; ed. Bossuat, *BHR* (VIII), 1946.
32. *Mystère de S. Barbe à 5 journées*; Paris B.N. fr. 976.
33. *Mystère de S. Barbe* (rôle); Soc. d'Hist. de la Maurienne; ed. Chocheyras, *Théâtre Religieux en Savoie*, Genève, 1971.
34. *Mystère de S. Crespin et de S. Crespinien*; (P); Paris B.N. n.a.f. 2100; ed. Dessalles, Chabaille, Paris, 1836.
35. *Mystère de S. Crespin et S. Crespinien*; (C) Chantilly, Condé 619.
36. *Mystère de S. Denis*; Paris B.N. fr. 1041 and Rothschild I, 1, 16.
37. *Mystère de S. Didier*; Chaumont, Bib.Mun. 159; ed. Carnandet, Paris, 1855.
38. *Mystère de S. Etienne Pape*; Paris B.N. Rothschild I-7-22A.
39. *Mystère de S. Genis*; Paris B.N. fr. 12537; ed. Mostert, Stengel, Marburg, 1895.
40. *Mystère de S. Louis de Gringore*; Paris B.N. fr. 174511; ed. Montaiglon, Paris, 1858.
41. *Mystère de S. Louis*; Paris B.N. fr. 24331; ed. F. Michel, London, 1871.
42. *Mystère de S. Martin*; Paris B.N. fr. 24332; ed. Duplat, *TLF* Genève, 1979.
43. *Mystère de S. Quentin*; Saint-Quentin, Bib.Mun. 100; ed. Châtelain, Saint-Quentin, 1909.
44. *Mystère de S. Rémy*; Paris Arsenal 3364.
45. *Mystère de S. Sébastien*; Paris B.N. fr. 12539.
46. *Mystère de S. Sébastien*; Paris B.N. n.a.f. 1051; ed. Mills, *TLF* Genève, 1965.
47. *Mystère de S. Vincent*; Paris B.N. fr. 12538.
48. *Mystère de la Destruction de Troye*; (P3) Paris B.N. fr. 1626;
49. *Mystère de la Destruction de Troye*; (P5) Paris B.N. fr. 24333;
50. *Mystère de la Destruction de Troye*; (P4) Paris B.N. fr. 12601;
51. *Mystère de la Destruction de Troye*; (P2) Paris B.N. fr. 1625;
52. *Mystère de la Destruction de Troye*; (P1) Paris B.N. fr. 1415;
53. *Mystère de la Destruction de Troye*; (E) Edinburgh, Nat. Lib. Scotland, Adv. 19.1.19.
54. *Miracle des Trois Pèlerins*; Paris B.N. n.a.f. 14062; ed. Ouy, *Pluteus* II, 1984.

55. *Mystères de Lille* (73 plays); Wolfenbüttel, Herzog August Bibl., Guelf. Blankenburgensis 9.
56. *Jeu des Trois Rois de Neuchâtel*; Chapitre de Neuchâtel 237; ed. Giraud, King, Reyff, Fribourg, 1985.
57. *Mystère de la Passion (rôle)*; Digne, Arch. Alpes de Haute-Provence C* 852.
58. *Mystère de l'Advocacie Nostre Dame*; Angers, Bib.Mun. 572; ed. Runnalls, *ZRP* (99), 1983.
59. *Mystère de la Passion de Harvard*; Harvard Thr. 262; ed. Elliott, Runnalls, Yale U.P., 1978.
60. *Estoire de Griselidis*; Paris B.N. fr. 2203; ed. Craig, Univ. Kansas, 1954.
61. *Mystère du Siège d'Orléans*; Vatican Reg. Cristina 1022; ed. Guessard, Certain, Paris, 1862.
62. *Jour du Jugement*; Besançon, Bib.Mun. 579; ed. Roy, Paris, 1902.
63. *Mystère de S. Bernard de Menthon*; in private hands; ed. Lecoy de la Marche, *SATF* Paris, 1888.

10. JETER DE LA POUDRE AUX YEUX

On a parfois prétendu qu'il y aurait solution de continuité entre le français du Moyen Age et le français moderne. Il s'agit d'une affirmation absurde. On serait d'ailleurs bien en peine de nous dire quand s'est effectuée cette rupture. Naturellement la langue française se transforme, se renouvelle. Des mots disparaissent, d'autres changent leur sens. Des nuances sémantiques se déplacent continuellement. Mais le français médiéval reste une langue vivante pour quiconque se donne la peine de le fréquenter journellement. Les éditeurs de textes dépensent beaucoup d'efforts pour offrir des matériaux fiables aux lecteurs. Et en particulier, A. J. Holden a acquis toute notre reconnaissance pour les belles éditions qu'il nous a fournies.

Dans *Ipomedon* de Hue de Rotelande (Holden, 1979) nous avons relevé, au v. 2143, *suffrer la pudre as oilz a auc.*, que le glossaire traduit par 'tromper, duper'. Dans ce texte, dont l'auteur utilise une langue très riche en proverbes et maximes populaires (v. introd. p.54), on n'est pas surpris de trouver la première attestation française de la locution qui s'est figée sous la forme *jeter de la poudre aux yeux*. Seul le verbe est différent, c'est, nous le verrons, l'élément qui a le plus varié au fil des siècles; *suffrer* y est une forme de *suffler* 'souffler'.

Dans le passage, le poète se livre à une réflexion misogyne sur le comportement des femmes et de son héroïne, la Fière. Cette dernière veut retarder le moment de se marier. A cette fin, elle a fait mander son oncle et suzerain, Meleager, qui viendra présider les débats. Le poète intervient alors et nous dévoile les pensées secrètes de la Fière:

> Je qui k'el se purverrat tant
> K'el *suffrerat la pudre as oilz*
> Et as josnes e as plus veulz.

('Je crois qu'elle fera tout pour duper les jeunes et les moins jeunes'.)

Le sens de 'duper' peut être appuyé par l'emploi quelques vers plus bas d'*engingner* (vv. 2148–49). Cette *pudre as oilz* prendra par la suite la forme d'un tournoi de trois jours, qui forme le coeur même du roman. On pourrait donc traduire 'utiliser des subterfuges pour se soustraire aux exigences de'. La métaphore est donc assez nettement perceptible.

En effet *pudre (poudre)* signifie 'poussière', sens habituel du mot au Moyen Age et qu'on trouve par exemple au v. 2709 d'*Ipomedon*.

Cette expression est très ancienne. Elle est déjà attestée en latin. Au 2e siècle, Aulu-Gelle dans *Les Nuits Attiques* (5, 21, 4) présente ainsi le comportement d'un grammairien, dont on veut croire l'espèce éteinte: 'Un impertinent censeur langagier qui avait très peu lu et seulement ce qui est rebattu dans la foule, qui possédait quelques rudiments appris par ouï-dire de la science grammaticale, les uns grossiers et ébauchés, les autres faux, et les jetait comme de la poudre aux yeux (*eas quasi pulverem ob oculos ... adspergebat*) de tous ceux qu'il avait entrepris'.

L'expression reparaît donc dix siècles plus tard, dans *Ipomedon*, composé peu après 1180. On peut affirmer qu'il n'y a pas emprunt; Hue n'a pas lu les *Nuits Attiques*. Des intermédiaires éventuels entre Aulu-Gelle et Hue manquent complètement. D'autre part, il y a incontestablement continuité et parallélisme entre *aspergere pulverem ob oculos* et *soffler la poudre aus ieuz*, même si le sens est légèrement différent ('chercher à en imposer'/'user de subterfuges pour se soustraire aux exigences de'); dans les deux cas les moyens utilisés se retourneront contre celui (ou celle) qui lance ou souffle la poussière.

A ma connaissance on ne retrouve l'expression que près de trois siècles plus tard. Pierre Michault, en 1466, dans le *Doctrinal du Temps Présent* (Walton, 1931, X, p.154) fait ainsi parler *Maistre Vantance*, qui donne à ses élèves des modèles de discours de vantardise à tenir:

> Car il fauldra qu'en guerre je me boute
> Et sy menray une si belle route
> Que je pourray a cop vanger mon dueil
> Et aux autres *mectre la pouldre en l'oeul.*

Le sens est cette fois 'l'emporter sur qn' avec une métaphore militaire très nettement perceptible. En effet, plusieurs textes se font l'écho d'une tactique qui consiste à mettre les ennemis face au soleil et au vent, pour qu'ils soient aveuglés par la lumière et la poussière. Au milieu du 15e s., Antoine de la Sale recommande qu'avant le combat l'on 'face tout son povoir de leur (aux ennemis) donner le solail, le vent et la pouldre au visaige en combattant' (Desonay, 1935, p.243). De même un général devait faire en sorte 'qu'il eust le dos au solail et la pouldre, qui moult estoit grant pour le fort vent' (Ibid., p.48). Jean de Bueil, militaire expérimenté, indique qu'il faut choisir 'champs et places les plus advantageux qu'ilz pevent pour combatre. Car on y gaigne le solleil, on y gaigne le vent pour envoier la pouldre droit a ses ennemys' (Favre/Lecestre, 1887, I, p.154).

Cette tactique est déjà antique. Tite-Live (22, 43, 11) note qu'à la veille de Cannes, Hannibal a eu l'habileté de choisir un lieu où les siens, 'le vent soufflant dans leur dos, engageront le combat contre un ennemi aveuglé par la poussière levée par le vent (*pulvere offuso*)'.

Rappelons aussi le passage de *Renart* où, dans son duel avec Isengrin, Renart 'li fait . . . De la poudre voler es euz' (R 8518; cf. FHS 15440 et M 6, 1300).

Ainsi l'expression populaire a pris un sens assez nettement différent du fait de son rattachement, probablement uniquement littéraire, à une technique de l'art militaire. Il s'agit là d'un des innombrables cas de remotivation d'une expression.

Quelques années plus tard, vers 1480, on a la preuve que l'expression peut s'employer, dans le même sens, sans cette métaphore militaire. On lit dans le *Mystère de saint Quentin* (Chatelain, 1908, v. 14560), dans la bouche d'un forgeron qui vante ses mérites professionnels:

> Je fay de fer ce que je veuil
> Et si ne crains diables d'enfer
> Qui m'en *boute la pourre en l'oeil*

Le sens est 'surpasser qn'.

Ce sens est appelé à se maintenir. Outre un intéressant exemple de Guillaume Crétin que nous commenterons plus bas, on le lit en 1551–2 dans Nicolas de Herberay, *Dom Flores de Grece*, f.143r (chap. LXXVIII): 'faites en sorte que l'autre ne vous puisse mettre la poudre es yeulx'. On le rencontre aussi dans Nicot (1606) (*Proverbes* p.22) qui définit ainsi *Jetter la poudre aux yeux*:

> Ceux qui anciennement couroyent pour gaigner le prix de vistesse, estoient ensemble egalement retenuz en une certaine ligne ou barriere, que les Latins appelloient *Carceres*: Et si tost que le signe de partir leur estoit donné, & ceste barriere ouverte, c'estoit lors à qui mieux doubleroit le pas, jusques à tant qu'ils peussent parvenir à la borne elevée & plantée au bout de la carriere, appelée des mesmes Latins *Meta*, & celuy qui premier y arrivoit estoit victorieux. Or d'autant que toute ceste carriere estoit bien applanie & semée de menu sable, il advenoit que les coureurs par la frequente agitation des pieds, excitoient une grande pousiere, de sorte que quiconque demeuroit, sembloit jetter ceste poudre aux yeux de ceux qui le suyvoient, ne pouvant courir si fort que luy. Doncques par metaphore ce prouerbe est usurpé, quand deux ou bien plusieurs entreprenans une mesme chose, on dict de celuy qu'on estime en

devoir venir mieux à bout: Il jettera à tous les autres la poudre aux yeux: Les Latins en usent en autre signification, quand ils disent: *Oculis pulverem offundere*.

On notera que le latin *oculis pulverem offundere* est en fait une référence à l'adage d'Erasme, cité plus bas; le latin, comme nous le verrons, disait *offundere tenebras*.

Nous avons ensuite de nombreux témoignages de ce sens de 'surpasser'. D'Aubigné emploie *mettre la poudre en l'oeuil à* 'vaincre au combat' (*Du debvoir mutuel des roys et des subjects*, 3), et Malherbe *mettre la poudre aux yeux à qn* 'surpasser qn (dans le domaine intellectuel)' (cf. Littré). On lit aussi dans Oudin (1640) *jetter de la poudre aux yeux à qn* 'surmonter une personne en quelque science, la vaincre en disputant'. Plus curieux, un auteur, le Sieur de l'Espine, emploiera (en 1609) la locution dans le sens même de la métaphore prétenduement étymologique: *mettre à qn la poudre aux yeux plus viste que devant* 'accélérer sa fuite devant qn qui vous poursuit' (cf. SatFrD 1, 37 ds FEW 9, 561b).

La documentation du TLF et le Littré nous ont fourni des exemples nets du sens de 'surpasser': 1623 *jeter la poudre aux yeux de qn* 'le surpasser' et *faire voler la poudre aux yeux de qn* 'rendre manifeste l'infériorité de qn' (tous deux, Auvray), 1645 *jeter de la poudre aux yeux de qn* 'id.' (Tristan l'Hermite), 1651–fin 17e 'le surpasser' (Scarron; Colletet; Mme de La Fayette).

On voit que dans cet emploi c'est le verbe *jeter* qui se généralise. Sa première attestation est plus ancienne encore. On la lit dans Amyot (cité dans Littré). Dans sa traduction de la *Vie de Cicéron* de Plutarque, en 1559, il écrit: 'Tu ne fus pas dernierement absouz en jugement pour ton innocence, mais pource que je *jettay de la pouldre aux yeux de tes juges*, tellement qu'ilz ne peurent voir la verité de ton forfaict' (Normand, 1927, p.25). Malgré le FEW 9, 561b et la notice historique du TLF, le sens n'est pas 'surpasser' mais bien 'utiliser des arguments fallacieux pour convaincre'. Il s'agit du retour à un sens voisin de ceux attestés chez Aulu-Gelle et Hue de Rotelande. L'image n'est pas exactement celle que contenait le texte grec de Plutarque. En effet, Plutarque prêtait à Cicéron cette moquerie adressée à quelqu'un qu'il avait défendu victorieusement lors d'un procès: 'Est-ce donc à toi-même, Munatius, que tu dois ton acquittement, et non pas à moi, qui ai répandu en plein jour une nuit profonde devant le tribunal? (οὐκ ἐμοῦ πολὺ σκότος ἐν φωτὶ τῷ δικαστηρίῳ περιχέαντος)' (éd. Flacelière et Chambry, 25, 2). Quintilien (II, 17, 21) attribue d'ailleurs au même Cicéron une image très voisine: 'Cicéron se fit gloire d'avoir versé des ténèbres (*tenebras offudisse*) lors du procès de Cluentius'. Amyot utilise donc une image existant dans la langue française (*jeter de la poudre aux yeux*) pour rendre une image gréco-latine (περιχεῖν πολὺ σκότος — *offundere tenebras*), que l'on traduirait en français moderne par *lancer un rideau de fumée*.

Pour le retour à un sens proche du latin il serait assez plausible d'admettre qu'Amyot se souvient d'une interprétation en usage dans les écoles, telle qu'Erasme la note dans ses *Adages* (2, 9): '*Pulverem oculis offundere*. Dicitur, qui de industria rem obscurat et adversario judicium eripit. Traductum videtur a militia'. On notera qu'Erasme souligne l'origine militaire de cette métaphore. Cependant on doit remarquer que la valeur originelle pourrait être restée sous-jacente car elle semble affleurer dans le passage suivant de Guillaume Crétin (Chesney, 1932, pp.295, 93), daté de ca 1525, où à propos d'une femme dont il est fait l'éloge, il est dit:

> Asseuré l'a quelcun que te sçait estre
> Sçavante assez pour *mectre pouldre en l'oeil*
> D'homme esloquent au tien plaisir et vueil.

Le sens est donc 'l'emporter sur' mais avec, me semble-t-il, comme l'écho de la valeur que nous avons relevée chez Aulu-Gelle mais dont aurait disparu toute nuance péjorative.

Dans la première moitié du 17e s. en tout cas, les deux sens coexistent. A côté des emplois du sens de 'surpasser', notés plus haut, la documentation du TLF présente: 1624 *tascher de jeter à qn la poudre aux yeux* 'présenter à qn une démonstration spécieuse' (Mersenne); 1625 *vouloir jeter à qn de la poudre aux yeux* 'id' (Naudé).

A la fin du premier quart du 17e s. la locution est définitivement figée au plan de sa forme qui est devenue *jeter de la poudre aux yeux*. En moins d'un siècle *jeter* a éliminé tous ses prédécesseurs (*souffler, mettre, bouter, faire voler*) et, simultanément, la préposition *de* s'est introduite entre le verbe et son complément d'objet. De même, *oeil* a retrouvé la forme du pluriel qu'il avait perdue, mais uniquement lorsque la locution signifiait 'surpasser'.

Une fois acquise la fixation de la forme, c'est son sens qui va s'unifier. Rien de plus instructif à cet égard que la mise en parallèle des définitions des trois grands dictionnaires de la fin du 17e siècle (Richelet 1680; Furetière 1690; Académie 1694).

> Richelet: '*Jetter de la poudre aux yeux*. Ce proverbe se dit des gens qui pour tout fond de mérite n'ont que de belles apparences. C'est tromper, c'est éblouïr par de belles apparences ceux qui ne se

connaissent pas bien aux choses. Ainsi on dira fort bien le Philosophe Launai jette de la poudre aux yeux des étrangers par son babil.'

Furetière: '*Jetter de la poudre aux yeux* c'est préoccuper les gens, les esblouïr par un faux mérite. Ce proverbe prend son origine de ceux qui couroient aux Jeux Olympiques, où l'on disoit de ceux qui avoient gagné le devant, qu'ils jettoient de la poudre aux yeux de ceux qui les suivoient, en élevant le menu sable et la poudre par le mouvement de leurs pieds: ce qui se dit figurément dans les autres occasions où il y a des compétiteurs.'

Académie: '*Jetter de la poudre aux yeux à quelqu'un*, le surpasser en quelque concurrence, le laisser loin derrière soy. On dit aussi d'un homme que *par ses discours, par ses manières d'agir il jette de la poudre aux yeux*' pour dire 'qu'il esblouit d'abord, qu'il impose' qu'il surprend l'esprit par des choses agréables 'et qui n'ont point de solidité.'

Furetière et Académie enregistrent les deux sens (*surpasser/éblouir*). Alors qu'Académie se borne à un constat sec qui donne peu de prise au commentaire (sauf pour la présence éventuelle du complément de destination, comme nous le verrons plus bas), Furetière donne déjà plus d'indications. Pour lui le sens premier, et le plus usuel, est 'esblouïr par un faux mérite' mais il éprouve le besoin de s'inspirer de Nicot pour une explication historique à la fin de laquelle il concède l'existence d'un sens figuré ('surpasser'). Richelet ne voit qu'un seul sens dont il donne une excellente définition qui montre comment s'est fait le mélange des deux sens. L'élément fondamental est l'idée de 'tromper' et d''éblouir' mais du sens de 'surpasser' vient la notation de l'infériorité de la victime ('ceux qui se connaissent pas bien aux choses'). Cette fusion est aussi très nette dans l'exemple fourni, où Launai triomphe et éblouit des auditeurs dociles par des propos peu solides.

Que cette réunification soit désormais faite nous en avons deux confirmations. D'abord par l'article de l'Académie (1718) qui a remodelé complètement sa présentation de l'expression: '*Jetter de la poudre aux yeux*, imposer, esblouir par ses discours et par ses manières'. Ensuite par les attestations extraites des textes du 18e s. et fournies par la documentation du TLF, où l'on trouve *jeter de la poudre aux yeux de qn* 'provoquer des illusions dans l'esprit de qn' (dep. 1714; Dacier; Lesage; Marivaux; Varenne). On peut noter que cette expression est typique de Lesage chez qui on en a déjà relevé au moins douze exemples: 4 fois dans *Gil Blas*, 3 fois dans *Guzman d'Alfarache*, 2 fois dans *Le Bachelier de Salamanque*, 1 fois dans *Le Chevalier de Beauchesne*, 1 fois dans *Estevanille Gonzales*, 1 fois dans *La Valise trouvée*. A titre de comparaison signalons que rares sont les auteurs français chez qui on la lit deux fois: Saint-Simon, Delecluze, Frapié, L. Daudet.

On notera un exemple particulièrement intéressant, et qui est très proche de la définition de Richelet, telle que nous l'avons analysée. Il figure dans Littré mais le contexte trop court ne permet pas d'en cerner toute la valeur. Saint-Simon décrit ainsi le duc et maréchal d'Harcourt: 'Le sophisme le plus entrelacé et le mieux poussé lui étoit familier; il savoit y donner un air simple et vrai, jeter force poudre aux yeux par des interrogations hardies, et quelquefois par des disparades, quand il en avoit besoin'. Le sens est donc à la fois 'convaincre' mais aussi 'éblouir'. La nuance n'est cependant pas aussi péjorative que dans Richelet ou, à plus forte raison, dans les autres attestations du 18e siècle. On est au point où l'on sent encore quelque chose de chacune des deux nuances de sens, attestées encore au début du 17e siècle.

On peut penser que l'évolution sémantique de l'expression est aussi liée à l'évolution sémantique du mot *poudre*. A l'origine il signifiait 'poussière'. On sait qu'à partir du 16e s. il est peu à peu concurrencé en ce sens par un mot, assez probablement régional à l'origine, *poussiere*, mot attesté uniquement en franc-comtois, lorrain et hennuyer jusqu'au 15 s.; voir l'article *Pulvis* de FEW 9, 561–73. On sait que Wartburg n'adopte pas entièrement la thèse de Jaberg, qui me paraît cependant comporter une grande part de vérité. Le seul point où elle ne me convainc pas est l'hypothèse que le sens de 'poudre à canon' a pu avoir une importance déterminante en provoquant une surcharge sémantique du mot *poudre*. Peu à peu le noyau sémantique de *poudre* va se déplacer du sens de 'poussière' à celui de 'poudre'. A coup sûr le 17e siècle est une période charnière dans cette évolution et la modification du sens de la locution nous paraît riche d'enseignements. Le sens de 'tromper, éblouir', qui réapparaît vigoureusement au milieu du 17e s., nous semble faire allusion à l'opération d'un charlatan, à la fameuse *poudre d'oribus ou de prelimpinpin* 'une chose de rien, un remède sans effet' (Oudin, 1640) cf. aussi *poudre de perlimpinpin* '(en parlant des choses qui n'ont aucune vertu)' (dep. Furetière, 1690).

Un emploi relevé par Oudin (1640) paraît encore apporter de l'eau au moulin d'une poudre magique. Il s'agit de l'expression *je commence d'avoir de la poudre dans les yeux* 'je m'endors'. Elle paraît venir de la croyance au *marchand de sable*, attestée aussi dans la lexicographie sous la forme: 'on dit proverbialement d'une personne qui s'endort que

le petit homme luy a jetté du sable sur les yeux, comme si cela l'obligeoit
à les fermer' (Furetière, 1690). On lit ensuite *avoir du sable dans les
yeux* 'éprouver une envie de dormir qui appesantit les paupières'
(Académie, 1798–1935).

Par ailleurs *poussière* lui-même a tenté un moment de s'infiltrer dans
l'expression au détriment de *poudre*, essentiellement au cours de la
première moitié du 17e siècle et dans les deux sens principaux. En voici
les exemples que fournissent la documentation du TLF et Littré: fin
16e s. *jetter de la poussiere aux yeux de qn* 'rendre manifeste l'infériorité
de qn' (Paré), 1623 *faire voler la poussiere aux yeux de qn* 'id.' (Auvray),
ca 1650 *jetter de la poussiere aux yeux à une armée* 'vaincre au combat
une armée (Guez Balzac), 1623 *jetter la poussiere aux yeux de qn*
'tromper par une démonstration spécieuse' (Garasse), 1625 — milieu
17e s. *jetter de la poussiere aux yeux de* 'id.' (Camus; de la Roque, Littré),
1627 *jetter de la poussiere aux yeux à qn* 'id.' (Sorel). Ces attestations
marquent clairement le moment où dans la langue générale *poussière*
supplante *poudre*. Mais cette tentative a échoué en ce qui concerne la
locution car *poudre* s'est soudée à *aux yeux* pour former une lexie
composée *poudre aux yeux* qui a pris un sens où *poudre* pouvait se
défendre face à l'envahissement de *poussière*. On verra que plus tard (au
19e s. et surtout au 20e s. cf. les ex. d'Amiel et de Morand, cités plus
bas) cette lexie composée en est venue à s'employer de façon autonome.
Cependant *poussière* a tenté un second assaut au cours du 18e s. On
relèvera cet exemple précieux, extrait des *Épîtres* de J.-B. Rousseau, cité
dans Guérin (1892): 'Un charlatan, sur Pégase monté, Nous *jette aux
yeux une vaine poussière*'. On voit que *aux yeux* possède toute son
autonomie par rapport à *poussière* qu'il précède (ce qui est une
innovation unique puisqu'on a toujours eu l'ordre *poudre (poussière)
aux yeux)* et que *poussière* est si peu clair qu'il a besoin d'être explicité
dans le contexte par son épithète, *vaine*, et même par le sujet de la
phrase *charlatan*; on retrouvera d'ailleurs ce même mot de *charlatan*
dans un exemple très intéressant de Montherlant, commenté plus bas.
Les lexicographes enregistreront encore *jet(t)er de la poussière aux yeux*
'éblouir par de beaux discours' (Richelet, 1737–59); 'id., éblouir par des
dehors pompeux' (Hautel, 1808).

Il reste maintenant à suivre dans les dictionnaires la description de
l'expression *jeter de la poudre aux yeux*. Au 18e siècle, les dictionnaires
campent sur leurs positions. L'Académie conserve sa définition. Les
dictionnaires de Trévoux se bornent à reproduire celle de Furetière.
Dans la première moitié du 19e s., les dictionnaires adoptent une
définition proche de celle de Richelet et proche aussi de celle de

l'Académie (1718): 'éblouir par de belles apparences, de beaux discours' (Boiste; Bescherelle).

Il revenait à Littré de réintégrer la dimension historique. Il établit deux subdivisions: d'une part 'éblouir, surpendre par ses discours, par des apparences', où les définitions correspondent aux exemples (Saint-Simon; Lesage) d'après lesquels elles sont partiellement forgées; d'autre part '(au 18e s. [mais il faut lire en fait *au 17e s.*]) éclipser, surpasser' où les définitions sont faites aussi d'après les exemples. Le second sens, dont Littré précise qu'il n'est plus usité, est suivi d'un commentaire historique textuellement emprunté à Furetière où 'de ceux qui couroient aux Jeux Olympiques' est devenu 'des coureurs' et où les imparfaits sont devenus des présents.

Le dictionnaire de Guérin (1892) copie d'abord l'Académie puis, pour le sens vieux, Littré, mais il ajoute aussi un exemple intéressant qui nous fait comprendre la valeur sémantique donnée désormais à *poudre*. Quand Musset écrit: 'les femmes aiment à avoir de la poudre dans les yeux; plus on leur en jette, plus elles les écarquillent, afin d'en gober davantage', on a l'impression qu'il pense effectivement à une *poudre de perlimpinpin*, poudre magique des charlatans et des magiciens. Cette interprétation peut être corroborée en outre par la phrase d'Oxenstiern qui sert de commentaire à l'expression dans les dictionnaires de Boiste et de Bescherelle: 'l'intérêt est comme la poudre que le démon jette aux yeux de l'homme, afin qu'il ne connaisse ni justice, ni devoir, ni honneur, ni amitié'.

Deux petits faits syntaxiques sont encore à souligner. Les exemples anciens se caractérisaient par le fait que l'on précisait aux yeux de qui était envoyée la poudre (*il lui jette de la poudre au yeux* ou *il jette de la poudre aux yeux de/à qn*). Le destinataire faisait défaut pour la première fois dans le dictionnaire de l'Académie (1694) (et encore seulement pour la locution qui a le sens moderne, puisque les auteurs opposent *jetter de la poudre aux yeux à quelqu'un* à *il jette de la poudre aux yeux*). Lesage offre une large majorité de tours où le destinataire est précisé, 10 emplois sur 12. A partir de 1740, les chiffres s'inversent et, dans la documentation du TLF après cette date, le destinataire n'est plus indiqué que dans 7 cas sur 18. Ainsi *yeux* est de moins en moins suivi d'un complément introduit par *de*. Parallèlement, à partir du 19e siècle le syntagme *poudre aux yeux* prend clairement son autonomie (v. déjà *avoir de la poudre dans les yeux*, Musset dans Guérin, cité plus haut). La documentation du TLF atteste le syntagme seul, sans verbe, dans Amiel ('Sa passion est pour la poudre aux yeux, le clinquant') et Morand

('. . . la cinquième avenue. C'est comme une préfiguration du luxe d'après-guerre. Poudre aux yeux, poudre d'or du Yukon et du Klondyke'), ainsi que *n'être que de la poudre aux yeux* (Alain-Fournier), *jeteur de poudre aux yeux* (L. Daudet) et le TLF a même relevé un emploi adjectival dans *opération poudre aux yeux*. Ces transferts grammaticaux indiquent que *poudre* doit être determiné, ce qui n'était pas le cas tant qu'était perceptible le sens de 'poussière'. On serait donc passé de *jeter de la poudre/aux yeux de qn* à *jeter/de la poudre aux yeux*. On comprend alors mieux l'introduction de la préposition *de* devant *poudre*. Elle amorçait la séparation entre le verbe *mettre, jeter* et son objet *poudre*. On pourrait penser que par compensation il fallait figer chaque élément en lui donnant une forme stable. On aurait donc le schéma d'évolution suivant:

(1°) Mettre (ou souffler, bouter, faire voler, jeter) la poudre // aux yeux de qn

(2°) jeter // de la poudre // aux yeux de qn

(3°) jeter // de la poudre aux yeux.

On remarquera dans cette optique le très significatif exemple, extrait de Montherlant, que fournit la documentation du TLF: 'jeter la poudre aux yeux du lecteur avec une explication de charlatan' (*Les Lépreuses*, Bibl. de la Pléiade p.517). On relève d'emblée qu'il s'agit du seul exemple depuis 1624 où le *de* partitif manque entre *jeter* et *poudre*. D'autre part, il appartient au tour, désormais largement minoritaire, où le destinataire (*du lecteur*) est indiqué. Il représente le schéma suivant:

jeter la poudre // aux yeux du lecteur // avec une explication de charlatan

Mais comme *jeter la poudre* n'a désormais plus aucun sens, il faut resémantiser la locution au moyen du complément circonstanciel, *avec une explication de charlatan*. Ce complément est lui-même remarquable. *Explication* coïncide avec le sens classique, explicité par la définition 'éblouir par ses discours' de la plupart des dictionnaires (Voir aussi l'ex. forgé dans Richelet 1680 et, déjà le contexte de la citation d'Amyot, cités plus haut), et *charlatan*, qui fait écho à *éblouir* de la définition citée, appuie l'interprétation que nous donnions plus haut à *poudre* (cf. *poùdre de perlimpinpin*) et rappelle aussi l'exemple de J.-B. Rousseau que nous avons commenté plus haut.

L'étude de cette expression me paraît intéressante et révélatrice. D'abord nous pouvons remonter sans véritable solution de continuité du vingtième au second siècle. Certes les attestations sont rares. Bien des siècles n'ont rien fourni et l'attestation chez Hue de Rotelande est

donc particulièrement importante. Comme souvent, nous avons une
grande densité d'attestations à partir du milieu du 15e s. Faute d'en
avoir disposé, le FEW n'a pu que donner une idée tout à fait fausse de
l'histoire de l'expression. D'autre part il faut prendre soin de suivre au
microscope les nuances sémantiques et les variations des constructions
que renferment les attestations des expressions. Dans le cas présent ces
fluctuations reflètent de façon indirecte les modifications sémantiques
qui affectent le mot de base. Mais on constate aussi que la valeur de la
locution a pu, malgré bien des turbulences de surface et en dépit du
changement de sens du mot *poudre*, rester étonnamment stable depuis
le 12e siècle (voire même depuis l'Antiquité). Dans un monde où tout
change si rapidement, d'après ce que serinent les porte-micro, c'est un
fait notable. Bref les locutions qui forment la chair même de notre
langue n'ont pas encore été étudiées avec un soin suffisant. Il y a
beacoup à faire et l'on ne pourra pas faire l'économie d'un dépouillement
général de toute la littérature française sous cet angle. Je voudrais
attirer, une fois de plus, l'attention des éditeurs de textes sur ce point,
trop souvent négligé dans leurs glossaires. Enfin nous avons pu constater
que les bons écrivains, dont notre langue ne manque pas à travers les
siècles, se révèlent dans l'emploi qu'ils font des locutions des linguistes
hors pair. Voilà bien de quoi inciter à la modestie les linguistes trop
disposés à *jeter de la poudre aux yeux*.

Références

Pour les dictionnaires on se reportera aux bibliographies usuelles du FEW,
du *Grand Larousse de la langue française* et du *Trésor de la langue
française* (TLF).

Chatelain, H. (éd.) (1908) *Le Mistere de saint Quentin*, Saint-Quentin.
Chesney, K. (ed.) (1932) Guillaume Cretin, *Oeuvres poétiques*, Paris.
Desonay, F. (éd.) (1935) Antoine de La Sale, *La Salade*, Liège-Paris.
Favre/Lecestre (éd.) (1887–89) Jean de Bueil, *Le Jouvencel* (2 vols),
    Paris.
Holden, A. J. (éd.) (1979) Hue de Rotelande, *Ipomedon*, Paris.
Normand, J. (éd.) (1927) Amyot, *Vie de Cicéron*, Paris.
Walton, Th. (éd.) (1931) Pierre Michault, *Le Doctrinal du temps présent*,
    Paris.

Philip E. Bennett

11. *LA GRANT EWE DEL FLUM:* TOPONYMY AND TEXT IN *LE PÈLERINAGE DE CHARLEMAGNE*

The itinerary followed by Charlemagne and his peers on their journey to the Holy Land in the first part of the *Pèlerinage de Charlemagne* has aroused as much scholarly debate as almost any other ten lines in the entire corpus of Old French epic poetry. The first two lines, which take the imperial pilgrims across France and Central Europe, seem clear enough, but the second half of the journey, which leads them apparently by a land route through Eastern Europe to Jerusalem without touching Constantinople, which they visit only on their return journey after visiting the Holy Sepulchre, seems confused and offers readings over which there has been little agreement. In a footnote to a paper published in 1984 and originally read at the Congrès International Rencesvals in Padua in 1982 (Bennett, 1984a, p.482), I offered a new interpretation of l.103: 'la grant ewe del flum passerent a la liee'. (Aebischer, 1965; all quotations from and references to the poem are from this edition unless otherwise stated). I did not at that time have space to develop all my arguments fully, and subsequent discussions with colleagues have suggested that there is still a need to do so. I would, therefore, like to take this opportunity to investigate this particularly obscure line in its context, and to draw from it some consequences for the ordering of the text at this point in the *Pèlerinage*.

Although the passage is well known in reconstructed critical editions it will serve to quote it here *in extenso* from the transcription made by Koschwitz, since that provides our sole surviving guide to the contents of the manuscript, and will help to avoid entering the discussion with any preconceptions supplied by modern editorial interpretations:

> Il issirent de frāce 7 burgoine guerpirēt
> Loheregne trau'sēt baiuere 7 hungerie
> Les turcs 7 les psaunz 7 cele gent haie
> La grant ewe del flum passerēt a la liee
> Cheuauchet li epere tres par mi croiz ptie
> Les bois 7 les forez 7 sūt ent^ez en grece
> Les puis 7 les mūtaines uirent en romanie
> E brochent a la t're u d's receut martirie
> Veient ierl'm une citez antiue. (Koschwitz, 1907, pp.6, 8)

(125)

Paul Aebischer's attitude to these lines was characteristically trenchant and dismissive:

> La description de l'itinéraire suivi par Charlemagne de Paris à Jérusalem a fait couler beaucoup d'encre, parce qu'on a estimé que l'énumération des pays traversés ne suivait pas un ordre rigoureusement géographique. En réalité, l'Orient que connaissait l'auteur se bornait à quelques notions sur la topographie de Jérusalem, et à quelques on-dit relatifs aux merveilles que recélait Constantinople. Après qu'il a fait traverser à ses pèlerins la France, la Lorraine, la Bavière et la Hongrie, noms qui constituent une suite logique, le poète invente, sauf dans le cas de *la liee* qui paraît bien devoir être une faute de copiste pour *Lalice*, soit Laodicée. Temps perdu, par conséquent, de prétendre identifier la *Croix Partie* ou le *Flum*. Temps perdu que de vouloir mettre de l'ordre dans les dénominations géographiques, réelles ou imaginaires, des vers 102–106. (Aebischer, 1965, pp.87–8)

Now while it is true that the jongleur's knowledge of the East does appear slight, and while his attitude to its topography appears cavalier (witness his having Constantinople struck by a north-west wind — *galerne* — blowing from the sea in ll.354–5), it would have been uncharacteristic of either the epic or the 'traveller's tales' tradition for him to have invented names rather than re-using inherited material. Our problems of identification lie both in the garbled form which a mixture of written and oral transmission may have given to exotic toponyms and in the subsequent mistreatments they may have suffered in the manuscript tradition of the poem.

At the heart of the problem lies the correction (usually deemed necessary) and interpretation of the segment *a la liee* (l.103). The way that this phrase dominates the whole context can be seen from Horrent's treatment of the question:

> Si le seul vers 102 a été transposé, il faut admettre que *La grant ewe del flum passerent a la lice* (sic), v.103, se rapporte à un lieu européen, qu'auraient connu les compagnons de Charlemagne avant d'atteindre la Grèce et la Romanie. Ce n'est guère possible, car *la lice* paraît bien indiquer une des Laodicées d'Asie Mineure. (Horrent, 1961, p.29)

In Horrent's thinking the conclusion dominates the argument. Because an interpretation has been determined *a priori*, the argument that should produce the conclusion is subverted to serve that interpretation. One can also note here the ordering of the elements *Grèce* and *Romanie*, presented not as a paronymic doublet but as geographically (because textually) sequential. The result of this approach is manifest in the next stage of Horrent's argument where he asserts, offering no proof, that *Romanie* is to be understood as that part of the Byzantine Empire situated in Asia Minor 'selon l'usage turc' (1961, p.30 n.2). Now, while there has been some attention focused recently on possible Moorish contributions to vocabulary, cultural, and even narrative features in Old French epic (Walker, 1979; Galmés de Fuentes, 1979; Bennett, 1984b) all such influences are adduced from possible contacts in Western Europe. The intrusion of this particular Oriental usage into *Le Pèlerinage de Charlemagne* is susceptible of no such explanation.

Horrent's hypothesis then becomes a given on which the following sentence is built:

> Charlemagne traverse une partie de l'Asie Mineure, franchit un bras de mer (v.103) pour atteindre Laodicée (Syrie) . . . (1961, p.30)

The internal logic of the argument has led to a drastic re-interpretation of *la liee* = *Lalice* as a town no longer in Asia Minor but in Syria. Consequently the *flum* has to be read as a firth or estuary (rather incongruously, although tentatively, identified with the Gulf of Alexandretta), whereas to cross from any conceivable port in Byzantine Asia Minor to Laodicea, considerably south of the port of Antioch actually used by Crusaders, a wide stretch of the open Mediterranean must be traversed. Thus, although Horrent's avowed aim is to produce a logical ordering of the manuscript text, the whole argument, including the interpretation of other crucial words in the text, is subordinated to the perceived need to confirm the meaning of *la liee* as 'Laodicea'.

This interpretation has been current, with problematic results, ever since Koschwitz's first edition of the poem (1880). Francisque Michel (1836) left the manuscript uncorrected and offered only a question mark as a gloss. Koschwitz hit on the ingenious solution of the scribal misreading and the identification with the Syrian Laodicea, but, even though his first edition aimed at being more or less diplomatic, his solution forced him to invent a 'missing' line between ll.101 and 102, printed in italics in his edition:

> *Lumbardie e Rumaigne, Puille e Calabre virent*

in which he exploits and re-interprets the elements *Romanie* and *croiz partie* from the manuscript. He then suppresses ll.104-6, the effect of which is to remove any possible reference to the route taken by the Second Crusade, or even by the principal participants in the First Crusade, and to construct a route used by the Third Crusade and minor elements of the First Crusade. This solution does have the advantage of explaining 'logically' the absence of any reference to Constantinople in the outward journey to Jerusalem, but only at the price of considering the manuscript wholly unreliable at this point.

In his second and subsequent editions Koschwitz abandoned this solution, although he kept the correction *Lalice* and its gloss as 'Laodicea'; he did, however, additionally introduce that re-ordering of the lines (100–101–105–106–102–103–104–107–108) which continues to find favour with Horrent and Madeleine Tyssens (1978, pp.4, 36) and which is intended to restore the logical sequence of Charlemagne's journey based now on the route of the Second Crusade. Most other modern editors and critics also accept this interpretation of *Lalice*, although not always accepting the modification in the order of the lines, being content to posit, like Panvini, that the second part of the itinerary is 'generico e vago' (1960, p.36). The problem none can escape, however, is that it is almost impossible to find a Laodicea whose geographical situation can be squared with the notion of crossing a great river. As we have seen, Horrent (1961) re-interprets *flum* as 'bras de mer'; for Favati (1965, p.147), quoting Voretzsch the river is the Lycus, a tributary of the Meander, neither of which could seriously be held to be a 'großer Fluß'. For Burgess and Cobby (1988, pp.35, 75), who dissent from the majority view in making *Lalice* refer not to a town but to the province of Lycia in southern Turkey, the *flum*, while being a 'river' in their translation becomes 'whatever waterway the author . . . would see as dividing Europe from Asia, perhaps here the Dardanelles' (p.76). In this respect at least, Burgess and Cobby adopt Horrent's view that a narrow stretch of sea is meant by *flum*. Other commentators are simply reticent about this, treating it almost as a formulaic element, as can be deduced from Picherit's comment (1984, p.77): 'As in most other French medieval *chansons de geste*, the poet uses here real and imaginary place-names without making any attempt at geographical accuracy.' However, in such a circumstance the formulaic element *sor mer* is far more likely to have come to the jongleur's lips to describe the situation of *Lalice* from his acquaintance with such epic locations as Larchamp/Aliscans, Narbonne, Lucerne, and Genves than is the complex reference we do have to crossing a mighty river.

In order to achieve a viable interpretation of l.103 it would, therefore, seem preferable to begin not with the highly dubious final element but to look for an acceptable gloss for the first hemistich, on the basis of which one may build a reasonable hypothesis about the second, more obscure one. The first consideration in tackling this problem has to be to determine what sort of waterway was designated in Old French by the word *flum*, after which one may try to pin down which waterway the poet may have had in mind.

Horrent's suggestion that *flum* might designate a stretch of the eastern Mediterranean, across the mouth of the Gulf of Alexandretta, is not supported by any twelfth-century source that I have been able to find. Saewulf (Brownlow, 1892), who sailed extensively round the coasts of Greece and Turkey in the course of his pilgrimage, and arrived in the Holy Land by sea uses only the word *pelagus* to refer to the Mediterranean. The Anonymous III and V (Stewart, 1894), writing in Latin, and Abbot Daniel, who travelled from Russia in 1106 (Wilson, 1888), all use terms equivalent to 'Great Sea', which, as *Grant Mer*, is also the expression used in the French account of Richard I's Crusade (Johnston, 1961). Nor indeed do Godefroy, Tobler-Lommatzsch, or the *Französisches Etymologisches Wörterbuch* give any references which would lead one to suppose that in Old French the word *flum* could designate the open sea.

The same is not totally true when one considers the suggestion that an estuary or tidal inlet may be in question, and in this connection one would equally need to consider the possibility of *flum* designating a strait such as the Dardanelles, whose aspect would easily assimilate it to the idea of a tidal estuary. However, there is again no indication that *flum* alone was ever used in this sense. The expression that is found to designate a firth or equivalent is *flum de mer*. Both Godefroy and Tobler-Lommatzsch give several examples of this usage including one from *Foucon de Candie*:

> Par moi avra la terre a un Escler
> Trente chastiaus selonc lo flum de mer (l.1979,
> Tobler-Lommatzsch, III, Cols 1957–8 *s.v.* Flum)

and this from Guillaume Guiart's *La Branche des Royaux Lignages*:

> Joignant de Cirice el fleuve
> Ou le flo de mer se treuve. (II, 10064, Tobler-Lommatzsch,
> III, Cols 1955–6 *s.v.* Flueve)

Both of these dictionaries do give references to *flum* unqualified in this sense, but always in a context where there is no possibility of ambiguity. Thus, in this quotation from Froissart:

> Haimbon siet droitement sus un bon port de mer et en va li fluns tout autour par grans fosses. (*Chroniques*, III, 357, in Godefroy, IV, 40b–c, *s.v.* Flum)

or this from the Continental redaction of *Bueves de Hantone*:

> Par ses jornees s'est li bers tant hastés,
> La mer costoie, dont li fluns estoit lés (II, 17,601, in
> Tobler-Lommatzsch, III Col. 1958, *s.v.* Flum)

In both these cases the word *mer* actually occurs in the immediate context of *flum* and is subsumed into the clause containing the latter word either by a pronoun (*en* in Froissart) or a relative (*dont* in *Bueves de Hantone*). One could not deduce from either text that *flum* could be used in total isolation to mean an estuary or tidal inlet. Von Wartburg (*FEW*, III, p.643a, *s.v.* Flumen) concurs in this view, and goes even further in restricting the expression *flum de mer* to a Picard usage, although the second quotation above must cast some doubt on that.

Our immediate conclusion must be that the type of watercourse indicated in l.103 of the *Pèlerinage de Charlemagne* will be a river, and one famous for its size, as may be deduced from the fact that the poet feels no need to name it but merely to emphasise its magnitude. Now, when a river is referred to without name in the context of pilgrimage texts it is usually the Jordan, as we see from the following lines of *Renaud de Montauban* (Michelant, 1862):

> Jusqu'en Costentinople connois je les barons
> Si alai au sepulcre et au flun a bandon. (p.253, l.18)

and *La Conquête de Jérusalem* (Hippeau, 1969):

> La riviere del flun sovent recherquerai (l.1076)

but it is out of the question that such can be the intention in our text.

There are, of course, many rivers to be crossed on the land route to Constantinople and Jerusalem, but there is no need to take most of them into account here. One which we should consider, however, is the Lycus, on which Laodicea stood, or perhaps more properly the Meander, of which the Lycus is a tributary. Odo de Deuil does give a graphic portrait of the difficulties encountered by Louis's army at the Meander during the Second Crusade. Odo describes the Meander as 'fluvius profundus et latus' (Berry, 1948, p.108) and stresses the effects of rain and snow in swelling not only this river but all the mountain streams that fed it. This description could have had a profound impact on our poet, and if he were working in the area of Paris or St Denis in the second half of the twelfth century, he could very easily have known, at least at second hand, a text composed by Suger's successor as abbot of St Denis. One must note, however, that there was no crossing of the Meander, that the reports of the running battles with the Turks completely overwhelm the description of the river in Odo's text, and the crossing of the Lycus does not even merit a mention. If, however, we do conclude that the Meander (probably rather than the Lycus) was the river alluded to, then we should have to agree with Koschwitz that ll.102–3 have been severely misplaced in the copying of the text. Before doing that it would be prudent to consider another possibility.

There is one river which regularly, one might almost say formulaically, calls forth an allusion to its size when it is mentioned in medieval writing. That river is the Danube. In Latin William of Tyre describes the early part of the Second Crusade's itinerary:

Transcursa igitur Bavaria et flumine magno Danubio apud
Ratisbonam transmisso . . . (Huyghens, 1986, p.741)

In French Wace refers to

Danube, un flum mult grant (Holden, 1970–73, *App.* v.171)

and the Middle English *Mandeville's Travels*, describing the route to the Holy Land, refers to the need to cross the Danube, adding:

This ryvere of Danube is a ful gret ryvere (Seymour, 1967, p.5)

The range of sources, learned and popular, as well as the persistence of the reference from the twelfth to the fourteenth century and beyond, shows how firmly embedded the idea of the Danube as *the* great river was in the medieval mind. Moreover, the passage in Wace from which a line was quoted above shows that the Danube was recognised in the mid-twelfth century as a frontier between kingdoms with a relationship, albeit vague, to Dacia:

> Une genz de Troie eschaperent . . .
> . . . de Danube, un flum mult grant,
> qu'Ester claiment clerc luisant,
> qui les regnes vet devisant . . .
> furent cil apelez Dani,
> qui estoient anceis Daci. (Holden, 1970–3, ll.165–76)

If we read l.103 of *Le Pèlerinage de Charlemagne* in this light, we find that it is quite in its correct place, the crossing of the Danube preceding the entry into the Byzantine Empire, referred to successively as *croiz partie* (from the legend of St Helen's finding of the relic of the True Cross?), *Grece* and *Romanie*, the mountainous terrain of which would be bound to strike any traveller heading south-east from the Danube basin to Constantinople (Obolensky, 1974, pp.35–8). While saving part of the text this interpretation does, however, raise problems with regard to both the expression *a la liee* and l.102. It is these problems that must finally be addressed.

One solution, the facile one, to the question of interpreting *a la liee* would be to revert to the manuscript reading, refusing any correction, as did Francisque Michel. This is a position which has also been proposed to me recently in a personal communication by Dr Burgess, who expressed dissatisfaction with his own, and with most other, published solutions. He suggested that an expression relating to joy or pleasure, or even to lying under the wind might be intended. This is, indeed, an elegant solution which removes all geographical difficulty, leaving the editor or critic only with a minor lexical problem. However, there is one other solution incorporating a toponym which should also be considered.

If the river indicated as being crossed in l.103 is indeed the Danube, then the order of ll.101–3 would again be faulty, on the assumption that Charles's pilgrims were following the route established by the First and Second Crusades. As we saw above all the crusading armies following the land route to Constantinople crossed the Danube at Ratisbon, before entering Hungarian territory, and, indeed, before completing their passage through Bavaria. However, the only way to correct the text in that case is to adopt Koschwitz's first solution, taking the Franks through southern Italy on the assumption that our manuscript is so corrupt that virtually none of the existing text can be saved. On the other hand, it is possible that the poet intended to keep the Franks on the left bank of the Danube for their journey through Hungary, and then to take them south down the valley of the Olt, in present-day Romania.

One has to confess that such an itinerary has left no trace in Western European sources, although it is well known in the East, and did constitute an important trading and military route for over a thousand years. The exact form to be given to the river's name in the twelfth century is in itself mildly problematic. Known to the Greeks from ancient times as the Ἀλουτα, it occurs in Latin as both Alutus and Aluta (Westermann, 1956, pl.38, 39; Shepherd, 1956, pl.39, 73). As the modern form shows, the name was stressed on the first syllable, which, together with the quality of the post-tonic vowel, poses a problem if we assume the name reached (or at least was reproduced by) our poet in the form *Alite* or *Alie*. However, these problems are more apparent than real, when one considers how extreme can be the corruption of alien proper names in medieval texts. For one thing the tendency of French speakers to assimilate latinate forms to the stress patterns of their own language was constant: the author of *Courtois d'Arras* rhymes *Te Deum laudamus: revenus* (Faral, 1961, ll.663–4); Villon rhymes *Domine: bonne heure né* and *balais: proles* in his *Epître à Marie d'Orléans* (Longnon and Foulet, 1966, ll.42:44, 106:108); while the Provençal troubadour Marcabru shows the same tendency in his famous song of the *lavador* rhyming *Domini: aujatz que di* (Hamlin, Ricketts and Hathaway, 1967, ll.1:3). This in itself could account for the adoption of an /i/ in the penult, to render the schwa of the post-tonic, especially if that helped maintain an assonance. Such deformation of foreign names and titles to suit purely poetic exigencies are commonplace in the epic, as we see from the following renderings of the Arabic *emir* in the *Chanson de Roland: amirafles, amurafles, amiraill* (Whitehead, 1942, ll.850, 894, 2615) and in *Maugis d'Aigremont: amirant, amiraut, amuafle, amustant, aumustant, amustandé* (Vernay, 1980, ll.1616, 1210, 6781, 104, 3911, 3941). Although the deformations of the Turkish proper names Kerbogha as Corbaran and Tugtigin as Dodekin in *Le Bâtard de Bouillon* (Cook, 1972, pp.305, 311) are not determined by rhyme or metre, they do show a reaction to vowel and consonant quality at least as erratic as that I posit for the shift from Aluta to Alite, which is also much less severe than that found in Caxton's *Godeffroy of Boloyne* in a passage in which, during the First Crusade, Bohemond warns Godefroy against wintering in Constantinople itself:

> 'Therfor I pray you/that ye withdrawe fro Constantinoble/And retorne to ward the plains of *andrenobe* or of *sympole* . . .' (Colvin, 1893, p.347: my italics)

which is a rendering via French of the following passage from William of Tyre:

> 'Cede ergo, si placet, urbe relicta ad partes *Adrianopolitanas* vel circa *Philipopolis* . . .' (Huyghens, p.173: my italics)

If we accept the possibility of this comparatively minor distortion of the name in, presumably oral, transmission, there remains the apparent obscurity of the route. This, however, is more evident than real. The valley of the Aluta provided the eastern *limes* of the Roman Empire in the second and third centuries AD, and along it was built a major road linking Roman Dacia across the Carpathians, the Danube and the hills of Sredni Gora to Philippopolis (Obolensky, p.38). In the twelfth and thirteenth centuries it marked the eastern border of the kingdom of Hungary, continuing to be a major trading route between Hungary and the Byzantine Empire (Philip, 1927, pl.32; Muir, 1911/1982, pl.19) and providing an important line of communications for all communities in the eastern Danube basin (Dunăre, 1963, pp.31–40, 413). Moreover, throughout the eleventh and twelfth centuries the area was a scene of intense military activity, the junction of the Aluta and the Danube marking also the meeting, and hence fighting, ground of the settled

Greeks and Bulgarians, the semi-nomadic Hungarians and Wlachs, and the nomadic and indomitable Petchnegs (Obolensky, pp.27–8). There is, then, the possibility of merchants carrying back information about this route, for, even if the travels ascribed to his *alter ego*, Tiacre de Cantorbiere, by Guillaume d'Orange in *Le Charroi de Nîmes* (McMillan, 1978, ll.1190–1202) do include an element of epic exaggeration, there is no doubt about the extent of mercantile activity throughout this area in the mid-twelfth century (Boulet-Santel, 1950). An even more likely source of information, however, would be mercenaries returning from service in the Byzantine armies. The role of the Varangians, Viking and Saxon, has been long documented, but one must remember that French knights also served in this way. The most notable of them being the general Hervé the Frankopole, who led the campaigns against the Petchnegs on the eastern Danube in the reign of Constantine Monomachos, inflicting on them the only serious defeats in the long history of their incursions into the Byzantine Empire (Grégoire, 1958, p.347).

There was, then, ample opportunity for the poet of *Le Pèlerinage de Charlemagne* to come by reports of this alternative route to the East and to incorporate it in his account of the Franks journey to Jerusalem. His motive for doing it, and for offering three obscure references to the Byzantine Empire, may be due to the approximation of his own geographic knowledge, but it may equally be due to his desire to camouflage the obvious weakness of his text: a journey using the overland route to Jerusalem which makes no reference to Constantinople. If we accept this explanation then the text of the manuscript is justified with the exception of l.102, which may have been misplaced, if not originally generated formulaically, albeit illogically, in the position in which we find it, under the influence of the reference to Hungary, Hungarians figuring so regularly in pagan armies in the *chansons de geste*.

Acknowledgements

I wish to express my particular gratitude to Dr Burgess and to Dr Cobby for their helpful comments, advice and communication of material at various stages in the elaboration of this essay. These scholars naturally bear no responsibility for the use to which their generosity has been put.

References

Aebischer, P. (1965) *Le Voyage de Charlemagne à Jérusalem et à Constantinople*, ed. P. A., Textes Littéraires Français 115, Geneva: Droz.

Bennett, Philip E. (1984a) '*Le Pèlerinage de Charlemagne*: le sens de l'aventure', in *Essor et fortune de la chanson de geste dans l'Europe et l'Orient latin*, Actes du IXe Congrès de la Société Rencesvals, Modena: Mucchi, pp.475–87.

—— (1984b) 'The Storming of the Other World, the Enamoured Muslim Princess and the Evolution of the Legend of Guillaume d'Orange', in W. G. van Emden and Philip E. Bennett (eds), *Guillaume d'Orange and the Chanson de geste*, Reading: Société Rencesvals, pp.1–14.

Berry, Virginia Gingerick (1948) Odo of Deuil, *De Profectione Ludovici VII in Orientem*, ed. V. G. B., New York: Columbia University Press.

Boulet-Santel, M. (1950) *L'Histoire du commerce*, ed. J. Lacourt-Gayet, tome 2, livre 2, 'Le commerce médiéval européen', Paris: SPID.

Brownlow (1892) *Saewulf (1102–1103AD)* ed. and trans. Rev. Canon Brownlow, London: Palestine Pilgrims Text Society IV.2.

Burgess, Glyn S. and Cobby, Anne Elizabeth (1988) *The Pilgrimage of Charlemagne (Le Pèlerinage de Charlemagne)* ed. and trans. G. S. B. with an introduction by A. E. C., Garland Library of Medieval Literature A7, New York: Garland Publishing Inc.

Colvin, Mary Noyes (1893) *Godeffroy of Boloyne or The Siege and Conquest of Jerusalem by William Archbishop of Tyre, translated from the French by Wm Caxton and printed by him in 1481*, ed. M. N. C., Early English Text Society extra series 64, London.

Cook, Robert Francis (1972) *Le Bâtard de Bouillon*, ed. R. F. C., Textes Littéraires Français 187, Geneva: Droz.

Dunăre, Nicolae (1963) *Arta populară din Valea Jiului*, ed. N. D., Bucharest: Editura Academici Republicii Populare Romîne.

Faral, E. (1961) *Courtois d'Arras*, ed. E. F., Classiques français du moyen âge 3*, 2nd ed., Paris: Champion.

Favati, G. (1965) *Il 'Voyage de Charlemagne'*, ed. G. F., Biblioteca degli Studi Mediolatini e Volgari 4, Bologna.

Galmés de Fuentes, Alvaro (1979) '*Le Charroi de Nîmes* et la tradition arabe', *Cahiers de Civilisation Médiévale*, 22, pp.125–37.

Gregoire, Henri (1958) 'Michel Attaleiates *Histoire*', traduction française par H. G., *Byzantion*, 28, pp.325–62.

Hamlin, Frank R., Ricketts, Peter T. and Hathaway, John (1967) *Introduction à l'étude de l'ancien provençal, textes d'étude*, Publications romanes et françaises 96, Geneva: Droz.

Hippeau, C. (1969) *La Conquête de Jérusalem*, ed. C. H., Geneva: Slatkine Reprints.

Holden, A. J. (1970–73) *Le Roman de Rou de Wace*, ed. A. J. H., Société des anciens textes français 93, Paris: Picard.

Horrent, Jules (1961) *Le Pèlerinage de Charlemagne, essai d'explication littéraire avec des notes de critique textuelle*, Bibliothèque de la Faculté de Philosophie et Lettres de l'Université de Liège 157, Paris: Belles Lettres.

Huyghens, R. B. C. (1986) *Willelmi Tyrensis Archiepiscopi Chronicon*, ed. R. B. C. H., Turnhout: Editiones Pontifici.

Johnston, R. C. (1961) *The Crusade and Death of Richard I*, ed. R. C. J., Anglo-Norman Text Society 17, Oxford: Blackwell.

Koschwitz, Eduard (1880) *Karls des Großen Reise nach Jerusalem und Constantinopel*, ed. E. K., Altfranzösische Bibliothek 2, Heilbronn: Henniger.

—— (1907) *Karls des Großen reise nach Jerusalem und Constantinopel*, 5th ed. revised by Gustav Turau, Altfranzösische Bibliothek 2, Leipzig: Reislund.

Longnon, Auguste and Foulet, Lucien (1966) *François Villon, Oeuvres* ed. L. A. revised L. F., Classiques français du moyen âge 2**, 4th ed., Paris: Champion.

McMillan, D. (1978) *Le Charroi de Nîmes*, ed. D. McM., Bibliothèque Française et Romane 12, 2nd ed., Paris: Klincksieck.

Michel, Francisque (1836) *Charlemagne*, ed. F. M., London: Wm Pickering.

Michelant, Henri (1862) *Renaus de Montauban oder die Haimonskinder*, ed. H. M., Stuttgart: Literarische Verein.

Muir (1911/1982) *Atlas of Medieval and Modern History*, London: George Philip and Son.

Obolensky, D. (1974) *The Byzantine Commonwealth*, London: Sphere Books.

Panvini, Bruno (1960) 'Ancora sul *Pèlerinage de Charlemagne*', *Siculorum Gymnasium*, nuova serie 13, 17–80.

Philip (1927) *Historical Atlas, Medieval and Modern*, by R. Muir and G. Philip, 6th ed. London and Liverpool: G. Philip and Son.

Picherit, Jean-Louis (1984) *The Journey of Charlemagne to Jerusalem and Constantinople (Le Voyage de Charlemagne à Jérusalem et à Constantinople)*, ed. J.-L. P., Birmingham, Alabama: Summa Publications Inc.

Seymour, M. C. (1967) *Mandeville's Travels*, ed. M. C. S., Oxford: Clarendon Press.

Shepherd (1956) *Historical Atlas*, 8th ed., London: George Philip and Son.

Stewart, Aubrey (1894) *Anonymous Pilgrims I–VIII (11th and 12th Centuries)*, trans. A. S., Palestine Pilgrims Text Society VI.1, London.

Tyssens, Madeleine (1978) *Le Voyage de Charlemagne à Jérusalem et à Constantinople*, trans. M.T., Ghent: Story-Scientia.

Vernay, Philippe (1980) *Maugis d'Aigremont*, Romanica Helvetica 93, Berne: Francke.

Walker, Roger M. (1979) '"Tere major" in the *Chanson de Roland*', *Olifant*, 7, pp.123–30.

Westermann (1956) *Großer Atlas zur Weltgeschichte*, Braunschweig.

Whitehead, F. (1942) *La Chanson de Roland*, ed. F. W., Oxford: Blackwell.

Wilson, Col. Sir C. W. (1888) *The Pilgrimage of the Russian Abbot Daniel in the Holy Land (1106–1107)*, annotated by C. W. S., Palestine Pilgrims Text Society IV.3, London.

Emmanuèle Baumgartner

12. *DEL GRAAL CUI L'AN AN SERVOIT*: VARIATIONS SUR UN PRONOM

Dans le *Conte du Graal* de Chrétien de Troyes et dans la majeure partie des textes de la fin du XIIe et du début du XIIIe siècle qui s'en inspirent directement — ceux dans lesquels Perceval reste le héros principal du récit — le motif du Graal est lié à celui des questions à poser. Comme l'a en effet justement rappelé Lévi-Strauss, la problématique des mythes 'percevaliens' est tout à la fois symétrique et inverse de celle des mythes oedipiens. Si ceux-ci 'posent le problème d'une communication d'abord exceptionnellement efficace (l'énigme résolue)', les mythes percevaliens traitent eux 'de la communication interrompue sous le triple aspect de la réponse offerte à une question non posée (ce qui est le contraire d'une énigme), de la chasteté requise d'un ou plusieurs héros . . . enfin de la *gaste terre*, c'est-à-dire de l'arrêt des cycles naturels' (Lévi-Strauss, 1982). La mission de Perceval, son élection, serait ainsi de poser la question libératrice, de réactiver une communication langagière, un échange verbal dont nous ignorons — peut-être est-ce là ce qui fonde les secrets du Graal? — quand, comment et pourquoi ils ont été rompus.

Or ces questions, que le jeune Perceval dans le *Conte du Graal* se formule nettement sans oser toutefois les articuler,

> Et li vaslez les vit passer
> et n'osa mie demander
> del graal cui l'an an servoit (Lecoy, 1972, 1975 vv.3231-3)

mais qu'énoncent dans la suite du récit la cousine et l'ermite, reçoivent de la part de ce dernier une réponse qui élucide une bonne part du mystère. Du mystère du Graal à tout le moins, sinon de la lance. L'ermite lève ainsi l'indécision du pronom *cui* en lui substituant le père du Roi Pêcheur:

> Quant tu del graal ne seüs
> cui l'an an sert, fol san eüs.
> Cil cui l'an an sert fu mes frere (vv.6197-9)

Il renseigne héros et lecteur sur le contenu, la nature (cette *tant sainte chose*) et la fonction du Graal: nourrir depuis quinze ans le vieux roi grâce à l'hostie qui *el Graal vient* (v. 6212). Il donne un point d'aboutissement au cortège qu'a vu passer Perceval en précisant que, depuis quinze ans, le vieux roi *hors de la chanbre n'issi/ou le graal veïs entrer* (vv. 6214-5), et il enlève du même coup toute pertinence à la question suggérée par la cousine:

> Demandastes vos a la gent
> quel part il aloient ensi? (vv.3554-5)

Les dialogues de Perceval avec sa cousine puis avec l'ermite, les deux reprises de la communication langagière, suppriment donc plusieurs énigmes: l'énigme du destinataire, le père du Roi Pêcheur, dont le caractère *esperitel* atteint celui du Graal, comme le souligne la rime *graax: esperitax* (vv. 6209-10); l'énigme du contenu du Graal: ni *luz ne lanproies ne saumons* (v. 6205), nourriture qui pourrait être procurée par l'activité diurne du Roi Pêcheur, mais une seule hostie; l'énigme sur le verbe *servir*: le Graal est (comme le *tailleoir* avec lequel il fait ici série) un 'plat de service' que l'on présente, que l'on 'sert' au vieux roi; l'énigme enfin du déplacement dans l'espace et de son point d'aboutissement: le Graal est porté jusqu'à la chambre où se tient son destinataire. Reste cependant non précisé le point de départ du cortège, le lieu d'origine du Graal: *D'une chambre an autre alerent* (v.3230). L'autre chambre est celle du vieux roi mais quelle est l'*une*? Reste également inconnue la provenance de la lance et de la goutte de sang qui perle à son sommet. Quant au mystère de la brisure de l'épée (à venir, selon les vv.3646-9), il n'est pas élucidé dans le *Conte du Graal*.

Les continuateurs du *Conte du Graal*, les auteurs de la *Première*, de la *Seconde* et de la *Troisième Continuations* ainsi que l'auteur du *Perceval en prose*, seuls textes que je prendrai ici en compte, se sont donc trouvés face à la tâche délicate de poursuivre le récit, la quête du Graal et, éventuellement, celle de la lance, de faire retourner le héros au château du Graal et de lui faire énoncer les questions attendues alors qu'il sait quelles elles sont et, au moins partiellement, quelles sont les réponses. Ce que je voudrais donc examiner ici, c'est quelques unes des solutions apportées à ce qui apparaît à priori comme une impasse narrative et comment, à travers les variations sur ces questions et le jeu sur les pronoms qui les introduisent, se reformulent le sens et la fonction du motif du Graal.

Un premier et essentiel déplacement est celui qu'opère l'auteur de la *Première Continuation* en supprimant le personnage du vieux roi, donc le destinataire originel du cortège du Graal. Choisissant d'autre part comme héros Gauvain, dont le sort est lié en priorité, depuis le *Conte du Graal*, à la quête de la lance qui saigne et réactivant un objet/un motif resté inemployé chez Chrétien, l'épée brisée, il rejette vers l'amont du récit l'ensemble des questions: pourquoi la lance saigne-t-elle, pourquoi l'épée est-elle brisée, d'où vient le Graal?

Gauvain, dans les différentes versions de ce texte, ne pourra sans doute satisfaire pleinement son désir de connaître *du Graal et de la lance/Le voir et la senefiance* (MS *T*, v. 1452). Puisqu'il a échoué à ressouder exactement l'épée, les secrets du Graal lui restent interdits, comme le lui déclare le roi son hôte dans la version longue et la version courte:

> Oï avez une partie
> Pour quoi si haute seignorie
> Ot li Graaus qui par lui sert,
> Et tant vos en ai descouvert
> Come je puis a ceste foiz.
> Li remananz si est segroiz
> Que je dire ne vos porroie
> Por nule riens, ne n'oseroie,
> Que n'avez pas l'uevre achevee
> Ne soudee la frete espee [MSS *MQU*, v.17743 *et ss.*]

Du moins apprend-il que la lance qui saigne est celle de Longin et que le Graal est le vase dans lequel Joseph d'Arimathie a recueilli le sang du Christ et qu'il a ensuite *translaté* en Angleterre. Les manuscrits *TVD*, la version 'mixte' de l'éd. Roach, ne donnent aucune élucidation sur le Graal mais assimilent la lance à celle de Longin. D'autre part, en supprimant le personnage du vieux roi, ce qui rend caduque la question *cui l'an an sert*, immobilise le cortège dans la salle où se tiennent le Roi Pêcheur et ses visiteurs, et bloque la trajectoire du récit, la *Première Continuation* recentre autrement la question sur la relique: ce qu'il importe maintenant d'élucider en priorité, c'est l'origine et la raison d'être de ce mystérieux pouvoir qu'a le Graal de servir *par lui*, de produire et de dispenser spontanément une nourriture qui semble inépuisable.

En s'interrogeant sur les propriétés intrinsèques du Graal plutôt que sur son destinataire, la *Première Continuation* me semble ainsi annoncer ce qui deviendra l'enjeu majeur des élus de la *Queste du saint Graal* et l'aventure réservée au seul Galaad: voir distinctement, à *descovert*, ce qui se produit, ce qui advient en son premier commencement à l'intérieur même du *vaissel*.

Si l'on s'en tient au texte édité par W. Roach à partir du manuscrit *E*, ce n'est pas cependant sur cette voie que l'auteur de la *Seconde*

Continuation engage son héros. Perceval doit en effet poser la question sous sa forme originelle, *del Graal cui l'an an servoit*; ce qu'il fait au reste à la fin du recit.

> Par foi j'orroie volantiers
> De ce Graal la verité . . .
> Cui an an sert et qu'an an fet (v. 32428 *et ss.*)

et au début de la *Troisième Continuation*:

> Biaux douz sire, fait Perceval,
> De la lance et dou Saint Graal . . .
> Me dites tout premierement
> Cui l'an an sert et dont il vienent (v. 32639 *et ss.*)

Et dont il vienent . . . La réponse qu'obtient alors le héros élucide en effet, comme dans la *Première Continuation*, l'origine et l'histoire des deux reliques de la Passion mais elle n'a pas pour effet de guérir le Roi Pêcheur puisque, au prix d'un autre déplacement, cette guérison ne dépend plus d'un questionnement sur le Graal ou sur la lance mais est liée au motif du Coup Douloureux, de l'Epée brisée et de la vengeance dont Perceval doit être l'instrument.

Dans la mesure cependant où le vieux roi, père du Roi Pêcheur, n'apparaît plus dans ces récits, le maintien tel quel de la question *cui l'an an sert*, qui revient aux vers 20972, 29118, 32433, de la *Seconde Continuation* et au vers 32645 de la *Troisième*, fait difficulté. Or, si l'on se réfère à la lettre du manuscrit on peut constater, comme l'indique au reste la note au vers 29118, que l'éditeur a systématiquement éliminé dans tous ces vers la leçon *que an an sert*, que donne *E*, et corrigé *que* en *cui* pour harmoniser le texte de *E* avec celui du *Conte du Graal*. La leçon *que l'an an sert/servoit* que donne tout aussi systématiquement le manuscrit *E* semble cependant tout à fait pertinente: elle prend acte de cette modification importante qu'est l'éviction du vieux roi et elle rend compte de la nouvelle orientation qui est ici donnée au motif du Graal et de la lance. Dans ces textes en effet la question ne porte plus (ne peut plus porter) sur le destinataire du cortège mais, à la rigueur, sur l'origine, déjà bien élucidée dans la *Première Continuation*, des deux reliques et, surtout, sur la nature même du service du Graal. A quoi sert-il? Qu'est-ce, finalement, que ce service?

La réponse que donne en son finale la *Troisième Continuation* n'est guère satisfaisante. Les manifestations du Graal dans ce texte — son service — restent liées à l'apparition d'une nourriture abondante et délectable, liaison déjà présente chez Chrétien et dans la *Première Continuation*, et que reprend au reste la scène initiale de la *Queste*, la Pentecôte du Graal. Il n'est pas question, dans les *Continuations*, de cette nourriture essentielle, de ce Pain de Vie qu'est l'hostie, qui vient se superposer, dans le texte de Chrétien, à la nourriture bien terrestre dispensée à Perceval lors de sa première visite chez le Roi Pêcheur. Peut-être faut-il cependant en retrouver comme un discret écho dans les derniers vers de la *Troisième Continuation*: Perceval, devenu prêtre, et assurant dix ans durant le *Dieu servise*, ne prend alors d'autre nourriture

> Fors ce que Diex li anveoit
> Par le Saint Graal qu'il veoit
> Et qui le servoit nuit et jor (vv. 42587–9)

Le Graal 'sert' ainsi Perceval pour l'aider à accomplir le 'service' divin . . .

Mais c'est sans doute dans le texte du *Perceval en prose* que se redéfinit et se renouvelle de façon décisive le motif du service du Graal et sa fonction. Ce récit, qui forme la troisième et dernière partie de la trilogie attribuée à Robert de Boron, s'inspire, comme on le sait, du *Conte du Graal* et de la *Seconde Continuation*. Mais il reprend et précise les données généalogiques mises en place dans le *Roman de l'Estoire dou Graal*, de Robert de Boron, puis dans le *Merlin en prose*: Perceval y devient le fils d'Alain le Gros et le petit-fils de Bron, le Riche Pêcheur, à qui Joseph a confié la garde de la relique; il est donc assimilé à ce troisième homme dont la venue est prédite dans l'*Estoire* de Robert, qui doit être le dernier gardien du Graal, celui par qui s'achèvera un récit conçu à la 'semblance' de la *benoite Trinité* (Nitze, 1927, v. 3373).

Le Roi Pêcheur du *Perceval en prose* s'inscrit ainsi, dans la succession des générations, à la place du 'vieux roi' de Chrétien de Troyes; mais comme le Roi Pêcheur de Chrétien, il est *mehaignié* et sa guérison est liée à la question que doit lui poser son petit-fils Perceval. Comme dans les *Continuations*, Perceval, ainsi que les autres quêteurs, sait en effet, dès son départ de la cour d'Arthur, qu'il faut questionner le roi, l'obstacle à surmonter étant ici de trouver la voie qui mène à sa demeure, puisque seul y parviendra celui qui *sera si essauciés sor tos homes, et ara le pris de le chevalerie del siecle* (p.151). Mais fait aussi difficulté, dans ce récit, le libellé exact de la question, comme en témoignent, tout au long du texte, les leçons embarrassées que donnent les deux manuscrits conservés, *E* et *D*.

Au début du récit, selon le manuscrit *D*, il *covendra que cil chevaliers* (Perceval) *demande de ce vessel que hon en siert* (sert). Selon le manuscrit *E*, Perceval doit demander *que on en fait et cui on en sert de cel Graal*; mais lorsque les chevaliers d'Arthur jurent d'entreprendre la quête, ils s'engagent à trouver la demeure du Roi Pêcheur et à demander *de quoi li Graaus sert* (p.151).

Le texte de *E* hésite donc d'abord entre la question traditionnelle, *cui on en sert*, qui n'a plus guère de sens dans ce récit, et la nouvelle question, déjà formulée dans la *Seconde Continuation, que on en fait* ou, plus nettement encore, *de quoi li Graaus sert*, quel en est l'usage. Evolution que semble confirmer la suite du texte puisque, selon le narrateur puis selon la soeur de Perceval, le héros aurait dû demander en voyant le Graal lors de sa première visite chez le Roi Pêcheur *que on en servoit* (p.209 et p.211), le texte de *D* étant encore plus explicite: *que l'en en fesoit* (p.211). Enfin, lors de la seconde visite du héros dans la demeure de son aïeul, la question libératrice est posée dans le manuscrit *E* sous la forme *dites moi que on sert de ces coses* (le Graal, la lance et les tailloirs) *que je voi illuec porter* (p.239), le manuscrit *D* donnant la leçon *je vos pri que vos me diez que l'en sert de cest vessel* (p.239).

On pourrait à la rigueur interpréter dans ces passages *que* comme l'équivalent de *cui*. La fusion qu'opère le *Perceval en prose* entre le 'vieux roi' de Chrétien et le Roi Pêcheur, comme la présence du Roi Pêcheur dans la salle même où se produit l'apparition du Graal, présence qui lève toute ambiguïté sur le destinataire, rendent peu plausible cette lecture qu'autoriserait la grammaire. La substitution de *que* à *cui*, commune donc à la *Seconde Continuation* (si l'on suit le texte du manuscrit et non la correction proposée) et au récit en prose, invite en revanche à reconsidérer la nature exacte du 'service' que rend le Graal, le déplacement opéré du *Conte* de Chrétien à ses continuations.

Tout se passe en effet comme si, à la faveur du changement de *cui* en *que/quoi*, l'auteur du *Perceval en prose* faisait glisser la question de son contenu concret, 'à qui est destinée la nourriture que dispense généreusement le Graal?', à une interrogation plus ambitieuse sur la fonction même de l'objet: à quoi sert-il?

Il va de soi que le *Perceval en prose*, pas plus que les autres textes, ne fournit de réponse explicite . . . Mais il semble bien que la formulation qu'il propose, à la suite de la *Seconde Continuation*, prenne enfin acte de la mutation qu'a subie le motif du Graal, de Chrétien aux textes des différentes *Continuations*. Poser, comme l'a fait Chrétien, la question 'à qui fait-on le service du Graal?', induit et invente un parcours, que configure en texte le cortège du Graal, et que referont à loisir, en l'amplifiant jusqu'à ses limites extrêmes (la 'naissance' du Graal, sa disparition et celle du monde arthurien) les récits ultérieurs,

Continuations en vers et proses du Graal. Confrontés à la nécessité de reformuler une question à laquelle l'élucidation de l'ermite enlevait une bonne part de son intérêt, les continuateurs ont trouvé comme solution, pour la poursuite du récit, l'interrogation sur l'origine, que suggérait au reste le texte de Chrétien . . . Récit d'origine que la grille chrétienne, les légendes concernant notamment Joseph d'Arimathie, leur a permis d'ancrer dans le temps et l'espace, le motif de l'épée brisée, du coup douloureux et de la vengeance qu'il appelle sous-tendant, dans les *Continuations*, la trame narrative et son devenir en lieu et place du questionnement sur le destinataire du Graal.

Mais recentrer l'interrogation sur l'origine et sur la fonction intrinsèque du Graal, supprimer, non sans hésitation et tâtonnements, le destinataire, remplacer en somme le 'cortège' du Graal par la 'scène' du Graal, la trajectoire de la quête par le temps suspendu de la vision, c'est aussi et définitivement arrêter (en prendre le risque) le cours du temps et le cours du récit. En posant la question attendue, le héros de Chrétien devait guérir le Roi Pêcheur de son infirmité, restaurer sa fertilité à la Terre Gaste, réintégrer les hommes et les choses dans le cours naturel du temps du monde, donner au récit un regain de vie. Dans le *Perceval en prose*, la question salvatrice guérit sans doute le Roi Pêcheur de son *enfermeté*, mais pour qu'il trouve enfin le repos dans la mort et l'au-delà. Et simultanément elle suscite toute une série de restaurations, de retours à l'état originel qui sont autant de blocages de l'aventure, de soudures du récit sur lui-même, comme le signifient et la soudure de la pierre faillée à la Table Ronde et la déréliction mortelle dans laquelle tombent les chevaliers d'Arthur lorsque Perceval a achevé sa quête. Poser la question sur le Graal et non plus sur le destinataire, entraîne ainsi désormais, en lieu et place d'une reprise de la communication langagière, la clôture du récit, la résorption de la parole dans la vision indicible des mystères. Mais ainsi s'énonce, dans les variations contradictoires sur un pronom, ce qui est sans doute l'enjeu même du motif du Graal, la possibilité qu'il offrait de retracer dans son déroulement ternaire/trinitaire le temps chronique des générations tout en fixant l'instant de la fusion dans l'un, le moment où la figure atemporelle du gardien du Graal s'image aussi bien sous les traits de Bron, le Roi Pêcheur, que sous ceux de son petit-fils, Perceval.

144   Emmanuèle Baumgartner

Références

Bogdanow, F. (1978) *La trilogie de Robert de Boron: le Perceval en prose* dans *GRLMA*, IV/I, pp.513–35.

Lecoy, F. (1972, 1975) Chrétien de Troyes, *le Conte du Graal*, 2 vols, Paris: *CFMA*.

Lévi-Strauss, C. (1982) *De Chrétien de Troyes à Richard Wagner* dans *Parsifal* de Richard Wagner dans *L'Avant scène*, 38–9, pp.10–15.

Nitze, W. A. (1927) Robert de Boron, *Le Roman de l'Estoire dou Graal*, Paris: *CFMA*.

Pickens, R. T. (1984) '*Mais de çou ne parole pas Crestiens de Troies*': *A Re-examination of the Didot-Perceval*; *Romania*, 105, pp.492–510.

Roach, W. (1949–83) *The Continuations of the Old French Perceval*, 5 vols, Philadelphia.

—— (1977) *The Didot-Perceval*, Philadelphia, 1941, Genève: Slatkine Reprints.

Tony Hunt

13. AN ANGLO-NORMAN MEDICAL TREATISE

There is as yet no general survey of Anglo-Norman medicine (but see Hunt, 1990) and the text printed in the following pages represents the first edition to have been produced of an Anglo-Norman medical treatise. Hitherto only short extracts made by Paul Meyer and miscellaneous receipts have been published (see Hunt, 1990; Goldberg and Saye, 1933), yet there exists much more manuscript material than is suggested by the cursory references in Vising's handbook of Anglo-Norman literature (Vising, 1923). There are three major receipt collections written in Anglo-Norman which became standard texts from which compilers borrowed heavily: the collection of prose receipts known as the 'Lettre d'Hippocrate' (Hunt, 1990; Södergard, 1981); the corpus in octosyllabic rhyming couplets known as the 'Novele Cirurgerie' (Hunt, 1987); and another versified collection, showing some contamination with the latter, which has been given the name 'Physique Rimee' (Hunt, 1990; Faribault, 1982). These texts, and other less-standardised receipt collections (often mingling Latin, French, and English), belong firmly to traditional or popular medicine, that is they are exclusively concerned with the therapeutic administration of naturally occurring *materia medica* and are of an entirely non-theoretical nature. The 'Novele Cirurgerie' exists in five witnesses (two are mere fragments), the most important of which is MS Oxford, Bodleian Library, Auct. F. 5.31 (S.C. 3637, *olim* e musaeo 120) written in England in the second half of the thirteenth century (Hunt, 1987, pp.271-3). It begins with two celebrated medico-botanical texts, the *Herbarium* of Pseudo-Apuleius (ff.1r-23r) (De Vriend, 1984) and the *Liber medicinae ex herbis femininis* (ff.23r-44r) (Riddle, 1981) and also transmits Galen's *Antibalomena* (ff.44r-57rb) and the well-known extract from the *Secretum Secretorum* which purports to be a letter from Aristotle to Alexander the Great 'de sanitate corporis conservanda' (Suchier, 1883, pp.473-80; Möller, 1963; Hirth, 1969; Manzaloui, 1977). Then come three vernacular texts: the 'Novele Cirurgerie' (ff.62vb-73va), miscellaneous prose receipts (ff.73va, 78va-79rb) (edited in Hunt, 1990), and part of a treatise (ff.73vb-78rb) covering the complaints *meneisun, thenasmon,* and *esmoroydes,* which is evidently acephalous

(145)

and ends with the explicit 'Ci finist le livret ki est apelé gardein de cors en verité'. Following a red rubric the text is somewhat inaccurately written in single columns with a number of rubrics rather randomly distributed (all rubrics are italicised in the edition below), more systematic use being made of red paragraph marks, and one in blue (not recorded in the text below). There is an opening blue initial. It is at once obvious that the treatise, like the so-called 'Euperiston' in MS Edinburgh, N.L.S., Advocates' Library 18. 6. 9 (s.xiv) ff.81r–146v, contains some discussions of aetiology and symptomatology as well as traditional cures which embrace both the use of simples from the *receptaria* tradition and the preparation of compound medicines as they frequently appear in the *antidotaria* (Jörimann, 1925; Sigerist, 1923). The main divisions under each malady, after the identification of the different varieties, are *causae, signa,* and *curae.*

While so many medieval medical texts remain in manuscript it is difficult to undertake exact or reliable source studies. Nevertheless, there is no doubt that the fragment printed below reflects Salernitan material found in the *Practica Brevis* attributed to Johannes Platearius II (*c.*1160), first printed at Ferrara in 1488 and more widely available in the print of 1497 (Platearius, 1497). This work is itself little more than a compilation and was duly plagiarised by other writers (e.g. in the *Practica Archimathaei* in de Renzi 5 pp.350–76 and the *De aegritudinum curatione* in de Renzi 2 pp.81–386). There is an extremely important Middle English translation in MS Cambridge University Library Dd. 10. 44 (s.xv) ff.1r–100r which transmits the prologue:

> Amicum induit qui justis amicorum precibus condescendit. I, Plateary, for love of my dyre frendys in þis treteys I am purposid forto shewyn the causes, cures and signes of sykenes, and not of alle sekenes, ffor why þe multitude and þe prolixite of wordys hathe distroblyd þe ferst froyte of whyse men herbefore, and also al þese and many other ben openlyche inow schewid and expouned in other bokys, save alone þe wyche I know best by experience and wyche I was wont most stedefastly to usyn and of wyche I hade most spede forto werk with. And ferst I begynne at the feverys.

The prologue is unfortunately missing in an even more important translation, in Old French, in MS Cambridge, Trinity College 0. 1. 20 (*c.*1250) ff.55r–194r (edited in my forthcoming *Anglo-Norman Medicine*). The Trinity text was copied from a deficient exemplar from which the opening chapters of the treatise were missing and begins in mid-sentence at Bk.1, ch.3 ('De febribus interpolatis et primo de flegmatica'). The text itself is disordered, again as a result of deficiencies in the exemplar, and the editor's first job is to re-order the sections of text in their correct sequence. The Trinity text appears to be a copy of a Franco-Picard translation written out by a number of insular scribes some of whom respectfully retained the Franco-Picard scripta of the original whilst the others typified Anglo-Norman at its most slovenly and idiosyncratic. On f.104v a prayer in Anglo-Norman has been incorporated. Whilst the lexicological value of the translation is very great, the work also usefully illustrates the difficulties facing editors of vernacular medical texts. It is valuable in itself, of course, to discover two Anglo-Norman witnesses to the insular fortunes of the *Practica Brevis* and it would also be interesting, though beyond the scope of the present contribution, to compare the two translations from a technical point of view.

Vernacular medical texts in the Middle Ages are almost invariably translations of Latin originals, but the originals themselves can rarely be reconstituted as definitive texts, since they were largely compilations which in their accretions, interpolations, omissions, and revisions display something of that 'mouvance' which characterises the Old French *chanson de geste* tradition. In other words, the element of improvisation was rarely absent. The central problem which faces the editor of a technical treatise, as opposed to a text of imaginative literature, is that of how to deal with the scientific accuracy of its contents. The translation may accurately render an attested reading of the source which is itself completely erroneous. Should the editor correct the translation in such a way as to preserve the scientific validity of its contents? When a simple palaeographical error, e.g. reading *minus* for *nimis* or *pecten* for *pectus*, is at the root of the problem the temptation is very great. Comparison with the Latin source is complicated by the fact that there are almost no critical editions of medieval Latin medical treatises. For example, the 1497 print of the *Practica Brevis*, which offers the only convenient way in which to read it, contains frequent errors and omits many passages found in the Trinity translation, whose editor must therefore acquaint himself thoroughly with the Latin MS tradition if he is even to recognise, let alone solve, problems in the translation. For example, on f.89r the Trinity translation describes the first type of dysentery 'si est dessous la ventosité des boiaus', which seems to be corroborated by MS B.L. Sloane 1124 which has *ventositas*, but which unfortunately makes very little sense. The 1497 print has *unctuositas*, which is equally unhelpful in the context, which demands the sense 'roughness'. The correct reading is almost certainly *villositas*. The room for error in the copying of medieval medical MSS is vast. First, there is the question of drug quantities, often missing and frequently represented by conventional signs ($\div$ = *uncia*; $\mathcal{3}$ = *drachma*; $\ni$ = *scrupulum*). These are often confused, as are the roman numerals which precede them. The enumeration of the materia medica is often subject to errors as the result of misreadings of the abbreviations for *ut, vel,* and *et.* The names of the ingredients are far from stable. Thus *storax calamite* is often copied as *storax, calamentum* and *aristologia ro.* [= *rotunda*] as *aristologia, rosa.* The uncomprehended often gives way to the incomprehensible, as in *luna epatis* for *sima epatis.* Botanical names are a hit-or-miss affair. Palaeographically induced error is particularly frequent, so that one finds scribal confusion of the type *salvia/saliva, menta/memita, mirra/mirta.* Here textual knowledge must be supplemented by pharmacological knowledge. I once wrestled with the plant name *grandin* in the *Alphita* until I saw that it was actually a faulty realisation of *grā dī* = *gratia dei.* Latin botanical names were so opaque to many vernacular translators that they would take over the Latin *tel quel* without any morphological adaptation to the syntax of the new context, the names often preserving the case in which they had been used in the Latin (often the genitive following an expression of quantity). The Trinity translation of the *Practica Brevis* contains on f.130r/v the reading 'les flors endarenge .i. centrum galli'. An attempt to recuperate the required sense from the Latin produces further confusion: *flores andragie .i. citranguli* (MS Sloane 1124); *flores curzange .i. centrum galli* (MS Sloane 420); *flores yringe, id est trianguli* (1497 print). These examples alone reveal confusion between the orange (Citrus aurantium L.), the rush (Juncus ssp.), sea-holly (Eryngium maritimum L.) and darnel/cockel (Lolium temulentum L./Agrostemma githago L.). The difficulty of correctly identifying plants by their popular names and hence judging the justification of their appearance in the text is not to be underestimated (see Hunt, 1989).

The text printed below represents the contents of the *Practica Brevis* Bk.IX (*De egritudinis intestinorum*), chs 3–8. Chapter 7 (on haemorrhoids) has been heavily interpolated. It is clear that at many points the Anglo-Norman text is closer to the readings of some of the Latin MSS than to the 1497 print and sometimes closer to the text of the *Practica Brevis* incorporated in the *De aegritudinum curatione* printed by Renzi. For reasons of space it has not been possible to indicate more precisely its relationship to the Latin.

[f. 73vb] Dissenterie, lienterie, diarie.[1]

Deus choses sunt dunt nus avum mut afaire, ceo est asaver li seaus de amur e li cercles de chasteé. Li seaus de amur est li lius dunt amur ad plus afere e si a nun nessance,[2] pur ceo ke par iloec nescent les flurs ky nescent a lur termes. De icés flurs ad l'um suvent trop, suvent trop petit. E de se surdent suvent diverses dolurs, mes de ceo n'ad vostre amy guarde, kar tel dolur ne vient mie a homme, mes as femmes afiert ke bien eiment. Li cercles de chasteté est li aneaus dunt amur n'ad ke feire. Par cel liu avinent diverses maladies. Ore en parlerum des treis, ceo est asaver ke la premere ad nun meneisun, l'autre ad nun thenasmon, la tierce ad nun esmoroydes.

Meneisun est quant li ventre se espurge a trop grant espleit parmi le anel de chasteé et cetera. De meneisun sunt treis maneres: dissinterie, lienterie, diarie.

Dissinterie est quant la buele est escorcee u quant la egestiun ist sanglante. Dissinterie avient en plusurs maneres: de cole, de melancolie, de sausefleme, de la feie, de mauveis buel. Si cest meneisun vient de cole, dunc ist la egestiun sanglante e jaune [u] entre deus; u partie verz, partie sanglante; [u] partie semblante ad a ruil de areim.[3] Si ele vient de melancolie, dunc est partie senglante, partie neire. Si ele vient de fleume, dunc est [le egestiun] partie [f. 74ra] sanc pur, partie pers ruge.[4] Si ele vient de la feie, dunc ist aucune fez sanc mut pur e sudeinement e aucune feiz espés.[5] Pur ceo quident esquanz ke ceo seit partie del feie ky ist, mes ne pot estre. E dunc ad l'um dolur del feie e del destre costé e desuz el ventrail n'ad gueres de dolur. Si ele vient de mauveis buel, ele ad treis maneres. Pur ceo sacez ke li boeaus sunt veluz par dedenz. La premere est ke la maladie ret cele veluesse e la egestiun recemble lavure de char grasse. La secunde manere est quant la maladie ret le buel meimes, si ke en la egestiun aperent unes peals cumme rarure de parchemin. Ceste manere guarist a peine. La tierce manere est quant par peicettes s'en issent li bueaus e en le egestiun apiert cumme partie de char e de veines e de nerfs. Ceste manere ne pot estre guarie. Derechief cele dissinterie ke vient del feie a peine garist u nule feiz. Derechief dissinterie que vient[6] de mauveis boel aucune feiz vient de la buele suvereine, aucune feiz de la buele desus. Quant ele vient de la buele desus, dunc sent l'em la dolur sur le numblil e semble ke ele seigne le malade e li sanc est mut medlé a l'egestiun. Si la dissinterie vient de la buele desuz, dunc sent li malade [f. 74rb] la dolur del numblil contreval sur le penil e sur les reins e dunc n'ad gueres de sanc medlez a l'egestion. Si ele est desus le numblil, celes mecines ki entrent par la

40 buche valent meus. Si ele est desuz contreval, dunc valent meuz
    mecines prisses par desuz. Bains e emplastres par desuz valent a l'un e a
    l'autre. Si le egestiun [ke] est de dissinterie piert verz u cumme ruil u
    neire, mortel signe i ad.
        Lienterie est quant li ventre curt par ceo que il ad le estomac, ceo est
45 le gisir, escrillant e la buele escrillant, si ke li mangers e li beivres i
    escrillent. E si s'en ist sanc sanz estre defit. Aucune feiz en ist li viande
    autreteus cumme ele entre. Ceste maladie pot estre de fleume gletuse ki
    pent el gisir cumme glu u en la buele. E si pot estre de dissinterie ki eit
    esté avant, ki ad par aventure res la buele. E si pot estre de clou qui eit
50 esté el gisier u de la buele ke est plaee e blessee. Si lienterie vient de
    dissinterie qui avant i fust, dunc ne pot la lienterie estre guarie, kar si le
    velu del buel est res ke dust li viande tenir, cele veluesse ne pot mie
    revenir.
        Diaria est quant li ventre curt e sanz sanc e nepurquant la viande est
55 defite. Diaria pot avenir de trop manger, [f.74va] de trop beivre, de
    viandes agues, de viandes puignans, de mauveis humurs ki descendent
    de la teste, de flemme, de trop grant plenté de flemme. En totes icés
    maladies purgent li fisiciens primes la matire, si trop en i ad, pus si funt
    mescines estreinanz. Plusurs en avez oï e asez en purrez oïr, quant vous
60 vodrez.
        Thenasmon est anguisse de aler a sele, anguisse de egestiun fere od
    grant esforz e od grant volunté. Thenasmon avient aucune feiz de cole,
    [aucune feiz de] fleume freide e glettuse. Si thenasmon vient de cole,
    dunc i ad en lui puingture e arsun e le egestiun a la fie jaudne e tient
65 aucune gutesces de sanc. Li malades vet suvent a sele. Aucune feiz [fet]
    petit, aucune feiz nient, aucune feiz sulement gutetes de sanc. Si
    thenasmon vient de flume, dunc sent li malades grevance e pesantime
    par desuz. L'egestiun recemble muse[7] e aucune feiz i ad gutetes de sanc
    medlees par rumpure de la veine que est rumpue par trop efforcer. Sanc
70 pot venir de cole, mes la cole fet arsun e puncture. Sanc pot venir de
    fleume. La fleume fet grevance e pesantume. La egestiun que veint de
    cole [f.74vb] est jaune. Cele ke vient de fleume est blanche e a fleume
    glectuse medlé. Cele maladie deit l'um guarir en haste, kar si ele n'est
    guarie tost, ele turne en dissinterie u en lienterie u en colike. Colon est
75 un buel gleste e freit u la viande entre primes, quant ele descent aval
    hors de gisier, e la est primes engluee, si ke ele pent ensemble. Sovent
    avient par surporter de aler a chambre ke la viande i ensechist e endursit
    e aucune feiz enneric ist e ne se pot l'um delivrer, si en morient li
    esquanz. E a plusurs avient ke il jettent parmi la buche autretel e tel
80 memes ke dust issir parmi le fundement. Ceste maladie ad nun colike.
    Si cele maladie dunt jo vus dis ki ad a nun thenasmon vient de cole,

dunc turne ele tost en dissinterie. Quant ele vient de fleume, si se change en colike.

[Cure].

Des mescines voil aucun mot dire. Cinc maneres sunt de mirabolans: citrins, kiebles, bellerins, emblins, indes. Dissinterie guarist l'um issi cumme orez. Jo vus dis ke dissinterie vient de buel u del feie. Dissinterie, si ele vient del buel, si purge l'um les humurus ke i mist en ceste manere. Pernez une unce u unce e demie u deuz unces de mirabolans citrinis solum la force del malade. Fetes pudrer l'espece, temprez la [f.75ra] pudre une nut en ewe rose e euue de plue u en mosge de chievre. L'endemain le culez e donez al malade icele culeure a bevre. Si la maladie dissinterie veint de fleume, as mirabolans citrins metez kieble une partie. Si melencolie i a, si metez ofoc[8] les mirabolans indes. Quant il les averat usé, guardez le sagement, ke il treit freit, e ke il ne manjuse ne ne beive ne ne dorme desque il seit purgez. Pus ordinez sa diete issi: pain de orge u de furment ovec ewe de plue u od eawe rose, la piere ematice od jus de plantein e teus choses estreignanz, greins de ris, petiz oisçaus, piés de porc, peires quites en ewe, sorbes, mezles, coinz. Beive euue[9] rose u euue de plue u quise mastic en euue. Si beive si il est feverus. Si il est sanz fevere, vin li purrez doner, mes que il seit eslaez de aucun de ces euues. Esperemenz oiez. Triblez semence de planteine e medlez odoc le aubun de un of e quisez sur une tiuuele chaude, si li donez. Furmage mut vieuz a trenché mut menu e quit en mel li vaut. Pocin rosti ofoke cire que seit dedens mise li vaut.

Encontre meneisun: Fetes secchir ferine de furment mut trés bien en une paiele de areim. Pus si i metez let, sil fetes buillir ensemble tant que il seit tenant cumme glu e mut trés bien tenant. E pus si i metez plus del leit e fetes rebullir en meimes la manere. [f.75rb] Pus si metez moeaus de ofeus e fetes buillir tant ke il vus seit avis en vostre curage ke li ofeus seint bien e naturelment endurci. Ceste viande li donez a manger. Sun pein fetes en tele manere. Sechisez ferine de furment e depecez menuement moeaus de ofs durs. Pus les medlez a la ferine. Pus pestriez tut ceo en aubuns [de] ofs crus e fetes pein, si li donez. *Autre.* Ardez corn de cerf deske en carbun e fetes en pudre, medlez ofoc gentil encens pudré e donez al malade chescun jur devant manger tant cum entreit en une cuillere. *Encontre meneisun.* Pernez le restebof, ki ad nun 'chammoc' en engleis, here terestre e cerlange e quisez en ewe e lavez les plantes des piés e les jambes desk'as genuil[s].

Pur garir lienterie. Fet l'em bolir ewe[10] ofoc semence de fenuil e en cele ewe temprez une nuit pudre de mirrabolans kiebles. Le matin le culez e donez a bevere al malade. E quant il serra purgé, donez li chaudes choses ki confortent cumme diaciminum e pus choses ki estanchent.

Diaria, si ele vient de trop manger e de trop bevere, ceo poez saver par
125 le malade. Si il vus dit ki il eit trop mangé,[11] amenusez sa diete, si garra.
Si il a mangé trop augues viandes, [dunez li] choses ki refreident
cumme sçurup violaz. Si ele vient de humurs descendant de la teste, ço
connutrez par le egestiun. [f.75va] Si il i a en la egestiun burbelettes e
escume, dunc li donez tanasye hu warence. Si ele vient de cole, si est le
130 egestiun jaune. Ceo devez purger[12] ausi cumme discinterie. Si ele vient
de dareite feblesse del cors, ceo verrez par ceo. Si les autres signes n'i
sunt mie cum cil [ki] n'a trop mangé avant, si lae egestiun n'a escume,
ele n'est trop jaune cume de cole ne trop blanche cume de fleume, dunc
n'i a si feblesse nun, dunc n'i a mester [de] purgation, dunc n'i a fors de
135 fere choses estreinantes, ausi cume dissinterie.

Thenasmon, si ele vient de cole, si purgez de la mescine que afiert a
dissinterie. Pus si le fetes baigner deskes al numblil e froter de mauve
quit en ewe e violé e uimalve ho en ferine de orge quit en euue ho en
semence de lin quit en ewe de pluie. E si li vaudra si vus li fetes
140 fumigaciun en tele manere. Querez un tuel ki seit a l'un des chief[s]
plus estreit ki a l'autre. Eschaufez un fer ardant u cele ordure del fer ke
l'um apele 'sinder' en engleis, kar cel vaut meuz. Si le metez en un pot,
si ke la chaline ne pusse issir. Cuverez cel pot de un es percié. Mette li
malades le tuel en cel pertus e l'autre chief en l'anel de chasteé, si
145 receive la fumee. Mes il deit esparpeiller aisil sur le fer chaud, dunc en
vendra bone fumee. Autretel poez fere de tiule eschaufee. Pus metez
cotun desus moilé en oille violat. [f.75vb] Fetes seim de siu de muton e
de siu de cheievre e de la gresse de geline e de ouue, si metez oille rosaz
e violaz e cire blanche. Si en fetes oignement e quant il serra teve,
150 muilez i une tente, si botez parfunt en l'anel.[13] Si thenasmon vient de
fleume, si la deit l'um purger cumme lienterie. Pus li fetes
suffumigaciun[14] par le tuel de foile de poreals bollez en vin. Autrement.
Fetes podre deliee de puliol e de ysope[15] e de organe, ceo est le erbe ke ad
nun 'seint Osipe uuert'. Pus la fetes builer. Pus fetes le malade efforcier
155 sei durement, si ke li buel isse parmi l'anel e ke li aneaus de chasteé li
seit reversee. Pus mette cele pudre. Mereveilles le cunfortera. Autre
mut esprové. Fetes oigndre les reins e tut deske la fin des eschines de
miel tenve.[16] Pus esparpeillez desus pudre de kersuns e de puliol e de
isope e de organe. E pus si liez de une bende. Ki ne pot tutes ces herbes
160 aver, prenge partie.

[Emorroides].

Emoreides sunt cinc veines ki asemblent en l'anel de chasteé dunt

vienent diverses passiuns. La une passion est emflure, l'autre retenement,
la tierce curs. Sacez ke humurs nescent tute jur e habundent en homme
55 e en femme. Mes humme deit estre plus chaud, si ke la chaline veinte
les humurs. Femme est plus freide, si li a nature dunee autre purgaciun,
cume ses flurs. [f.76ra] Ore pot avenir ke a humme faut sa naturele
chalur u a femme sa naturele purgaciun. Si nescent e habundent les
humurus, si avelent deskes en cele cuntree e depicent celes veines,
70 si en issent[17] e par ceo est li cors defenduz de diverses maladies. E
curent ces emoroides en diverses manieres: u el meis une feiz u el meis
deus feiz u une feiz en demi an. Si eles curent trop, si en vienent
diverses maladies. Ces emoroydes a plusurus sunt si turnez[18] a nature
ke sanz ceo ne purreient il estre seins e nomément quant vielles sunt.
75 Dunt Ypocras dist 'Ki guarist emoroides anciennes, il entysic u ydropic
u autre maladie en avera'.[19] Neis en la nuveaté, si femme les eust, si
lorrei ge ke ele feit primes revenir ses flurs, kar si ele eust plenté de
cele purgaciun, si purreit estre le plus seurement l'autre estancher.

Enfleure avient suvent de ceo ke les humurus ki descendent as veines
80 sunt espesses cum lie.[20] E pur ceo cloent e engrossissent e espessisent la
buche des veines, si ke eles ne poent despecer e de ceo se estendent e en
emflent. Aucune feiz avent de[21] la matire ki est trop secche ki estrecist[22]
les veines, aucune feiz avent de ceo ki li surigien les ardent e pus suivent
sursanure[s].[23] Celes ne porent ja pus estre uvertes, si ne seit par
85 aventure, par grant force e par grant peine. [f.76rb] Retienement, ceo
est ke li curs est clos e les humurs retenues. Ceo aveint de messmes la
reisun u de l'espeisse de sanc. Li curs si aveint aucune feiz e chiet sanc
par la force de la nature que depiece[24] les veines pur le cors purger.
Aucune feiz avient par force de la maladie, ceo est ke les humurus sunt
90 trop aigues u les veines trop ufertes.

Enfleure, si ele i est, ceo saverez par le[25] malade ki la sent u par veue,
ke vus purrez veir le[s] chief[s] des veines engrossis. Le retienement
conustrez par ceo: si li malades vus dit ki il ne ad mie [purgaciun][26] as
termes k'il sout aver; e par autres signes, cume par dolur de la teste, la
95 face pale e fade, pesantume des reins e del penil e des quisses, kar si
nature les vousist aver e ne pot, dunc i ad mal del retenir, ceo est
retienement. Li curs est legiers a cunustre par le sanc ki en ist. Cil sanc
est aucune feiz tut purs, aucune feiz neirz, aucune feiz jaunes, solum la
diverseté des humurs.
100 Sacez ke meint humme sunt enginné ki unt emoroides e quident aver
dissinterie u thenasmon, e tel ad dissinterie u thenasmon ke quide aver
emoroides. Mes cil [ki] ad emoroides se delivre de sanc sanz ceo ke li
ventres ne curt ne ne mot. Ceo ne fet pas cil ky ad dissinterie. [f.76va]

Derechief cil ki ad emoroides les ad sanz efforcier e sanz grant travail e
205 anguisse de aler a sele. Ce ne avient mie a homme ki ad thenasmon, kar
cil ad grant talent e suvent sanz rien fere. Un sages humme dist
emoroides est aornement e uverture de la veine ki est en l'anel de
chastitee, dunt li sanc curt de plusurs sainz [?] aures asises.[27]

Dunt emorois vient. Emorois vient a la fie de grosses humurs e de
210 tenanz cume glu ki sunt dedenz le buel ki descendent deske as nages e
par iloc issent. Si en vient emorois e clos e plaies. Aucune feiz vient[28]
emorois de humurus aguz e pungnant. Emoroides funt tut jurs la colur
del malade jaunes e numément si eles sunt ancienes, si funt destresse
del piz,[29] dolur del dos, pesantume en jambes e en quises e emflure des
215 costez. Emoroides ki sunt de grosses humurs e[n]glués[30] burbelent e
enflent li ventre, ceo est de la matire ki est crue pur le estomac, ki est
froiz pur le sanc, ki est destemprez. Emoroides, si eles sunt ague de
grosses humurs, dun[en]t ja mal as nages e dulur, e aucune feiz
thenasmon, e quide li malade ki deive[31] aler a sele quant il n'i a rein. Ceo
220 vient de thenasmon, ceo n'est mie adreite de emoroides.

[Cure].

Contre enflure e arsun des emoroides. Fetes seigner [f.76vb] vostre
malade de la veine ki est desuz le talun e desuz la keville del pié par
dehors, ke pur emoroides seignerez par dehors, pur la marize, par
dedenz. Pur le mal de la mariz le quel qu'il eit, u trop u trop poi des
225 fleurs, si vaht la seignee de la keville par dedenz. Pur le mal des
emoroides par dehors fetes li suffumigacion, sicume jo dis la sus, ovoc
vostre tuel, de puliol, de sel nitre, de saugemme quit en vin, kar en ceste
manere u eles depecerunt u eles secherunt. Autre manere. Esparpeillez
le aubun de un of sur un drap linge e metez u entur u sur la buche des
230 veines e quant il serra bien ensecchi, si l'en trehez en haste, lors
depecerunt les veines e overunt[32] les buches des veines. Autre mut
bone. Uns miens amis aveit iloc endreit pur defaute de curs de emoroides
u pur trop grosses humurus un aposteme, ço est 'un clo' en francés. Il ne
saveit le quel, un clo u enfleure. Il mist la racine de chenlange el feu e la
235 fit quire mut bien. Lores fu mol cume bure. Pus la bati, si l'eschaufa
tant chaud cum il la pout suffrir, si en [fit] emplastre a sun cucher.
Quant li emplastre fu refreidiz, si l'eschaufa une feiz u deus, pus si
dormi, si le lessa tute la nut, si ke unkes n'i mist bende, mes il a cele
cuntre grosse e grasse[33] [f.77ra], si la retint bien. L'endemein fu tut
240 | seins. [. . .][34] N'eez mie ceste herbe en despit, kar ele est bone e vaut a
mutes choses. Je vi un produmme ky aveit mal en une de ses meins, lors
i mist cest herbe, si wari mut bien.

Retienement. Cuntre retienement u retentiun des emoroides fetes le
seigner de la veine dunt jo vus dis, ki est sur la kiville del pié par dehors.

245 En tutes ces choses se treit bien e sens ke l'em cumençast de purger par
mescine la matire dunt trop i a. Si le deit³⁵ l'um purger ad mirabolans,
kar l'em n'i deit doner nule mescine trop ague sicumme est aloe. Doner
li poez trifere, e le grant e la menur, pur ceste retenciun. Si les
emoroides sunt retenues, bon est ki il seit ventosé as nages. Si les

250 emoroides sunt de humurus agues, ce poez saver par le arsun e par le
anguisse. Lors estoet restrendre l'anguisse par seigner del braz de la
veine del feie u de ambedeus les jambes desuz la kiville dehors. E si la
veine est si deliee ke ele ne seigne mie bien, si metez en ewe chaude, si
seignera meuz. Pur le anguisse³⁶ ke il ad a la feiz. Pernez gresse de

255 geline e oille violat, cire blanche, la meule de veel. Si vus n'avez del
veel, pernez de bof e aubuns de oufs e fetes oignement, cest l'eswagera.
Autrement. Pernez leit de femme e oile violet, morele e jubarbe e
destemperez [f.77rb] ensemble e muilez cotun par dedenz, si i metez. Si
les emoroides sunt dedens le cors, fetes une tante mole de lin u de cotun

260 u des deus ensemble,³⁷ sil metez sovent dedenz ovec vostre oignement.
Autre manere bone. Si il ad grant anguisse, u de emfleure u de
retienement, si est bon cunseil de retra[i]re les emoroides e fere les
cure, si s'en ira l'enflure e aswagera la dolur. Pur attreire, si frez ceste
[es]list fumigaciun. Jutez en un pot ces herbes, kersuns de more e

265 kersuns ortolans, averoigne, mente e mentastre, e chescune manere de
ache, puliol real e autre, persil, fenoil. Ces choses i valent sengles e
mieuz ensenble. Quant li pot serra plein de ces herbes, pus emplez le de
ewe, si le estupez entur de arcille, pus si quisez ses herbes mut bien.
Quant le herbe va as funs, ço signefie ke ele est bien quite. Pus metez

270 vostre tuel al pertus de l'es,³⁸ si le oignez bien dehors de arcille. L'autre
chief del tuel metez a l'anel de chasteé aukes parfund e fetes bien oigdre
le tuel par dehors ainz ke il seit mis en l'anel de chastitee. E si le fetes
lungement receivre la fumee. E tant cum il i serra, fetes oindere le anel
entur pur la chaline. Ci il volt ço suffrir, les emoroides li vendrunt asez

275 menues la nut u mut tost. [f.77va] Quant en avra asez eu e vus le
wodrez estancher, fetes quire mut bien confire e cunsolde e warance, ço
est en engleis 'mader', plantein, esscorce de chesne, ço est tant secchi,
escorce de purnelier ki porte les purneles e les foiles, si vus les avez, si le
fetes baigner deske al numblil, si estancherat, pus si metez vos

280 oingnemens.
Ore avum dit de l'emflure e de retinement. Ore dium des cures des
curs. Li curs, si il vient de force de nature ki par sa pruesse se purge,
dunc ne curt si a mesure nun. Dunc nel fet mie bon estancher,
numément si mut ne seit nuveauls e si il ne se fie bien en autres

285 purgaciuns cumme si li homme est jofnes e crest en naturele chaline e si

ço est femme ki bien se pust fier de ses flurs. Si li curs vient par force de
la maladie, ço saverez par la feblesse del malade.[39] Dunc les cuvent
destreindre l'estanchisun. Ki jo vus dis ore de cunfire e des autres
herbes i est bone. Autre. Fetes lui suffumigaciun ovec vostre tuel de
290 foiles de poreaus quites en vin. Autre. Pernez le tendrun de la runce e
del ceu, si les batez mut menu ausi cume a sause fere. Pus le destemprez
ovec oile ki seit fet de mueaus de ofs. Mueilez[40] lens cotun, si le metez
desus. Autre. Pernez ço ki est dedens la pomme de pin ovec peiz
[f.77vb] de neif, si les metez sur vif carbuns, si en receive la fumee ovec
295 le tuel, si estanchera. Autre. Si vostre ami ad emoroides, metez au fu
waide dunt l'em teint dras. Ne vus esmaiez mie si la chose ne seit trop
duce. Metez la al fu sur un tes u sur une tuwele, ki meiuez vaut, e
arosez le de vin u de eisil, ki meuz vaut, e tut sanz vin vaut mut, mes ne
mie tant. E quant il serra bien chaud, si en fetes plastre sur le cercle de
300 chasteé u en quir u en parchemin. Ceste estanche la maladie e tot la
dolur e la anguise. Sire Johan de seint Mertin[41] entent ki ceste chose
vaut cuntre curs e cuntre enfleure[42] e cuntre la retencion[43] e en tutes
maneres. Aucune feiz avient ke hors del cercle de chasté pendent les
emorodes cume mameleittes e si eles curent trop, si solent li sirugien
305 estancher les, ne mie tutes, mes une partie, par lur fer ardant. Cirugien
sunt li mire ki ovrent de fu e de fer, mes estanchen[t] mie voluntieres ke
aukun ne remaingne. Tutes les mescines qui sunt cuntre dissinterie i
valent a estancher. Si les mecines ki jo vus ai dit sa sus ne valent nient,
kar pot cel estre les emoroides sunt trop fruissés e perciees si ke quiture
310 en ist, dunc sacez ke il n'i ad garisun si par cirugie nun, ço ert par ceus
ki ovrent de fu e de fer. Galiens [f.78ra] dist emoroides fruscés
resemblent roseals — overz sunt dedenz e dehors ausi cume festre. Ne
poent garir si par la mein nun al cirugien. Si il aveint ke il eit as nages
clo, si i metez choses ke tost meurisent le clo cume oignun chaud u le
315 limasun od tute sa escale. Jo me fi mut en la racine de chienlange[44] dunt
dis la sus. Si vus es nages[45] sentés arsun, si i metez cel oignement dunt
vus avez oÿ. Emoroides purreient estre si jefnes ke par aventure, si la
matire fust bien purgié, ke eles secchereint del tut. Pur purger freit bon
prendre sis jurs u set oximel simple e surupe acetus meslé. Pus aprés
320 prendre mescine solum la force del malade: mirabolans unce e demie al
plus fort humme, al fieble homme demi unce, destempré en euue u rose
seit boilé o en ewe de pluie u en mosge de cheivere. Mes gardez ke tut
seit freit.[46] Si n'i metez fors plein petit hanape mut petit, tel dunt l'em
beit vin en plusurs lius. Si le lesez la hors tute nut [u] al serein. Le matin
325 le culez, si lui donez a beivre tut ausi pur dissinterie. Sacez ke mut freit
grant bien de user chescun jur aprés manger fenoil tant cume vus

tendrez en vos treis deis u entre vos quatre. Fenoil est mut bone chose: ele abate ventosité e la dolur des costez. Sacez ço est trop grant folie de surporter de aler a chanbre, [f.78rb] kar de ço nescent mutes maladies.

330 Autre mescine ke ne fet mie a oblier contre enfleure ke veint des veines estendues: un prudume aveit les nerfs engurdiz en une des meins e les veines si engrossies ke une veine i ut en sa mein dehors plus grosse ke dei que jo aie sanz puseier e les autres veines cume mis petit doit. De cest mescine fetes forment tribler rue e frire en seim ovec tut sun jus e

335 pus culer parmi un drap e pus prendre salgieme bien triblee en pudre deliee e esparpeiller de vostre mein le sein tant cumme il est chaud. Gardez cel oignement,[47] si en oingnez le liu. Si li aneaus de chasteé s'en ist sovent e chet de sun liu aval hors del cors, ço avient des humurus dunt trop i a u des humurus ki sunt escrilanz u esculurjables.[48] Si trop i

340 a des humurus, si enpesantissent cele partie la aval. Si ço vient des humurus escrillanz, si a l'em en l'anel une glette e une freidur. Si il i a trop humurus, purger les covient. De quele chose ke la maladie vienge, si lui vaut cist bainz: fetes quire maruil, aloingne, plantein, hyeble, wymawe, mauve e fetes le baingner dedenz.

    CI FINIST LE LIVRET KI EST APELE 'GARDEIN DE CORS' EN VERITÉ

Select Glossary

[The glossary includes only names of ingredients of receipts and other words not easily recognisable from Old French "francier" usage. Grammatical abbreviations follow the conventions used in the Anglo-Norman Dictionary. Verbs are normally entered under the infinitive.]

ache s. 266 wild celery, smallage (Apium graveolens L.)
agu, aigu, augu a. 56 sharp, pungent
aisil, eisil s. 145 vinegar
aloe s. 247 aloes
aloingne s. 343 wormwood (Artemisia absinthium L.)
anel, aneaus (de chasteé) s. 12 anus, anal sphincter
aposteme s. 233 aposteme, ulcer
arcille s. 268 clay
areim s. 18 brass, bronze
arsun s. 64 burning sensation
aubun s. 102 albumen
averoigne s. 265 southernwood (Artemisia abrotanum L.)
avinent 8, 6 pi AVENIR, to occur
bende s. 159 strip, bandage
burbeler v.n. 215 to bubble

burbelette s. 128 bubble
cercle de chaste(t)é s. 2 anus, anal sphincter
cerlange s. 117 hart's-tongue fern (Phyllitis scolopendrium (L.) Newm.)
ceu s. 291 willow (Salix)
chaline s. 143 heat
chammoc (ME) s. 117 cammock, restharrow (Ononis repens L.)
chesne s. 277 oak (Quercus)
ch(i)enlange s. 234 hound's tongue (Cynoglossum officinale L.)
cirugien, sirugien s. 183 surgeon
cloent 180 pres. ind. 6 of CLOER to close, block up
clo(u) s. 49 aposteme, ulcer
coinz s. 99 quince (Cydonia oblonga Mill.)
cole s. 15 bile
colike s. 74 colic
colon s. 74 colon
confire, cunfire s. 288 comfrey (Symphtum officinale L.)
corn de cerf s. 114 hartshorn
culeure s. 91 strained, sieved matter
cunsolde s. 276 consound, comfrey (Symphtum officinale L.)
curs s. 186 flux, flow, discharge
defire v.t. 46 to digest
dei s. 328 finger
delié a. 336 fine (of powder), delicate
depi(e)cer v.t. 169 to unblock, burst; v.n. to burst
destreindre v.t. 288 to restrain, inhibit
diaciminum s. 122 electuary made with cumin
dissinterie s. 12 dysentery
egestiun s. 14 excretion
e(s)moroides s.pl. 10 haemorrhoids, piles
emorois s. 209 haemorrhoid
encens s. *gentil e.* 114 incense
enginné p.p. 200 deceived, mistaken
engurdi p.p. 331 numbed, numb
ennercir v.n. 78 to turn black
enpesantir v.t. 340 weigh on
entysic s. 175 lung disease, asthma
es(percié) s. 143 (pierced) plank
escale s. 315 shell (of snail)
es(s)corce s. 277 bark
escorcer v.t. 14 to strip the surface of
escril(l)ant a. 45 slippery, slimy
esculurjable a. 339 slippery, slimy
eslaer v.t. 101 to dilute
eslist a. 264 select, excellent
espeiss s. 187 thickness, density
esquant pr. 22 some
estancher v.t. 123 to staunch

estanchisun s. 288 staunching
estrecir v.t. 182 to narrow, constrict
estrei(g)nant a. 59 constringent
estuper v.t. 268 to stop up, block
eswageru, aswageru 256 3 fut. ESWAGER, to soothe
euue, ewe s. 90 EWE ROSE, rose water
fade a. 195 pale
fenoil, fenuil s. 119 fennel (Foeniculum vulgare L.)
festre s. 312 fistula, ulcer
fleume, flemme, flume s. 20 phlegm
fl(e)urs s.pl. 3 menses
freit a. 75 cold
freit 318 cond. 3 of FERE to do, to make
fruscer, fruisser v.t. 309 to break open
fumigaciun s. 140 suffumigation, treatment with
   aromatic fumes
fundement s. 80 anus
geline s. 148 hen
gisi(e)r s. 45 stomach
gleste a. 75 viscous
glette s. 341 phlegm
gle(c)tus a. 47 viscous, phlegmatic, covered with slime
grevance s. 67 physical discomfort
gutesce, gutete s. 65 droplet
here terestre s. 117 ground ivy (Glechoma hederacea L.)
hyeble s. 343 danewort (Sambucus ebulus L.)
jubarbe s. 257 houseleek (Sempervivum tectorum L.)
kersun (ortolan) s. 158 garden cress (Lepidium sativum L.), *k. de more*
   water cress (Rorippa nasturcium-aquaticum (L.) Hayek)
keville s. 222 ankle
lie s. 180 lees
lienterie s. 13 lientery, form of diarrhoea
limasun s. 315 snail
lorrei 176 cond. 1 of LOER to advise
mader (ME) s. 277 madder (Rubia tinctoria L.)
mameleitte s. 304 little breast or udder
marize s. 223 womb
maruil s. 343 horehound (Marrubium vulgare L.)
mastic s. 99 mastic
mauve s. 137 marsh mallow (Althaea officinalis L.)
me(s)cine s. 84 medicine
meneisun s. 9 diarrhoea
mentastre s. 265 horsemint (Mentha sylvestris L.)
mente s. 265 mint (Mentha)
mereveilles adv. 156 wonderfully
meule s. 255 marrow
mezle s. 98 medlar (Mespilus germanica L.)

mirabolans (citrins, kiebles, bellerins, emblins, indes) s.pl. 85 fruit of varieties of Terminalia incl. citrina, chebula, bellerica etc.
moeal s. 108 yolk of an egg
morele s. 257 black nightshade (Solanum nigrum L.)
mosge de chievre s. 91 whey of goat's milk
mot 203 3 pi MOVOIR to move
muse s. 68 mucus
nages s.pl. 210 buttocks
nessance s. 3 vulva
numblil s. 35 navel
odoc, ofoc prep. 93 with
o(u)f s. 102 egg
oig(n)dre v.t. 157 to anoint
oille rosat s. 148 oil of roses, attar of roses
oille violat, violet s. 147 oil of violets
ordure de fer s. 141 scoria, slag, cinder
organe s. 153 marjoram (Origanum vulgare L.)
ouue s. 148 goose
oximel s. 319 oximel, wine flavoured with honey and spices
peiz de neif s. 294 naval pitch
penil s. 38 pubes
persil s. 266 parsley (Petroselinum crispum (Mill.) Nyman)
pesantime, pesantume s. 67 heaviness
piere ematice s. 97 haematite
planteine s. 102 great plantain (Plantago maior L.)
plu(i)e s. 90 rain
pomme de pin s. 152 pine cone
poreal s. 152 leek (Allium porrum L.)
puignant, pungnant a. 56 pungent, sharp
puingture, puncture s. 64 stinging sensation
puliol, p. real s. 153 penny royal (Mentha pulegium L.) or wild thyme (Thymus serpyllum L.)
purnele s. 278 sloe (Prunus spinosa L.)
purnelier s. 278 sloe tree
pus adv. 58 then
puseier s. 333 thumb
quiture s. 309 pus, discharge
rarure s. 28 scrapings
res 49 pp RERE to shave, erase, scrape away
restebof s. 116 restharrow (Ononis repens L.)
ret 26 pres. ind. 3 of RERE to scrape (away)
retenciun s. 243 retention
retenement, retinement s. 163 retention
reverser v.t. 156 to turn inside out
ris s. 98 rice
rue s. 334 rue (Ruta graveolens L.)
ruil s. 18 rust; t. d'areim Verdigris 18

salgiemme, saugemme s. 227 rock salt, sodium chloride

sausefleme s. 16 saucefleme, 'salt phlegm'

sçurup violaz s. 127 syrup of violets

seaus de amur s. 1 vulva

seigne 36 subj. pres. 3 of SEINDRE to constrict

seignee s. 225 bleeding, blood letting

seigner v.t. 221 to bleed

seim s. 147 animal fat, grease

seint osiᵽe uuert (ME) s. 154 'St Osyth's wort', identity uncertain
  (? marjoram, ? wild thyme)

sel nitre s. 227 saltpetre

sele, aler a sele 65 to go to stool, evacuate the bowels

sengles adv. 266 individually, singly

serein s. 324 evening

sinder (ME) s. 142 scoria, slag, cinder

siu s. 147 animal fat

sorbe s. 98 fruit of the service tree (Pyrus domestica L.)

suffumigacion s. 152 suffumigation, treatment with aromatic fumes

surporter v.n. 77 to do excessively

sursanure s. 184 scab, cicatrice

surupe acetus 319 syrup of vinegar

suverain a. 34 upper

tanasye s. 129 tansy (Tanacetum vulgare L.)

tenant a. 210 sticky

tente s. 150 tent (med.), roll or pledget for cleansing and holding open
  wound

tes s. 297 (shard of) earthenware pot

teve, tenve a. 149 tepid

thenasmon s. 9 tenesmus

tiu(u)(e)le, tuwele s. 102 tile

tot 300 pres. 3 of TOLIR to take away

trifere s. 248 soothing medical preparation (Grk. trypheron)

tuel s. 140 tube, pipe

veel s. 255 calf, veal

velu s. 52 rough texture or surface (of bowel)

velu a. 25 rough (of texture, surface)

veluesse s. 26 roughness, rough coating (of bowel)

ventoser v.t. 249 to cup or bleed

ventrail s. 24 intestines

waide s. 297 woad (Isatis tinctoria L.)

warance s. 129 madder (Rubia tinctoria L.)

wuimauve, wymawe, uimalve s. 138 marsh mallow (Althaea officinalis L.)

ydropic s. 175 dropsy

ysope, isope s. 153 hyssop (Hyssopus officinalis L.)

Notes

1 I have italicised those red rubrics or underlines which appear in the
   MS.

2 For another attestation of the sense 'vulva', see the gynaecological
   treatise in MS Cambridge, Trinity College 0. 1. 20 f.222v 'Sor les
   carbones mist ceste medicine,/sor la sele patie [corr. percié] fist
   s[e]oir la roine,/ensi qu'en la nassance la fumee venist . . . Dame que
   tel mecine vodra fere sovent/doit oindre sa nassance de ole rose
   devant.'

3 The original Latin is here compressed, 'entre deus' (the Trinity
   translation has 'l'un et l'autre) corresponding to 'quoddam modo'. The
   second set of symptoms stems from *colera prassina*, the third from
   colera eruginosa.

4 MS = *s.p. partie le egestiun pers ruge*. The colour-adjectives *pers* and
   ruge do not accurately reflect the *subalbidus* (var. *subpallidus*) of the
   Latin.

5 MS = *d. est a. f. mut sanc e sudeinement est pur sanc a. f. e.*

6 MS = *veient.*

7 Apparently a hapax in Old French, see FEW 6, 181a.

8 MS = *of od.*

9 MS = *enuue.*

10 MS = *eoile.*

11 MS = *u ki il leit trop m.*

12 MS = *ceo deous purgeret*. The text omits *flegma* as a source of
   diarrhoea, but since it is treated with the same purgative employed for
   lienteria, not *dissinteria*, it is unlikely that MS *deous* = 'deus'.

13 i.e. anus.

14 MS = *fuffumigaciun.*

15 MS = *ypope.*

16 MS = *tendue.*

17 MS = *si fenisent.*

18 MS = *turnez e a n.*

19 The Trinity translation (f.97r) and the 1497 print have no reference
   to Hippocrates, but the text in Renzi's *De aegritudinum curatione*
   does.

20 The Latin has *spisse et feculente.*

21 MS = *ke.*

22 MS = *estrencist*. The Latin has *coartante.*

23 MS = *si iiienent sursanure.*

24 MS = *de qus piece.*

25 MS = *le le malade.*

26 MS = *il nes ad mie as t.*

27 This sentence is not in the *Practica* and remains obscure.

28 MS = *vient is e.*

29 MS = *des esperiz.*

30 MS = *egluses.*

31 MS = *deivez.*

32 MS = *voerunt.*

33 The sense is obscure. Something seems to be missing.

34 Some material has obviously fallen out.

35 MS = *les deit.*

36 MS = *anguissie.*

37 MS = *u ensemble dedens*.
38 The abrupt introduction of the plank suggests that an earlier reference has dropped out.
39 MS = *de la malade*.
40 MS = *uiueilez*.
41 I cannot identify this figure, who does not appear among the medical practitioners listed in the works of Wickersheimer, Kealey, and Talbot and Hammond.
42 MS = *enfleiure*.
43 MS = *retencinon*.
44 MS = *chienlangle*.
45 MS = *si li a enages*.
46 MS = *fieit*.
47 MS = *dignement*.
48 MS = *esculuriiables*.

References

De Vriend, H. J. (1984) (ed.) *The Old English Herbarium and Medicina de Quadrupedis*, EETS 286, London: Oxford University Press.
Faribault, M. (1982) 'La Chirurgie par rimes: problèmes de la compilation de recettes médicales en français', *Fifteenth-Century Studies*, 5, pp.47–59.
Goldberg, A. and Saye, H. (1933) 'An Index to Mediaeval French Medical Receipts', *Bulletin of the History of Medicine*, 1, pp.435–66.
Hirth, W. (1969) *Studien zu den Gesundheitslehren der sogenannten 'Secretum secretorum' unter besonderer Berücksichtigung der Prosaüberlieferung*, diss. Heidelberg.
Hunt, Tony (1987) 'The "Novele Cirurgerie" in MS London, British Library, Harley 2558', *Zeitschrift für romanische Philologie*, 103, pp.271–99.
—— (1989) *Plant Names of Medieval England*, Cambridge: D. S. Brewer.
—— (1990) *Popular Medicine in Thirteenth-Century England: Introduction and Texts*, Cambridge: D. S. Brewer.
Jörimann, J. (1925) *Frühmittelalterliche Rezeptarien*, Zürich: C. Hoenn, repr. 1977.
Manzaloui, M. A. (1977) (ed.), *Secretum secretorum*, EETS 276, London: Oxford University Press.
Möller, P. (1963) *Hiltgart von Hürnheim, Mittelhochdeutsche Prosaübersetzung des 'Secretum secretorum'*, Berlin: Akademie-Verlag.
Platearius (1497) *Practica Jo. Serapionis dicta breviarium . . . Practica Platearii, expl. Impressum Venetus mandato et expensis nobilis viri domini Octaviani Scoti civis Modoetiensis per Bonetum Locatellum Bergomensem 17 kal. Januarias 1497*.
Renzi, S. de (1852–9) *Collectio Salernitana*, 1–5, Napoli: Tipografia del Filiatre-Sebezio.
Riddle, J. M. (1981) 'Pseudo-Dioscorides' Ex herbis femininis and Early Medical Botany', *Journal of the History of Biology*, 14, pp.43–81.
Sigerist, H. E. (1923) *Studien und Texte zur frühmittelalterlichen Rezeptliteratur*, Leipzig: J. A. Barth.

Södergård, Ö. (1981) *Une Lettre d'Hippocrate d'après un manuscrit inédit,*
    Stockholm: Alquist.
Suchier, H. (1883) *Denkmäler der provenzalischen Literatur und Sprache,*
    1, Halle a.S: M. Niemeyer.
Vising, J. (1923) *Anglo-Norman Language and Literature,* London: Oxford
    University Press.

INDEX